## 'You are very, ~~w~~ ~~pung,~~ my beautiful Letty.'

Nicholas looked into her eyes, his own strangely sad, and then, with a muffled sound very like a groan, his mouth sought for and captured hers. Their lips clung, the painful pleasure sheer ecstasy, and then Letty felt her mouth being forced open and an extraordinary sensation took possession of her whole body. A strange longing seized her, but she had no idea what it was she longed for.

With an abruptness which startled her, Nicholas regained control. He raised his head and gave her a twisted sort of smile. 'Do you know what you do to me when I hold you in my arms?' And as she hesitated, uncertain of his meaning, he went on, 'No, of course you do not—you are a well-brought-up young lady. But what would I not give to be the one who teaches you! Oh, Letty, why did we not meet sooner?'

MIKE'S FAMOUS
BOOKSTALL
FOR
PAPER BACK BOOKS

Alison Greenway has always been mad about history and has had several historical novels published. Living in Suffolk is a constant joy because of the ancient villages and beautiful half-timbered houses. Her chief interests, apart from writing, are reading, walking, Scottish dancing and, last but not least, her grandchildren. *White Nights* is her first historical novel for Masquerade.

# WHITE NIGHTS

## Alison Greenway

MILLS & BOON LIMITED
ETON HOUSE   18-24 PARADISE ROAD
RICHMOND   SURREY   TW9 1SR

*All the characters in this book have no existence outside the imagination of the Author, and have no relation whatsoever to anyone bearing the same name or names. They are not even distantly inspired by any individual known or unknown to the Author, and all the incidents are pure invention.*

*All Rights Reserved. The text of this publication or any part thereof may not be reproduced or transmitted in any form or by any means, electronic or mechanical, including photocopying, recording, storage in an information retrieval system, or otherwise, without the written permission of the publisher.*

*This book is sold subject to the condition that it shall not, by way of trade or otherwise, be lent, resold, hired out or otherwise circulated without the prior consent of the publisher in any form of binding or cover other than that in which it is published and without a similar condition including this condition being imposed on the subsequent purchaser.*

*First published in Great Britain 1990
by Mills & Boon Limited*

© Alison Greenway 1990

*Australian copyright 1990
Philippine copyright 1990
This edition 1990*

ISBN 0 263 76796 5

*Set in Times Roman 10 on 11 pt.
04-9004-79410 C*

*Made and printed in Great Britain*

# CHAPTER ONE

IT SEEMED to Letty that the train had been pounding across Europe ever since she could remember, yet they had only boarded it yesterday. Even the boat trip from Harwich to the Hook of Holland, in itself an adventure, now seemed remote, like something that had happened last week, or even a month ago. As for the quiet home in the Cathedral Close at Ely, where she had been born on April 25th 1890 and had spent almost exactly twenty unadventurous years since, she could scarcely believe it continued to exist. So Cinderella must have felt when the Fairy Godmother transformed her with a wave of her magic wand.

In the opposite corner her own particular Fairy Godmother slept uncomfortably upright, her smart grey travelling hat still firmly in position above the curled fringe of suspiciously black hair, her mouth slightly open and her chins neatly folded one over another upon the boned lace of her high collar.

'I never sleep properly in a train,' Mrs Kemp had announced last night, when they were waiting in the corridor, while the attendant removed the spotless white daytime coverlets of coarse cotton from the dingy brown seats smelling of ancient dust. As soon as the smooth, equally spotless sheets were in place, they returned to the compartment and each lady began to make preparations for bed, modestly removing as little as possible of her clothing.

To Letty, whose train journeys had consisted only of trips to Hunstanton on the Norfolk coast, and rare visits to London to visit an aunt, it was all novel and tremendously exciting, so much so that she had not slept well either in spite of the comfortable berth. She was paying for it now with drooping lids and a slight headache which was making her wish she could take her hat off. The brown silk toque with its spray of small greenish feathers standing straight up in front was a little tight where it pressed on her forehead, though it sat easily enough at the back where it was supported by the coil of red gold hair.

If only she had someone to talk to, the time wouldn't seem so long.

For no reason at all Letty found herself thinking of the young man they had seen on the boat, who had bowed to Mrs Kemp and received a slightly distant inclination of the head in reply. The polite removal of his hat had revealed dark curling hair, worn rather long. His overcoat, broad-shouldered and tight-waisted, was a little long, too, and the whole effect was vaguely military. A pair of diamond-bright grey eyes glanced briefly at Letty and then the elegant figure moved on.

'Count Nicholas Namorov,' Mrs Kemp said, her tone a mixture of pride because she was acquainted with the aristocracy, and an odd disapproval. 'The Namorovs are a very old Russian family and distantly related to the Tsar.'

Letty had glimpsed the young man again when they were boarding the train, but Mrs Kemp had been too occupied with heaving herself up the high steps to notice him. Later, she had half hoped to see him in the first-class dining-car, but his mealtimes were apparently different from theirs.

The train rattled noisily over a bridge and the sleeping figure stirred a little, but gave no sign of waking up. Letty sighed and allowed her thoughts to wander. How strange that as recently as two weeks ago she had never heard of Mrs Kemp, now her trusted travelling companion. But for her, Canon Mayfield would never have allowed his younger daughter to leave home and travel so far. She would have remained a prisoner in the comfortable and claustrophobic world which revolved round the Cathedral; 'working' at her embroidery, doing the flowers, practising the piano and producing insipid watercolour pictures with a slapdash speed which pained her art teacher. It had not even been possible to enliven matters by fancying herself in love with either him or her music master, since both were middle-aged and conspicuously lacking in male attractiveness.

Sometimes Letty thought seriously of becoming a suffragette and running away to London to chain herself to railings and shout, 'Votes for women!' She was genuinely on their side, but the prospect of imprisonment terrified her. Besides, she had no money of her own and she had heard that the suffragettes preferred wealthy supporters.

Edward, her brother, who, being a man, could have escaped easily, had no desire to leave his comfortable home. Tall, thin and, already at twenty-five, with a scholar's stoop, he had never given his parents a moment's worry. He was content to spend his time in a shed at the bottom of the long, secluded garden, where he conducted vague scientific experiments. He would blow them all up one day, Letty thought sometimes, and wickedly half hoped it might happen. At least it would be exciting!

'Why cannot you be more like your brother, Letty?' the Canon's wife would ask despairingly. 'What have I done to deserve *two* such restless daughters? One would have been bad enough, but at least Marina has the excuse of a great talent. To have a second girl with so much energy—it is too much! I declare that at times even to be in the same room with you wears me out.'

Charlotte Mayfield was French, the daughter of a professional actor. The Canon had met her while touring the Continent as a young man, fallen in love with her fragile prettiness and married her as soon as possible. It was the only impulsive thing he had done in his whole life and, if he had ever regretted it, he gave no sign. Charlotte bore him a son and two daughters and then relapsed into vague ill-health, asserting herself only to make sure that Edward, Marina and Letty grew up bilingual. To talk in her own language with her family remained her only link with France and the Bohemian life she had known there.

'Poor Mama!' Letty bent to pick up the despised embroidery from the floor. 'You will just have to hope that some suitable young man comes along and asks for my hand in marriage.' Unconsciously she sighed and the large hazel-green eyes were wistful as she bent her bright head over the traycloth she was working on. 'I can't imagine where such a one is to be found in Ely. They are all either married already or of such a fearful dullness that I could not tolerate any of them in the role of husband.'

Her mother's cheeks flushed slightly and she made a very French gesture with her thin hands. 'You don't know what you are talking about, Letty. Dullness is a most desirable trait once the first...er...enthusiasm has ended. Dull men are dependable and that is a good thing when one has a home to run and children to care for.'

Letty's full red lips curved into a rebellious pout, but she knew better than to argue. Sometimes, though, she dared to do verbal battle with her father.

Canon Mayfield was tall and thin, like his son, and his hair had receded so far as to be almost invisible. He had a comfortable private income and could indulge his taste for ancient books. The study was lined with them, and the room smelt so strongly of parchment and old leather that Letty sometimes felt she could hardly breathe, but if she wanted to talk to her father she was obliged to put up with his background.

Perched tautly on the edge of a high-backed chair, she poured out her frustration and longing for a more interesting life. 'You believe in having girls educated to the same level as boys, Papa,' she pointed out passionately, 'but what good is my education? I shall never make any use of it in this dull little town.'

The Canon peered at her over the pince-nez perched on his high-bridged nose and frowned disapprovingly. 'My dear Letty, a good education is *never* wasted. Instead of complaining, you should make use of your own to enrich your life and——'

'I shall never be able to do that in Ely!' Suddenly she was on the verge of tears. 'You let Marina leave home, Papa—it's not fair to deny me the same chance.'

'It's ridiculous to compare yourself with your sister. Marina was singularly gifted and had a burning ambition, so that she carried us all before her. I believe it would have been actual cruelty not to let her follow her chosen career, much as both your Mama and I disapproved of it at the time.' His tone softened. 'Believe me, I understand how you feel, my dear, but, if I allowed you to leave home, where would you go and what would you do?'

It was the unanswerable question with which he always defeated her. Letty was aware that she had no particular talents in spite of a quick brain. The only career open to her would be that of governess, which would certainly be a lot worse than staying at home. 'I'm sorry, Papa,' she said glibly, standing up and moving towards the door. 'I know I have much to be thankful for and it's very wrong of me to be such an ungrateful daughter.'

The Canon gave her a keen glance and raised his eyebrows slightly. Knowing that her apology had not rung true, Letty hurried from the room. She would go for a walk across the fields which lay beyond the Cathedral Close and use up some of her boundless energy.

The bright spring morning was invigorating and she walked at a good speed, careless of her long skirt sweeping the dew-wet grass. By the time she had tramped through three fields and the whole length of a drove, as the local people called the narrow lanes used by cattlemen, she felt refreshed in mind and body. Sauntering back, she gazed admiringly at the lantern tower of the great Cathedral which sparkled in the sunlight, magnifying it a thousandfold. All around it the slate roofs of the tight little town perched above the Fens were shining too, giving an illusion of beauty and light which faded rapidly as Letty approached.

By the time she reached the row of Georgian houses lined up near the Cathedral and inhabited by clergy, from the Dean downwards, the brightness had gone and everything was ordinary again. The only liveliness came from the boys of the Choir School, who had been let out after morning classes. They laughed and shouted and chased each other, and Letty smiled as she paused to watch them.

'Morning, miss.' It was the postman, making his second delivery. 'Just put a whole handful of mail through your letter box,' he volunteered. 'There was one with a foreign stamp on it—reckon it'd be from your sister.'

'Marina!' Letty gave a little skip of excitement. 'Thank you for telling me, Postman. I'll hurry home at once. We have not heard from her for some time.'

He nodded, touched his cap with its twin peaks fore and aft, and went whistling on his way. Letty resisted the temptation to break into a run and approached the house at a sedate pace suitable for Canon Mayfield's daughter. A letter from Marina was an important event, to be savoured to the full by every member of the family.

But Letty had absolutely no premonition of how very much more than ordinarily important this particular letter would turn out to be.

By the time she reached the hall the letters had already been picked up by the parlourmaid and placed on a silver salver. Canon Mayfield was standing by the hall table, glancing through them.

'I met the postman and he told me there's one from Marina,' Letty burst out. 'Do open it quickly, Papa!'

To her astonishment he held out the letter towards her. 'It is not for me to open it, Letty. It is addressed to you.'

'To me?' Colour flooded the fair skin, which always freckled in summer because she refused to use a parasol. 'But she only writes to me for my birthday and that isn't until next April.'

'Nevertheless, she has written to you now. You had better open it quickly if you want to be the first to hear her news. Once your mother knows there is a letter from Marina she will be quite unable to control her impatience no matter to whom it is addressed.'

Letty's fingers trembled as she slit open the foreign-looking envelope and unfolded the thin paper. There was only one page and the writing looked as though it had been scrawled in a hurry. She read it quickly, frowning over a badly written word now and then. By the time she came to the end her heart was pounding so fiercely she could hardly speak.

'Well?' The Canon was unusually impatient. 'How is your sister? In good health, I trust?'

'She—she says not—at least——' Letty hastened to correct herself, distressed by the look of alarm on his face. 'She isn't actually ill, Papa—only a little out of sorts, which is unusual for her. She says, too, that she is homesick, and that's also unusual, as far as we know. She longs to see a member of her family and—oh, Papa—she wants *me* to go and visit her!' Letty seized his arm, gazing imploringly into his face. 'Please, please let me go!'

The letter had fluttered to the floor, and the Canon bent to retrieve it, gently disengaging himself as he did so. 'My dear Letty, do try to calm yourself. There is no need for so much excitement. As for your question, I cannot possibly answer it until I have read the letter for myself, and probably not even then since there is a great deal to be considered and, in addition, your mother to be consulted.'

'She's sure to say it's impossible,' Letty exclaimed tragically, her eyes wide and despairing. 'You are my only hope, Papa!'

He smiled. 'So much passion deserves a more serious subject.'

'You don't think it is serious that Marina isn't well?'

'I did not mean to imply that, but in my opinion the letter was written in a moment of depression such as your sister has probably often experienced before. So far from home, she must, at times, long to see someone from her own family.' He held out the sheet of paper. 'Take it to your mother and see what she has to say, but don't be too hopeful, my dear.'

Letty was not hopeful at all. The tremendous upsurge of excitement which she had felt on first reading the letter had quickly faded. Her parents would never let her go all the way to St Petersburg to visit Marina; her mother would probably faint at the mere suggestion.

It was quite a while before she could even mention the matter. At first Charlotte Mayfield could think only of her much loved elder daughter, unwell and alone in a distant country, and the fact that the younger one had been invited to visit her hardly seemed to register at all. When she was finally persuaded to think about it, her reaction was exactly as Letty had feared.

'It is out of the question! How could we possibly allow a young girl to travel so far by herself? Just think of all the terrible things which might happen!'

'What exactly do you mean, Mama?' Letty asked, momentarily diverted.

'Nothing that I could possibly discuss with a girl of your age,' Charlotte said hurriedly, as a slight flush crept up beneath the light rouge on her cheeks. The other Cathedral wives very much disapproved of the delicate make-up but most of them endeavoured to be charitable because 'she's French, of course, and one must make allowances'.

'Would you let me go if Edward would agree to escort me?' Letty demanded.

'Oh, dear—I really don't know. You must ask your father.'

Letty asked her brother first and received the answer she had expected. In Edward's opinion Marina was probably making a fuss about nothing. She had been away from home for years and had long got past the stage of suffering from homesickness. 'In any case,' he added, 'I could not possibly get away just now. My scientific experiments have reached a critical stage and an interruption might prove disastrous.'

'You don't think it's disastrous that Marina is ill and unhappy?'

'My dear Letty——' his tone was maddeningly superior '—you are exaggerating as usual.'

There followed a week of argument, tears and temper which turned the house upside down, and at the end of it Letty was no nearer her objective than she had been at the beginning. Nevertheless, she left the letter unanswered in the apparently vain hope that she might be able to reply to it in the way that both her heart and her restless spirit dictated.

And then Mrs Kemp came to tea.

She was visiting a niece married to one of the minor clergy, and at first Letty did not recognise her Fairy Godmother in the short stout lady dressed in purple velvet and wearing an immense hat on which exotic birds perched uncomfortably. It was the invalid hostess who, unwittingly, steered the conversation in the right direction.

'How long do you propose staying in Ely, Mrs Kemp?' Charlotte enquired politely, presiding over a tea table laden with massive silver, wafer-thin sandwiches and plum cake.

The visitor accepted the eggshell-thin cup of china tea which Letty handed to her. 'I have only another week in this delightful little town and then I must return to my poor neglected husband. I am afraid he has been left on his own for far too long, but I have had such a round of visits to make while I have been in England. I do like to keep in touch with all my relatives and letters are not quite the same as a personal visit. Do you not agree?'

Letty darted a glance at her mother, but Mrs Mayfield was concentrating on pouring tea for the silent niece.

Mrs Kemp took a sip of tea and continued her monologue. 'My husband is a banker and we have lived abroad for most of our married life. First we were in Paris and then Rome, but for some years now we have been resident in St Petersburg. It is such a lovely city and——' She broke off and looked across at her hostess. 'Forgive me, Mrs Mayfield, but is something wrong?'

Charlotte had put down the heavy silver teapot with a slight bang which slopped a little tea on to the immaculate lace-trimmed cloth. She said hastily, 'I'm so sorry if I startled you—I fear I have very little strength in my wrists. Letty, my dear, will you pour the other cups for me, please?'

Letty pulled herself together and obeyed. She had been as taken aback as her mother, but had concealed it better.

An uncomfortable silence had fallen on the lovely elegant drawing-room with its white paint, gilt-framed mirrors and numerous graceful ferns. The shyly murmured, 'Thank you,' with which the younger guest received her tea made no impact at all. Well-trained in social poise, Letty knew someone simply *had* to say something. She resolved to take the conversation into her own hands.

'Did you say you lived in St Petersburg, Mrs Kemp?' The quiet voice gave no indication of her wildly beating heart beneath the tight bodice of her high-necked cream shirt-blouse, trimmed with hand-made lace.

'Yes, indeed I did, Miss Mayfield. There are a great many English residents in the city, you know. Some, of course, belong to the diplomatic circle, but mostly they are there for business reasons. My husband, being, as I said, a banker, is equally at home in *all* circles and consequently we have a great many friends. Our social life is at times really quite exhausting, and in spite of all the travelling about I feel I have had a comparatively restful time in England.'

Letty glanced at her mother, hoping she had recovered from her shock and would re-enter the conversation, but Charlotte remained silent. She was pale and her hands were trembling slightly. It was clear there would be no help there.

Unconsciously Letty tilted her head defiantly. 'What you have been saying is extremely interesting, Mrs Kemp,' she told the visitor, and hoped no one would notice the slight tremor in her voice. 'You see, I have a sister in St Petersburg.'

'Really?' Mrs Kemp put down her cup and gave Letty her full attention. 'I wonder if I know her? She is married, I take it?'

'No, she's not, and so her surname is still Mayfield, but that is not the name by which she is known now.' She paused and her air of defiance became more pronounced. She did not glance at her mother. 'My sister is a dancer, Mrs Kemp—a member of the Imperial Russian Ballet, and her name is Marina Varaskaya. Perhaps you have seen her perform?'

There was another silence, this time so filled with blank astonishment that Letty had to repress a hysterical giggle. Mrs Kemp sat motionless with a tiny sandwich halfway to her mouth and stared at her. The niece gave a small nervous cough and hastily pressed a lace-edged napkin to her lips.

The stout lady in purple velvet recovered rapidly. 'How very interesting, Miss Mayfield! I'm afraid my husband and I do not patronise the ballet, but it is, of course, immensely popular in St Petersburg, and indeed world famous for the high standard of its dancing. Your sister must be quite remarkably talented to have been accepted into the company.'

The sentence had ended on a slight rising note and Letty had no difficulty in guessing the questions which the visitor was too polite to put into words. She glanced again at her mother, but Charlotte was looking down at her tightly folded hands and had plainly withdrawn from the conversation. Recklessly, Letty plunged into an account of Marina's career.

'She always loved dancing, even when she was a small child. She is two years older than me, but I can just remember her kicking off her slippers and dancing on the lawn from sheer joy in movement. With her long golden hair and blue eyes, she seemed just like a fairy to me.' She broke off and coloured, aware that she had allowed herself to get carried away.

Mrs Kemp said carefully, 'Your sister must have had a long and arduous training to have become a professional dancer. Was that not something of a problem in Ely?'

'Indeed, yes.' Letty's mind flew back to those difficult days when Marina had announced her intention and clung to it through every kind of opposition. Hands had been flung up in horror and heads had been shaken round the tea-tables of the Cathedral Close. Charlotte had wept and pleaded, and the Canon had taken a firm stand.

None of it had been any good. The slender eleven-year-old child had defied them all. It was her father who had ended it all with a sudden capitulation, and because he was loved and respected in Ely they had weathered the storm.

'At first Marina went to a local dancing class,' Letty went on. 'The teacher was so impressed with her talent that she encouraged her to think about taking up dancing as a career, with the result that she eventually went away to London for proper ballet training.'

This time Mrs Kemp made no attempt to hide her astonishment. 'That must have been a very difficult decision for your parents to make—a young girl leaving home by herself——'

The implied criticism brought Charlotte back into the conversation. 'Naturally we were extremely worried, but we were assured that Marina would be perfectly safe as a resident at the Ballet School, where the children were carefully supervised. In addition, I have a sister living in London who promised to see her regularly—a promise, I may add, which she kept faithfully, right up to the time my daughter went abroad.'

Letty could not resist a half-hidden smile. It was hardly surprising that Aunt Eugenie had been so willing to help. She had been a dancer herself, on the Paris stage, a piece of family history hidden from the ladies of Ely. She had met her husband while visiting her sister Charlotte and now, widowed, childless and well-off, took a great deal of interest in the niece who had inherited and improved on her own talent.

But she mustn't think about her aunt now. Nothing, absolutely nothing, must be allowed to deflect her from snatching at this heaven-sent opportunity. Taking a deep breath, Letty made her appeal.

'Mrs Kemp, I believe you said you were shortly returning to St Petersburg? I wonder if you would be so kind as to permit me to travel with you? I am most anxious to visit my sister, who is unwell, but my parents would certainly not allow me to travel alone.'

She heard a faint gasp from her mother and ignored it. Her large, hazel-green eyes were fixed on the visitor's face in desperate appeal. It was clear that she had administered yet another shock, but Mrs Kemp quickly rallied and allowed her kind heart to show briefly beneath the social veneer.

'But, of course, you can come with me, my dear! I should be delighted to have your company on that tedious journey. Do you think you can be ready in ten days' time? I cannot delay my departure any longer.'

With difficulty Letty restrained herself from flinging her arms round the stout figure. 'Thank you,' she said sedately, but with so much warmth no one could doubt her sincerity. 'I am truly grateful. You may rely on me to be ready when the time comes.'

And ready she was. With all her battles behind her and a letter to Marina announcing her coming already in the post, she climbed into a 'ladies only' compartment at Ely station and turned her head to take one last look at the great Cathedral on its hilltop.

It was to be a long time before she saw it again.

# CHAPTER TWO

They were crossing a bridge over an immense river and the altered sound of the train wheels awakened Mrs Kemp. She yawned, concealing it behind a gloved hand, and looked across at Letty.

'What would I not give for a good strong cup of English tea!'

'Shall I go along to the samovar and ask for tea to be brought here?' Letty, glad of something to do, was already springing to her feet.

'Thank you, my dear. It will be better than nothing, though I don't much care for the stuff they serve in trains. In Petersburg we have no difficulty at all in obtaining our favourite brand sent out from England.'

Letty smiled and slid the door shut behind her. As she turned to walk along the corridor she saw that the way ahead was blocked by a young man standing with his back to the samovar and staring out of the window. With a tiny tremor of excitement she recognised him. It was Count Nicholas Namorov, the man who had bowed to Mrs Kemp on the boat.

He really was amazingly handsome in a foreign sort of way, so very different from the young men at the tennis club and the minor clergy attached to Ely Cathedral!

Hoping he would sense her approach and move out of the way, Letty slowed her steps, but he continued to stare out at the passing view, which at that moment consisted of an immense lake surrounded by birch trees. Letty had long ago become satiated with forests and lakes; she much preferred pretty red-roofed villages or mediaeval castles perched on rocky crags. She suspected the Count's thoughts were not on the melancholy scene outside, but fixed on some private matter. The start he gave when he at last became aware of her presence seemed perfectly genuine.

Should she say, 'Excuse me' or *'Excusez-moi'*? Mrs Kemp had told her that educated Russians—and particularly members of the aristocracy—spoke French, and even preferred it to their native tongue.

It was not necessary to say anything. He immediately moved out of the way, said, 'Forgive me,' in perfect English and asked if he could be of any assistance.

'I...I only wanted to order two glasses of tea to be brought to our compartment.' Impulsively, Letty added, 'How did you know I'm English?'

He smiled, his grey eyes dancing. 'I assure you it was not at all difficult, but it would be hard to say *how* I knew without going into personal details which one does not normally discuss with a young lady—unless one knows her very well indeed. Let it suffice to say you *look* English.'

Letty felt herself flushing. No doubt he meant her clothes weren't smart enough, though they were the best that the tailoress at Ely could provide, and her tightly fitting grey flannel coat and skirt had cost a great deal of money. Before she could think of a suitable reply he turned to the attendant and relayed her order.

There was a moment's pause while the woman busied herself with her samovar and then the Count continued talking.

'You are travelling with the excellent Mrs Kemp, I believe, and that means that your objective is probably St Petersburg. If that is so, we are very likely to meet again. Permit me that I introduce myself. I am Nicholas Namorov.' And as Letty inclined her head without saying anything, he added smoothly, 'Am I allowed to know *your* name?'

She was blushing again and angrily aware of it. Guiltily, she thought of her mother's horror if she could overhear this conversation with a strange young man. Nevertheless, throwing caution to the winds, she told him her name was Letty Mayfield.

'Letty?' He repeated it slowly and frowned. 'It is perhaps quite a common name in your country?' And then, noting her astonishment, he added hastily, 'Forgive me—I should not have asked such an impolite question.'

'My name is short for Letitia,' Letty said a little stiffly, 'and it is not as common as some. Have you never heard of it?'

Before he could answer, which he seemed in no hurry to do, the tea was ready, served in two tall glasses in metal holders, and there was no longer any excuse for lingering. With a slightly frosty smile and a formal bow, she turned and preceded the attendant down the corridor.

Nicholas Namorov looked after her thoughtfully, his eyes appreciating the slim figure and vivid colouring. There was something about her face which was vaguely familiar, and then there was her name, but even added together they meant very little and he dismissed them from his mind with a shrug.

'You've been a long time,' Mrs Kemp commented as Letty appeared.

'I came as soon as the tea was ready.' Letty glanced out of the window at a flat featureless plain with no sign of life. 'Do you know where we are?'

'Not precisely. Somewhere in Poland, I presume.' She tasted her tea, grimaced and then drank it thirstily.

'I was wondering if we were getting near the Russian border.'

Mrs Kemp consulted the small diamond-studded watch pinned to her ample bosom beneath her jacket. 'If the train is running to time we should reach there in about two hours. Unfortunately we shall then have to waste about four hours while the train is transferred to a different set of rails. For some unknown reason, the Russians use a broader gauge than other people—so tiresome of them, but unfortunately they have a great many strange ideas.'

Almost exactly two hours later, Letty climbed down the steep steps and stood for the first time on what she liked to think of as Russian soil, even though the earth was covered with paving. High above her head there was a huge domed roof of dirty glass, and all around men in loose blouses and baggy trousers tucked into high boots rushed about, shouting to each other in the most foreign-sounding language she had ever heard. Although it was daylight outside, the station was murky with evil-smelling smoke and great billowing clouds of steam which belched forth from behind the giant wheels of engines. Gas lamps flared in the gloom, doing little to lighten it, and the noise of many trains clattering over points was mingled with the panting of stationary engines and the varied human sounds all around.

Canon Mayfield would probably have likened it to the mouth of hell, but Letty experienced a sort of savage excitement caused by the noise and confusion. She was disgusted by it and at the same time stimulated.

Mrs Kemp, who had endured it many times before, felt quite differently. 'Dreadful place!' she exclaimed, holding a lace-edged handkerchief to her nose. 'Let us make our way to the restaurant and see what they have to offer. At least it will pass the time.'

'Shall we have a Russian engine now instead of a German one?' Letty asked as they threaded their way slowly along the crowded platform.

'My dear, I have not the faintest idea. It can be any nationality, for all I care, so long as it takes us safely to Petersburg.'

The restaurant seemed almost as large as the station, but at least it was clean and much more brightly lit. The white tablecloths were stiffly starched and the waitresses wore floor-length black dresses with spotless pleated aprons and white streamers fluttering from their caps as they hurried about under the eye of a major-domo with fierce moustaches. In spite of so much activity, the meal was a long time coming and by the time it arrived Letty was starving. She thoroughly enjoyed the strange red soup served with dark bread rolls covered with poppy seeds, and was not disposed to criticise the nameless meat with its tiny helping of vegetables.

They had now been in each other's company for more than forty-eight hours and conversation, which had flowed easily for most of the time, was beginning to drag a little. Glancing round the vast restaurant in search of inspiration, Letty thought she discerned a curling dark head in a far corner and, on an impulse, changed her mind about telling Mrs Kemp about her meeting with Count Namorov.

Before she was halfway through she had begun to regret it. Mrs Kemp's plump face was filled with dismay.

'I hardly think your dear mother would have approved,' she said severely when Letty had finished. 'A young girl alone cannot be too careful and it really was most unwise of you to encourage the young man.'

'I didn't encourage him,' Letty protested earnestly. 'I was only being polite. And I wasn't really alone because you were only a few yards away.'

'I'm afraid the Count would be more than likely to take politeness for encouragement. One must always be on one's guard with these dashing young aristocrats and this particular one belongs to a family with a bad reputation where women are concerned. So different from the Tsar and Tsarina, who set such an excellent example and have brought up their four daughters so very strictly. Such *sweet* girls.'

'Do you know them?' Letty asked with interest.

'Er—not personally. The Imperial family does not take much part in social life. It is said the Empress actively dislikes it.'

The topic lasted them for the remainder of the meal, and after that they did not have to wait long before resuming their seats in the train. Mrs Kemp went to sleep again almost immediately and Letty tried to make the time pass more quickly by thinking about her sister. There had been no time for a reply to the letter she had written before starting out, but she felt sure Marina must be as excited as she was at the prospect of a meeting.

It was at least five years since they had seen each other and the infrequent letters written in St Petersburg had not been very satisfactory. There had been plenty of news about the ballet—how she had been promoted to dancing a cygnet in *Swan Lake*, followed by good supporting roles in other ballets. The letter which announced that she had been chosen to dance *Coppelia* had been full of excitement and Letty now thought of it as the last 'normal' communication they had had from her.

None of the letters had contained any information whatsoever about Marina's private life.

The train pounded on through increasing darkness and Letty could now see nothing but her own reflection when she tried to look out of the window. An overwhelming sleepiness engulfed her and within a few seconds she had joined Mrs Kemp in peaceful slumber. For some time they were completely undisturbed.

Their awakening was sudden and violent. With a protesting shriek from the brakes and a loud grating sound, the long trans-continental train began to slow down, at a rate which flung the mostly dozing passengers from their seats and piled them up on the floor in a tangle of arms and legs.

Worse was to come. In the midst of the general turmoil a tremendous crash was followed by the noise of splintering wood and shattered glass, and the train finally came to a halt. But it was too late to save some of the coaches from disaster. Slowly, but with a terrible inevitability, they rolled over, their wheels spinning uselessly in the air, and came to rest on their sides, thus rendering even more horrific the frightful confusion inside.

The coach containing Mrs Kemp's and Letty's compartment was one of these, and to add to the terror the lights failed completely, plunging them into total choking darkness.

Letty could hear people screaming—one of them quite close. That must be Mrs Kemp. Although she was sick with fear she felt no desire to scream herself. It was much more important to try and control her dazed mind and find some way of getting out. Apart from a pain in her ankle—not serious—and something warm and sticky trickling down her face, she didn't seem to be hurt. And presumably Mrs Kemp was all right too or she would not be making such a noise.

She called her companion's name loudly and the screaming stopped. Two groping hands clutched one of hers, the rings pressing painfully into her flesh. A quavering voice reached her through the blackness.

'Letty! Thank God you are safe! What a dreadful thing to happen so near home——'

'Yes indeed—I think we must have run into something—perhaps another train.'

Letty stood up slowly and felt above her head for the door into the corridor which she guessed must be where the ceiling was before the accident. If only she could manage to slide it back and somehow climb up, she would at least be nearer the outside world instead of imprisoned in the horrible darkness full of splintered wood and dangerous fragments of glass.

In actual fact, she now realised as she stared upwards, it was not as dark as it had seemed. A small amount of light was filtering in from above and—even more encouraging—she could hear men's voices.

'Either some passengers have managed to get out,' she said cheerfully, 'or we are in a station. There are definitely people about outside.'

'There are a number of small stations near Petersburg.'

Suddenly Letty knew what she had to do. 'If I haul myself up by the luggage rack, I think I can reach the door. I'm going to try anyway.'

'Do be careful!' Mrs Kemp cried anxiously.

Letty was not listening: her mind was wrestling with an important decision which had to be made. If she removed her long skirt, the black silk underskirt and her white petticoat decorated with broderie anglaise and climbed up in her bloomers, she would find the ascent a great deal easier. But caution prevailed. She might not be able to put her garments on again before she was seen by some gentleman, and that would be unthinkable.

So, much encumbered by her skirts, she slowly and painfully hauled herself upwards, using the rack as a sort of ladder. Eventually she reached the door, discovering at the same time that the glass down below had come from its window. It required an enormous effort to slide it back but somehow she managed it. There was fresh air on her face and she gulped it in eagerly before struggling through into the corridor. Sitting on the wall of it, which was now the floor, she found herself looking straight up into the night sky, faintly sprinkled with stars.

If she stood up and carefully put her head through the space where the window had been, now framed in jagged glass, she would be able to see their surroundings. Slowly, with infinite care, she achieved this.

She had been right when she suggested they might be in a station. She could see it just ahead, a tiny place dimly lit by oil lamps. There were also a number of bobbing lights which puzzled her until she realised they were lanterns carried by the men she had heard shouting, but whether they were railwaymen, villagers or travellers she could not guess.

The engine lay on its side in a cloud of steam and at least four of the coaches behind it had also toppled over, but the back part of the train had remained upright. Serious as it was, it might have been much worse.

Letty was so absorbed in taking it all in that she did not notice that a solitary lantern had detached itself from the mêlée round the station and was swinging along towards her. Suddenly a voice spoke from below in English.

'Miss Letty Mayfield, I believe? You appear to be in a somewhat perilous position.'

Apart from Mrs Kemp, only one person on the train knew her name. With a leap of the heart, not entirely due to the relief of meeting another human being who could speak English, Letty recognised Count Nicholas Namorov. What a blessing she had refrained from removing her clothing! Although he could only see her head, she could never have stood there and conducted a conversation with him wearing only bloomers below the waist. It was bad enough that she had lost her hat and her hair was half falling down.

For a moment she was on the verge of hysterical laughter. Not that there was anything amusing in the present situation—except perhaps her own appearance, with her untidy head stuck out of a broken window—but there had to be some reaction to shock, and laughter was better than tears.

To steady herself she switched her thoughts to the other people on the train—those in the forward part. Many of them must have been hurt, perhaps killed. Her voice shaking a little, she asked the Count if he had any news of them.

'Judging by the noise they have been making, I think most of the passengers have survived without serious injuries. The driver has probably suffered more severely, and the fireman, too, but as they are still trapped in their cab no one yet knows their fate.' He paused, staring up at her, his face pale in the lantern-light. 'Are you enjoying the view from up there, Miss Mayfield?'

'Of course I am not! But it's better than being down in the compartment like poor Mrs Kemp.'

'Ah, Mrs Kemp. For a moment I had forgotten your companion. I trust she is not hurt?'

'I don't think so, but she could not possibly climb up as I have done. Oh, dear—however is she going to be got out?'

'The first necessity,' said the Count calmly, 'is a ladder.'

'I still don't see——'

'It will all be revealed to you in due course, and in the meantime, I'm afraid you will have to be patient.'

Mrs Kemp was calling from below and Letty withdrew her head to reassure her. When she looked out again the Count had vanished, but she felt confident he would return before long, having obtained a ladder from somewhere. If she could manage to open the heavy outer door, everything would be simpler. Trying the lock, she felt it move under her fingers and, miraculously, the door did not seem to have jammed, but to push it open upwards was a heavy task. Crouching in her confined space, desperately afraid of slipping back into the compartment from which she had so painfully climbed, Letty needed all her youthful strength. But at last she was rewarded with a moment of triumph when the door reached the halfway position and its own weight sent it crashing back against the carriage.

She was resting her trembling arms and trying to get her breath back when the Count returned. 'Capital!' he exclaimed. 'I never would have thought you had the strength. Now we will soon get you both out.'

Looking down, Letty saw he had not only obtained a ladder but had brought two men to carry it. He supervised the placing of it against the coach and then climbed nimbly up to join her.

'Allow me, Miss Mayfield,' he said courteously, holding out his arm. He might have been escorting her into dinner instead of helping her on to the top of a ladder leaning against a fallen train.

Letty ignored the outstretched arm. 'What about Mrs Kemp?' she demanded. 'How is she to be rescued?'

'I'm sure we can safely leave that to these two fellows——'

'I shan't move until you explain to me how it is to be accomplished.' She set her lips into a firm line and faced him courageously.

'It's really quite simple. Once you are safely on the ground, they will both climb the ladder and then draw it up after them. It will then be inserted into your compartment and one of them will go down to help the lady to ascend. After that the process will be reversed.'

'Oh,' she said in a small voice. 'I had not thought of that. As you said, it is quite simple.'

But halfway down the ladder she suddenly stopped and looked up at the Count. 'Our luggage—what is to become of it?'

'I have given the men instructions that all your possessions are to be brought up as well. Have you trunks in the van?'

'Yes—one each.'

'That, too, will be attended to,' he stated.

A moment later she stood beside him on the ground, and as they waited for Mrs Kemp to be got out—a process which took some time—all the elation at having escaped from that horrible prison abruptly left her. She ought to be making a little speech of thanks but instead of that she was suddenly overwhelmed by fear of the immediate future.

Where were they? She had no idea. How were they to reach St Petersburg—and when? It would probably not be until tomorrow, and that meant they would have to find somewhere to sleep. The difficulties loomed immense and her tired mind felt quite incapable of coping with them.

Mrs Kemp arrived at the top of the ladder in tears, and came down it with little shrieks of terror. But as soon as her neat buttoned boots felt solid ground beneath them she was herself again.

'It was so kind of you, Count, to organise our rescue,' she told him in her best society manner.

Not wishing to be thought discourteous, Letty added her own thanks and finished imperiously, 'Please thank the two men for us as well. They have done a great deal of hard work.'

He looked astonished. 'I assure you they will not expect any thanks, Miss Mayfield. They are workers from one of my family's estates and it is their duty to assist.'

'Then you know where we are?' Mrs Kemp exclaimed.

'Oh, yes. This whole district has been familiar to me since childhood.' With an expansive gesture he included the little station and all the dark countryside beyond it. 'We are at Liev, about twenty miles from Petersburg.'

'Oh, dear—I had hoped we might be nearer——'

'No doubt you are concerned about accommodation for the night,' he swept on smoothly. 'It is no problem, Mrs Kemp. It so happens that a member of my family— my great-grandmother, to be exact—lives nearby and I have already sent a message telling her to expect guests.'

Letty heard herself give an audible gasp, and Mrs Kemp burst out, 'Oh, but we could not possibly——'

'You have to sleep somewhere and you will be a great deal more comfortable at the house of my aged relative than in the station waiting-room, which is probably the only alternative.'

'But my husband——' Mrs Kemp was nearly in tears again. 'He will be meeting the train and when he hears about the accident he will be frantic with worry.'

But the Count had a solution even for that. 'You have only to write a message telling him you are safe and I will see it is sent by telegraph to St Petersburg.'

'A telegram? At this hour?'

'There is a small post office here.' His tone showed signs of impatience. 'The postmaster will not hesitate to open it at my request. Have you any other objections?'

'N-no.' She was suddenly a very tired and bewildered lady long past her first youth. 'I'm sure we are both very grateful.'

'And you, Miss Mayfield? The arrangements I have made meet with your approval?'

Letty was not at all sure that they did. She was grateful to him for the efficient way he had organised their rescue, but she resented the high-handed manner in which he had taken charge of them since. Besides, it scarcely seemed fair that they should turn their backs on the scene of horror at the station and go off to spend a comfortable night in some grand house. If she had been alone she would have refused outright and stayed to see if she could be of any assistance, but it was impossible to imagine Mrs Kemp helping the injured and it was only right that the older woman should be considered.

Consequently, she said mechanically, 'Oh, yes, of course, Count Namorov. It's very good of you to offer us hospitality.'

But as they threaded their way through the confusion, past labouring men and rows of casualties lying on the ground, Letty was conscious of one thing only—an intense longing for her own comfortable bed, far away in Ely. There she would be safe from experiences such as she had just endured; safe, too, from the dangerous attraction which she sensed Nicholas Namorov could turn on and off at will.

And then, as she waited for Mrs Kemp to write her telegram, her mood changed again. She had longed for adventure and would doubtless soon do so again if she were miraculously whisked back to her home. She should not complain because she had received more than she had bargained for!

# CHAPTER THREE

TWENTY minutes later they stood in the entrance hall of the great house of Liev. At least, Letty assumed it was great, although they had been able to see very little of it as they approached through the darkness. She would have expected numerous lighted windows, but at first there seemed to be no lights at all, and then, as they drew nearer, she discovered a few tiny glimmers suggesting that the place might be inhabited after all, which she had seriously begun to doubt.

The carriage—procured as mysteriously as the ladder had been—halted, and the Count ran ahead of them up some steps and pushed open a massive front door, shouting as he did so. Following him in, Letty saw a big lofty room with shadowy corners and a black and white tiled floor. A huge white porcelain stove painted with flowers gave out a welcome warmth, and ornate oil lamps—only two of which were lit—provided a reasonable amount of light. Happening to glance upwards, she was horrified to see that the ceiling was draped with cobwebs.

Before she had recovered from the shock, a tapping noise caught her attention and an aged crone, dressed in rusty black with a shawl over her head, hobbled in with a stick. Presumably the great-grandmother. She was attended by two wide-eyed country girls, their hair hidden by kerchiefs. They had broad faces with high cheekbones, and stared at the visitors in shy amazement.

The Count was shouting again, into the old lady's ear, and she said something to the two maids who promptly vanished. Now, surely, he would introduce them and explain their presence.

But he made no attempt to do so. Instead he put his hand into his pocket and pulled out a small battered object, its pretty feathers broken and bedraggled. 'Your hat, I believe, Miss Mayfield.'

Deeply ashamed, Letty took it from him and wondered what to do with it. She had not failed to notice the amusement in his eyes and knew he must be laughing at her beneath the veneer of courtesy. And indeed she must present a ludicrous figure, with her hair falling down in spite of her efforts to restrain it, and her clothes torn and dusty. Mrs Kemp, on the other hand, looked reasonably tidy and even had her hat still firmly in place. No doubt she was disgusted at finding herself in the company of such a disreputable creature; she certainly had a shocked expression on her face.

But Mrs Kemp's expression had a much kindlier base than disgust. 'My dear!' she exclaimed, 'You seem to have cut your head. There's blood all down one side of your face.'

That would just about complete the picture. Letty remembered the warm trickle she had felt long ago and groped for a handkerchief. 'It's nothing,' she said hastily. 'Just a scratch which is already drying up.'

'Nevertheless it should be attended to.'

'I will give instructions to the servants who will take you to your rooms,' the Count interposed as the two girls returned with wine and glasses, and a plate with a few stale-looking biscuits on it. 'But first, I'm sure you would like a little refreshment.'

It seemed a century since they had eaten at the border town and Letty was starving. She thought suddenly of the roast beef, Yorkshire pudding and crisp potatoes served every Sunday at home. How she would love a plateful now! Pushing the thought aside, she accepted a biscuit—which turned out to be as stale as it looked—

and a glass of wine. Perched on the edge of a stiff, uncomfortable chair, she sipped and nibbled delicately, and tried to ignore the black eyes of the old lady who stood leaning on her stick and observing their every movement. It was eerie, the way she just stared at them without saying anything. As an aristocrat she ought to be able to speak French, but perhaps she was so old she had forgotten it all.

The Count had swallowed his wine as though it had been water and was now holding out his glass to be refilled. As though he had read Letty's thought he said casually, 'Does either of you speak Russian?'

'I know a little, just sufficient to give orders to my own servants,' Mrs Kemp told him.

'That should suffice.' He accepted a fresh supply of wine without saying thank you, and continued. 'My great-grandmother, of course, speaks French but you are unlikely to see her. She is ninety-five and keeps strictly to her room.' He smiled. 'There is a joke in the family that she died years ago and no one noticed.'

Mrs Kemp's expression was showing plainly that she considered the remark in very poor taste and unworthy of a distant relative of the Tsar, but Letty's face made only too clear the blank astonishment she was feeling.

Once again the Count seemed to read her thoughts. 'Perhaps you imagined Katya to be my grandmother? Certainly she is nearly as old, but she is only the housekeeper, however formidable she may look.'

What a gift this man had for making her feel embarrassed! Hiding her mortification as best she could, Letty brushed aside the information and reverted to the previous conversation.

'Should we run into any kind of language difficulty, Count, I presume you will be here to assist if necessary?'

'I am afraid not.' He glanced at an elaborate gilt clock on a dusty side table. 'I am not accustomed to going to bed as early as this and I propose to take advantage of this unexpected opportunity to visit a—er—friend living on the estate. It may well be we shall sit late over a game of chess. Katya will see you are conducted upstairs and settled comfortably for the night, and all that remains for me to do is to wish you pleasant dreams.' With a quick bow he opened the front door and vanished.

'Extraordinary!' Mrs Kemp snorted. 'Never before have I stayed in a house with an invisible hostess and a host who removes himself elsewhere. It really is a most unusual situation.'

'A train crash is unusual in itself. As for the Count, perhaps he has a passion for chess.'

'My dear——' Mrs Kemp's tone was motherly '—you are too young and innocent to understand these matters, but in my opinion Nicholas Namorov has no more intention of playing chess than you or I. His passion is likely to take a very different form.' Clearly feeling she had said too much, she buttoned up her mouth and rose from her chair.

Letty stood up too and they both looked expectantly towards Katya, taking it for granted she would now give instructions regarding their rooms. But the old woman, with a look of scorn, only muttered something and then hobbled slowly out of the room. She was followed by one of the maids who almost immediately returned carrying two candles in tarnished silver holders. Both girls now took up positions at the foot of an ornately carved staircase and said something in Russian. Seeing that they had been understood, they ran lightly up the curving stairs and waited at the top.

Letty could have run up as quickly but she was obliged to remain behind Mrs Kemp's wearily plodding form. Nevertheless, she was the first to notice and exclaim at the sight which met their eyes when they reached the gallery. Neatly piled along the wall was a collection of luggage, including the two trunks. It had certainly not travelled with them in the carriage, so how had it got here?

'The whole district probably belongs to the Namorovs,' said Mrs Kemp, panting on the top step. 'No doubt the Count had only to lift his finger to get it transported here by some serf.'

'Serf? Doesn't that mean a sort of slave? I thought they had all been freed some time ago.'

'Oh, yes, they were, but I do not imagine it made much difference to the majority.'

They each searched for and found the two small Gladstone bags which contained their overnight necessities, and then turned expectantly towards the maids, hoping to be shown to their rooms. But the girls were arguing together, apparently unable to decide which rooms should be given to the guests. They flung open doors, it seemed at random, revealing furniture shrouded in dust-sheets which gleamed ghostlike in the candle-light, and huge four-poster beds with heavy old-fashioned hangings.

'I really cannot think why that old woman downstairs did not give them proper instructions,' fumed Mrs Kemp.

'Can you understand what they're saying?' Letty asked.

'Not very well. They speak so quickly and have a strange local accent——' She broke off as a newly opened door showed them a room that looked habitable, with the bed actually made up. 'I think they want me to take this one, dear. Almost certainly the bed will be damp but at the moment I am too tired to worry about it.' She moved thankfully towards the doorway. 'I do hope they will soon find one for you. Among so many bedrooms there surely must be another that is habitable.'

Letty hoped she was right. The girls were arguing again, one of them pointing towards a door which she thought had not yet been opened, though in the con-fusion she couldn't be sure. The second girl shook her head but eventually allowed herself to be overruled. The result, to Letty's relief, was the opening of the door to the disputed room.

Peeping in, she saw it was larger and grander than the one given to Mrs Kemp. The vast bed was draped in dusty crimson velvet, and huge pieces of furniture loomed in the dim light provided by one flickering candle. It almost looked like a state room and perhaps was kept for important guests.

Letty was too weary to care. She smiled at the maids, receiving beaming smiles in return and gestures which she interpreted as meaning they would bring her water for washing.

While they were gone she wandered round, curious in spite of her weariness and wrinkling her nose because of the musty smell. There were enormous cupboards and chests, and an immense washbasin, big enough to bath at least two good-sized babies. She came to the bed last and gazed at it in wonder. It was wide enough to accommodate three or four persons, and, as she touched one of the curtains to examine a crest high above, the cloud of dust made her sneeze.

Eventually the maids returned, one carrying a large but threadbare towel, and the other a copper jug with a small quantity of lukewarm water in it. With smiles and curtsys, they deposited their burdens on the washstand and withdrew.

Letty washed quickly, shivering a little for, although there was a stove nearly as big as the one downstairs, it was icy cold. When she had finished she inspected her face in a large gilt-framed mirror. But the glass was spotty and the candle flame made her familiar features look strange and ghostly. With a shudder she plunged into her long-sleeved, high-necked flannelette nightgown and approached the bed. It was definitely one for climbing on to rather than merely getting into, and she scrambled up with difficulty, impeded by her voluminous garment.

The mattress was a feather one, soft and warm, and she sank into it with a sigh of relief. The long hard day was ending at last. Tomorrow they would be able to resume their journey. Tomorrow she might see Marina.

She lay so deep among the feathers that her body made scarcely a curve, and as was her custom she had pulled the top covering over her head so that the vast bed appeared to have no occupant at all. For a moment her tired mind registered the muffled sound of a cantering horse and then she fell into a deep dreamless sleep.

Nicholas had found it impossible to awaken the groom, who was apparently lying in a drunken stupor, and had had to saddle his mount himself, which had annoyed him considerably. It now seemed possible he might not reach the dacha—a tiny cottage hidden in the woods—until after its occupant was in bed, and it was a relief to see a light shining through the trees as he approached the clearing.

'Nicholas!' A tall, slender girl with her hair in two long fair plaits left him in no doubt about her welcome. 'I thought you were in England attending to your mysterious business interests.'

'There is nothing mysterious about running a shipping company, but I did not come here to talk about such mundane matters——'

'You broke your journey at Liev specially to see me?'

He laughed wryly. 'Not exactly. The interruption was not of my choosing, delighted as I am to see you. Fetch me that bottle of fine brandy I left here and I will tell you of my adventures.' Supplied with a large glass of cognac, he gave her a brief account of the train crash, adding casually that he had brought two English passengers to spend the night at the big house.

'That was kind of you.'

Nicholas shrugged. 'I doubt if the old lady will be aware of the visit.' Across the top of his glass his eyes studied her face. 'You look tired. Are you not sleeping?'

She flung out her hands in a dramatic gesture. 'How can I sleep when there is so much to torment my mind? So many doubts and fears and prickings of conscience——'

'You have been here only a few days. Once everything is—arranged, you will feel more at ease.'

'I doubt it,' she said bitterly.

The warmth of the small room was combining with the brandy to make Nicholas feel sleepy, but in an effort to cheer her he stayed much longer than he had intended. It was past two o'clock when he allowed his horse to find its own way home.

This time Letty was so sound asleep that she heard nothing of the hoof beats. Nevertheless, she awoke suddenly a little later, her heart thudding with fear. The room was full of quivering light and for a moment she wondered if she had forgotten to put out the candle and it had somehow managed to set fire to something.

And then, before she had managed to force her sleep-weighted eyes wide open, the light was extinguished. Even more strange and terrifying, the bedclothes covering her stirred, there was a rustling sound and a twitching which quickly subsided into stillness. Silence again took possession of the room.

Except for the sound of human breathing.

Letty was so frightened that her own breathing almost stopped. Was the room haunted, and was that why the maids had not wanted her to sleep there? But surely ghosts did not need to breathe like people who were still alive?

Her own need for air was becoming urgent. She took a deep breath and discovered, imposed on the damp and musty atmosphere, the unmistakable smell of brandy.

Somehow it gave her courage. Sliding out of bed, she groped for the matches and relit her own candle.

Although she was more than half prepared for the sight which met her eyes, she had to repress a scream. A man lay stretched out on the far side of the bed, his dark head comfortably supported by the other end of her bolsterlike pillow, and his feet, still in boots, protruding from the bottom edge of the coverings.

They stared at each other, the girl in her long nightgown, her shining hair hanging to her waist, and the man almost speechless with astonishment.

Nicholas Namorov was the first to speak and it was impossible not to notice that his voice was slightly slurred. 'Miss Mayfield, I believe,' he said politely, and then with more force, 'What the devil are you doing here?'

Letty's heart was racing and her mouth felt dry. Her experience of gentlemen who had taken too much brandy was limited but she had been given to understand that they sometimes behaved very badly indeed towards ladies. In what way, she had no idea, and the mystery surrounding it made it all the more frightening.

Pulling herself together as far as possible, she said with as much dignity as she could manage, 'I was under the impression this was to be *my* bed for the night. I—I demand to know why you have invaded my privacy in such a despicable manner.'

She had spoken bravely but the candle in her hand shook alarmingly. Shadows chased each other across his face, at one moment leaving his eyes hidden in depths of blackness and the next revealing a twinkle in their grey depths.

How *dared* he find the situation funny!

Letty stamped her foot, but owing to the fact that her feet were bare, it went unnoticed. The Count still lay stretched out comfortably, with absolutely no sign of removing himself.

'If you have any decency, sir, I beg you will get up and go!' she exclaimed passionately.

'But I always sleep in this room when I come to Liev,' he said calmly. 'Those silly girls should not have assumed I would stay the night with my friend, and given it to you.' He raised himself slightly, leaning on his elbow. 'What we have to discuss is how the situation should be resolved. The obvious solution, of course, is to...er...leave matters as they are. The bed is enormous and I am fully dressed. I am also very tired and somewhat under the influence of some very good brandy, though not to any serious extent, I assure you. At the moment my only desire is for sleep.'

Letty could scarcely believe her ears. Colour flooded her face and seemed to spread over her whole body, right down to her toes. The effrontery of the man! Even she, in her sheltered and claustrophobic life, had learnt that it was terribly wicked for a man and woman to share the same bed unless they were married.

Before she could gather herself together sufficiently to answer him, he gave an enormous yawn. 'You have my solemn promise that you would be perfectly safe with me,' he murmured. One eye suddenly opened wider and again she saw that mischievous twinkle. 'In spite of your very fetching appearance in that delectable garment, Miss Mayfield.'

Letty was past being embarrassed. The hot colour faded and, in spite of the fact that her legs were shaking, was replaced by a frozen calm. 'Since you apparently have no intention of behaving like a gentleman,' she said icily, 'it appears that I shall have to be the one to move.'

'Not my fault,' he told her sleepily.

'You may not be to blame for the situation arising,' she conceded, hurriedly collecting an armful of clothes. Burdened also with the Gladstone bag, she somehow managed to pick up the candle as well. 'But it's most certainly your fault that I—a guest in your grandmother's house—am forced to flee in the middle of the night from the room allotted to me.'

Rather pleased with that exit speech, she opened the door and swept out. Closing it softly behind her, she stood irresolute, staring first left and then right along the dark silent corridor. Which was Mrs Kemp's room? She had already forgotten, but, in any case, she had no intention of imposing herself on her travelling companion.

With a hysterical giggle she wondered what Mrs Kemp would think if she knew the girl she was chaperoning was wandering about the house in her night-clothes looking for a bed. The whole incident would shock her beyond measure and she must certainly never hear of it.

Finding another bed was becoming urgent, for Letty was beginning to shiver with cold as well as tension. She began to wander aimlessly down the long corridor, trying to make up her mind which door to open first. The flame of her candle gave very little illumination and barely held the shadows at bay. And suddenly she realised that the house was not silent after all. There were little creakings and rustlings, the scamper of tiny feet behind the panelling, and once something ran over her bare foot, almost making her scream. Even the portraits which lined the walls between doors seemed to lean out from their frames menacingly as she passed, as though angry at this invasion by an alien girl of the stronghold of the Namorovs.

With a sob of sheer panic, Letty opened the next door she came to and peered fearfully into the room. The shrouded furniture was weird and ghostly, but the bed loomed up in the candle-light, a haven of refuge. It was not made up, but when Letty scrambled up on to it she discovered a rug beneath the dust-sheet. Rolling herself into a sort of cocoon, she soon felt warmer and slowly she began to relax.

But it was a long time before she fell asleep, and, even when she did manage it, she slept uneasily, troubled by crazy dreams which, when morning came, she was glad to find rapidly fading.

The heavy curtains at the window were undrawn, but the glass was covered by an elegant blind of cream ruched silk, through which daylight easily penetrated. Immeasurably thankful that the night was over, Letty jumped down from the high bed and went to look out, not at all surprised to discover that the silk was split and dusty. She saw at once that the trees through which they had driven last night were part of an immense forest stretching as far as she could see. Spring was not as advanced as in England and, in spite of the new green leaves, the general effect was gloomy and secretive.

She dressed quickly, longing for hot water and wondering whether some had been taken to the Count's room for her use. The maids would be surprised, but she felt sure he would be quite equal to the occasion.

It was a relief to find that her coat and skirt, attacked vigorously with the small clothes brush in her overnight bag, looked passable and the only real problem was the lack of a hat. Unthinkable that she should continue the journey without one! There were others in her hat-box, but none so suitable as the small toque. Peeping cautiously out into the corridor, she discovered it to be deserted and went quickly along to the pile of luggage.

She had just selected a pretty pale blue felt with a brim, trimmed with bunches of forget-me-nots, when she heard a door open. Fearful that it might be the Count, Letty spun round and was delighted to discover Mrs Kemp, who greeted her like a long lost daughter.

'How did you sleep, dear?' Luckily not waiting for a reply, she went rushing on to give an account of her own night which, she declared, had been most unrestful. 'What with the damp bedclothes and the cold musty room, and nothing to eat, I suppose it is a miracle that I slept at all,' she finished.

'Do you think we shall get any breakfast?' Letty asked as they went downstairs.

'I sincerely hope so, and even more important is to discover what arrangements—if any—have been made for conveying us and our luggage back to the station.' Staring disapprovingly round the empty hall—which looked a great deal worse in daylight than it had done the previous night—she continued, 'We don't even know if the Count returned after his game of—chess.'

Letty could have told her, but she had no intention of doing so. The appalling experience she had had last night was just a little more bearable if no one else knew about it.

With a purposeful air, Mrs Kemp marched across to an antique bell-pull and tugged it. To their mutual astonishment, it was answered almost immediately by one of the maids who beamed, curtsyed and said something in her strange tongue. Receiving an order, and apparently understanding it, she nodded vigorously and went off again.

'I have instructed her to bring breakfast,' Mrs Kemp announced. 'It is not, naturally, my custom to give orders in someone else's house, but, in this most peculiar situation, I feel it is excusable.'

'Yes, of course,' Letty agreed mechanically, a faraway look in the wide greenish eyes. Bacon and egg, sausages, kidneys, fried bread. Most of these had been available daily at home, and she had taken them for granted. At that moment she did not think she would ever do so again.

Ashamed of her mind's fixation on good English food—yesterday it had been roast beef—when she ought to be thinking about the coming meeting with Marina, she went to see if she could open the massive front door. It was neither locked nor bolted and swung inward in response to a good strong pull. Outside the sun was breaking through clouds and the world looked a great deal less gloomy than it had done from her bedroom window.

But it was not at the weather that Letty stared. At the bottom of the steps, the patient horse half-asleep, there waited the shabby old carriage in which they had arrived the previous evening.

'Well, at least that is one of our questions answered,' said Mrs Kemp, when she had relayed the information. 'Provided our luggage appears as miraculously as it did yesterday, we can set off for the station as soon as we are ready. It will not matter at all if the Count does not join us.'

They were both greatly cheered by the discovery, and even registered a stoical resignation rather than disappointment when their breakfast turned out to consist of black bread and tea. There was butter as well and some nameless jam, and they made the best of it. Halfway through, the sound of creaking wheels sent Letty again to the door and she reported jubilantly that she had seen a farm cart laden with their luggage going past, presumably on its way to the station.

Breakfast finished, Letty was frantic to get away. Although her companion commented acidly on the fact that there was no one to see them off, she was only too thankful. Very likely the Count had decided to stay on for a few days, she thought hopefully.

'Never have I been so glad to depart from anyone's house,' declared Mrs Kemp, settling herself in the carriage. 'Though I have to admit,' she added grudgingly, 'that the Count has been very efficient behind the scenes in organising both our rescue and our transport to and from his grandmother's residence. One must give credit where credit is due.'

'It was easy for him,' Letty burst out. 'He only had to give orders and other people did the work. I don't see we need be all that grateful.'

Mrs Kemp looked surprised at her vehemence, but all she said was, 'I'm very glad to note, dear, that you do not appear to have been bowled over by the young man's good looks and charm. A girl with your sheltered background might so easily have been deceived.'

Letty said nothing, but her thoughts were busy. Yesterday, she was obliged to admit, she had been just a little in danger of being taken in. But not any more. Not after last night.

## CHAPTER FOUR

IN THE bright light of a sunny morning they were shocked to see the devastation at the station. The huge engine lying on its side was a terrifying sight, and it seemed scarcely believable that so much power had been reduced to utter helplessness in a matter of seconds. The first and second coaches had been more severely damaged than their own and for a few minutes they were both silent as they realised the full extent of their good fortune.

The relief train sent out from St Petersburg was waiting a short distance up the line and the stranded passengers were making their way to it with difficulty, stepping from sleeper to sleeper if they were gentlemen and unimpeded by skirts, and slowly and painfully if they were ladies past their youth, like Mrs Kemp.

A railwayman was making signs to them to climb up the steps to a first-class compartment and the older lady began to labour up with much effort and panting. About to spring up behind her, Letty had her attention caught by the sound of galloping hoofs. A rider came into view, flung the reins to someone and began to stride along the track towards them.

Mrs Kemp was still struggling up the steep steps and giving her whole attention to the effort required. Letty yearned to speed up her ascent by giving her a push so that she herself could gain the shelter of the train before Nicholas Namorov reached them, but all she could do was to keep her head resolutely turned away from the approaching figure. Perhaps he would not see them at all in his hurry to board the train, or maybe he would merely say, 'Good morning' and pass on.

Neither happened. In fact it almost seemed as though the Count had hurried for the special purpose of accosting Letty.

'Miss Mayfield!' he called urgently. 'A word with you, if you please.' And then as she reluctantly looked down, he added more calmly, 'I will only detain you a moment.'

If only Letty could have controlled her blushes she would have been better able to face him. All she could hope for was that the brim of her hat would provide some protection.

'I can think of no possible reason for conversation between us, Count,' she said, the iciness of her tone contrasting violently with the warmth of her cheeks.

'I hardly think this brief exchange could be deemed a conversation,' he pointed out curtly. 'My only purpose is to tender you an apology for my behaviour last night. It was unpardonable and my sole excuse is the excellence of the brandy I had consumed.'

'To me that does not constitute an excuse at all,' Letty told him loftily.

'Nevertheless, I'm afraid it will have to suffice.'

His tone had changed and, in spite of her resolution not to look directly at him, Letty found herself studying him suspiciously. Was it possible that the steel-grey eyes actually harboured a *twinkle*? Could it really be that in the cold light of day and a state of sobriety, he found last night's episode *amusing*?

She wrenched her eyes from the handsome aristocratic face and dark curling hair. 'I'm sorry, Count,' she flung back at him. 'I find your apology quite unacceptable. My only hope is that we never meet again.'

With a swirl of skirts she turned and entered the coach, and behind her she heard quite distinctly a drawling voice saying casually, 'The new hat is charming, Miss Mayfield. I prefer it to the other one.'

Mrs Kemp looked at her curiously when she entered the compartment. 'You appear very flushed. Did I hear you talking to someone?'

'Oh—er—the Count arrived on horseback and paused to—to say good morning.'

'Did you thank him for his hospitality?'

'It never entered my head,' Letty told her frankly.

'You should have mentioned it, my dear.' Mrs Kemp suddenly revealed that she, too, could harbour a twinkle. 'But I must admit I am glad that you did not!' They both laughed, and the older woman went on, 'I wonder how long we shall have to wait for this train to start. I must confess I am becoming increasingly impatient to reach Petersburg and see my own house again.'

Strange she did not mention seeing her husband, Letty reflected, but perhaps that was taken for granted. Aloud she asked, 'What time do you think we shall get there if the train starts soon?'

'In plenty of time for lunch, I hope.'

At that moment the train gave a jolt and, with a great deal of creaking and rattling, began on its journey to the capital. It travelled very slowly and frequently stopped outside small stations, but with every mile that passed Letty felt her spirits rising. Gradually the nightmare of her experience at Liev receded into the background, and the immediate future to which she had so much looked forward began to dominate her thoughts.

'It's so kind of you to invite me to stay with you, Mrs Kemp,' she said earnestly, 'but I hope I shall not have to impose on you for very long. I think my sister has a small apartment and I'm sure she will want me to stay with her.'

'You *think* she has an apartment? But surely you have an address to which you send your letters?'

'Well, no, actually we don't have one. Marina had all her mail sent to the Mariensky Theatre because it will always find her there. She wouldn't want a letter from home to go astray because she had moved or—or something.'

Mrs Kemp made no comment, but Letty could see she still thought it rather unusual. She didn't know, of course, how very rarely Marina wrote home. She probably imagined letters flying backwards and forwards between Ely and St Petersburg every other week, instead of only once in three or four months. Marina could easily change her address and her family know nothing about it for some time.

Beyond the window the eternal birch trees, which had marched beside them all the way from Liev, were beginning to give way to patches of cultivated land with peasants working in the fields. Letty knew little about agriculture, but even she could see that the tools they were using looked as though they belonged in a museum. Before long there were rows of small houses with brightly painted gables and steep roofs. 'So that the snow slides off,' Mrs Kemp informed her.

For a moment Letty tried to imagine this strange foreign country under deep snow, with sleigh bells jingling and people all wrapped in furs. She would never see it like that, of course, and a good thing too. If she had had to bring all her warm clothes her luggage would have reached unmanageable proportions.

Suddenly she gave a little squeak of excitement. The cottage-type houses had given place to a fully built up area. There were rows of mean houses and great blocks of what looked like flats, all very dreary-looking and depressing, but every now and then the dark scene was brightened by gaudy onion-shaped domes—green, gold and sometimes wonderfully striped. This, surely, must be the beginning of the city she had travelled so far to reach and endured so much.

'The churches are very ornate here.' Mrs Kemp got up to adjust her hat—quite unnecessarily—in the mirror, but Letty continued to stare from the window, her nose almost pressed to the glass like a child. 'I understand the services are most peculiar with people wandering in and out and lighting candles, and the whole place reeking of incense. I don't know what your dear father would think of it all.'

Receiving no reply, she glanced out at the much larger houses they were now passing. 'We shall be stopping in a few minutes, dear. I do hope my husband is there with the motor.'

How wonderful it would be if Marina were there at the station to meet them! Knowing it to be impossible, Letty concentrated on assembling her hand luggage, and a moment later she stepped down on to the platform in time to see Mrs Kemp being chastely saluted on the cheek by a stout middle-aged man wearing the frock coat and striped trousers of a British businessman. He held his top hat in his hand as he turned to greet Letty and as she smiled at him she had to repress a start. With his neatly trimmed beard, aquiline nose and portly figure, he was the image of King Edward the Seventh, whom she had seen once.

'Welcome to Petersburg, Miss Mayfield,' he said cordially, his eyes between puffy lids taking note of her trim figure. 'It will be a great pleasure to have you staying with us.'

'It's very kind of you both,' she murmured, not much liking the stare of those pale blue eyes under bushy brows.

'Oh, Albert, we have had such a dreadful journey!' Mrs Kemp was on the verge of tears now that it was all over. 'I simply cannot tell you how glad I am to be here.'

'And I am glad to have you back, my dear,' he said smoothly, summoning a porter with a lordly gesture. 'We will set out for home the moment your luggage is collected together and put into the motor car.'

The operation took some time, with the chauffeur and two porters working hard. But, at last, they were off, gliding quietly out of the station yard. Letty had scarcely ever been in a car and certainly never in such an elegant limousine. She was torn between appreciating the experience to the full, and staring about her as they drove through St Petersburg.

Soon they came to a wide straight thoroughfare lined with shops, which seemed to stretch into the far distance where a slender golden spire stuck up into the sky like a finger. The pavements were crowded with people, most of them smartly dressed, though some wore the loose baggy clothing of peasants.

'Look, Letty,' Mrs Kemp cried, gesticulating with a plump hand. 'There is the English shop, where we buy our tea. You can get everything English there, even Pear's soap and bicycles and typewriters.'

'This is a very famous street,' Mr Kemp informed her. 'It is called the Nevski Prospect, but we shall not drive all the way down it today. Our house is in a quiet avenue just past St Isaac's Cathedral.' He patted her gloved hand in a fatherly way. 'I hope you will enjoy your stay in Petersburg, my dear. You may rely on my wife and I doing everything in our power to ensure a happy time for you. It will be delightful to have someone young in the house, do you not agree, Edith?'

'I don't think I can be entirely happy until I have seen my sister,' Letty said soberly. 'Though you are both most kind,' she added hastily.

'Ah, yes, well—we must arrange for you to visit her at the earliest possible moment. You have her address, I presume?'

Letty repeated the information she had given his wife. 'I shall have to make contact with her at the theatre,' she explained.

He frowned, his over-red lips pursing up dubiously beneath the dark moustache. 'That will be much more difficult for you, since you do not speak Russian. We must see what can be arranged.'

'Thank you.' Letty wondered whether to make it clear, here and now, that she was ready to tackle a whole theatre of Russian-speaking people if it meant she would at last meet her sister, but she decided it was more tactful not to show too much independence at this stage. 'Have you seen Marina dance, Mr Kemp?' she asked instead.

'Er—no, I am afraid not. My wife and I are not admirers of the ballet. We prefer musical comedy, which is so much livelier and has such splendid catchy tunes. There was an English company here with a charming piece called *The Merry Widow*.' He glanced at his wife— who had been more silent during the last ten minutes than Letty would have believed possible—and addressed her directly. 'A pity you missed it, Edith. You would have enjoyed it, I am sure.'

'I saw it in London.' Mrs Kemp leaned forward as they drove through the huge empty square where the Cathedral stood, and showed signs of excitement. 'We shall be there in a moment, Letty, and I don't think I have ever been so thankful.'

'You enjoyed your stay in England, surely?' her husband said.

'Yes, of course, but just now that is somewhat overshadowed by our experiences last night.'

'Ah, yes—the accident. It was certainly most regrettable, but you are both obviously quite unhurt and I presume you found somewhere to spend the night?'

'We were the guests of an aged relative of the Namorovs.' Ignoring his exclamation of astonishment, she looked across at Letty as the car swept ponderously round a corner and entered a tree-lined residential street. 'Here we are! That house over there with the wrought-iron gates.'

Letty was busy staring about her. She had never seen so many trees in a city before, and there were glimpses of water where the road crossed a pretty canal with a graceful bridge ornamented with dolphins. As the car paused while a servant ran to open the gates, she turned her attention to the house which was to be her home for—how long? She had no idea, but presumed it would only be for a few days.

She could not have been more wrong.

Untroubled by premonition, she gazed admiringly at the large porch supported by Corinthian pillars and the tall windows discreetly veiled with lace. It was more of a mansion than an ordinary house and she reflected that an English banker in St Petersburg must be extremely wealthy to afford it.

The chauffeur drew up noiselessly at the foot of some wide stone steps and sprang out to open the door. At the top of the steps the double front doors were opening too, as though by magic, though she caught a glimpse of white-gloved hands. When she looked into the wide hall she was for a moment reminded of Liev, for the floor was black and white marble, but there the resemblance ended. Here everything shone with polish, and instead of oil lamps there was gas, each separate outlet encased in an elaborate glass shade, and near the foot of the double staircase an intricate glass chandelier twinkled and glittered in a ray of sunlight penetrating from some window higher up the stairs.

In a bemused state, she followed a maid up to her room on the first floor. It was large, luxurious and prettily feminine, with a great deal of pink muslin trimmed with frills. A smiling maid brought her hot water which really was hot and she treated herself to a leisurely wash and a complete change of clothing, taking her time over it. When, much later, she ventured downstairs clad in a dark green cashmere dress ornamented with silver buttons all down the front, she felt completely restored.

There was no sign of her hostess, but Mr Kemp was sitting in a wing-back chair reading a several days old *Financial Times*. He greeted her with rather overdone pleasure and invited her to sit opposite him. Talking interestingly about St Petersburg, he kept her entertained until his wife came in and announced that luncheon would be ready in a moment.

As they sat at an oval table in the very English-looking dining-room, waited on by a man and two maids—one each, Letty reflected naughtily—she seized the first opportunity which occurred to bring up the subject which lay closest to her heart.

'I'm simply longing to see my sister. How far away from here is the theatre where the Imperial Ballet performs?'

Mr Kemp considered, beating an absent-minded tattoo on the white starched tablecloth with perfectly manicured fingers. 'Within walking distance for someone as young as you, but you could not possibly go alone, of course.'

'Out of the question,' his wife put in.

'Oh!' Letty was dismayed. 'I'm quite used to going out by myself,' she protested. 'I should feel most distressed if I had to trouble someone to come with me.'

'St Petersburg is very different from Ely,' said Mrs Kemp firmly. 'I am sure you were quite safe at home, but here you are in a foreign city and unable to speak the language, which might make things very difficult for you if—er—any sort of unpleasant incident should arise.'

'It would be a very great error on our part if we should allow such a charming young lady to wander about by herself,' Mr Kemp told her with an air of gallantry which did not suit him. He helped himself from a large dish of elaborately shaped ice-cream and began to spoon it up with obvious enjoyment.

Letty, who had been served first by the manservant, was finding it delicious, too, but it did not deflect her from her purpose. She was wondering what line to take in the argument without offending her kind hosts, when Mr Kemp began to speak again.

'You see, Miss Letty, there is a great deal of unrest in Russia just now, and particularly here, since this is the capital. The working classes are discontented and resent what they have the audacity to consider the unnecessarily autocratic rule of the Tsar, and consequently——'

'One cannot really blame them, Albert. Compared with the workers at home they are dreadfully downtrodden——'

He raised his bushy eyebrows and looked coldly at his wife. 'Dear me, Edith—I had no idea we were harbouring a revolutionary in our midst!'

'Of course I am not a revolutionary,' she said crossly, 'but I have lived in Petersburg long enough to know that there is room for improvement in the way this country is run.'

'You know absolutely nothing about these matters, my dear. I suggest that you leave discussion of them to *men*, who at least know what they are talking about.'

Horrified at the turn the conversation had taken, Letty kept her eyes on her plate. What would the suffragettes think of Mr Kemp with his old-fashioned ideas about women? It seemed to have completely escaped his notice that times were changing.

She had not taken to him from the first moment, though she had to admit he had kept her interested before lunch when he was talking chiefly about the history of the city, and how Peter the Great had created it out of a muddy swamp. It had made her feel she wanted to explore every bit of it and not merely confine her outdoor activities to a saunter along the Nevski Prospect. And even that they probably wouldn't let her undertake alone, she thought despairingly.

Mrs Kemp did not seem to be particularly put out by the ticking off she had received. Perhaps she was used to it? She was looking quite composed and now pointed out calmly that they were getting away from the subject under discussion. 'Have you any suggestions to make regarding Letty's visit to the theatre?' she enquired, looking at her husband.

'Not merely a suggestion, but a solution. I have on my staff at the bank a most able and responsible young man named Gerald Sheldon, who is a fluent Russian speaker. I propose to lend him to you for the afternoon, Miss Letty, to act as escort and overcome any language difficulties.'

'Oh, thank you, Mr Kemp—that is really kind!' Her heart warmed towards him, though she would still have liked to go by herself. 'What time shall I be ready?'

He pulled out the gold watch from his waistcoat pocket and pressed the catch which opened the cover. 'It is now nearly two o'clock. I should think arrangements can be made for Sheldon to call for you about three. Will that suit you?'

'Very well indeed,' she said joyously.

But the wait seemed interminable and she was ready long before her escort arrived. Wearing a light fawn coat over her dress and a straw hat to match, she sat tautly in a small room opening off the hall which Mrs Kemp referred to as the morning-room. Her hostess and her husband had settled themselves comfortably in the drawing-room, apparently intending to take an after-lunch nap since he had tucked a white silk handkerchief into the front of his stiff collar so that the starched edge would not cut into his neck. Glad to be relieved of their company in her present state of tension, Letty resisted the temptation to walk up and down and tried to control her impatience by clasping her gloved hands tightly together.

Gerald Sheldon had been summoned from the bank by telephone, a procedure which Letty still found magical, even though her aunt in London had one. Mr Kemp had told her it was worked by batteries, which left her very little wiser though she knew that the front door-bell at home was operated in the same mysterious way.

The shrilling of an electric bell cut sharply into her thoughts and she leapt to her feet. Peeping into the hall, she saw a young man as correctly dressed as his employer except that he wore on his head a tall hat of astrakhan which had a very Russian look. As soon as he saw Letty he swept it from his head, revealing thick brown hair. His eyes were brown too, she noticed as he greeted her and introduced himself, and his skin had a healthy outdoor colour, unusual in a city worker.

'It is very kind of you to take me to see my sister,' Letty said politely as they left the house and began to walk along the leafy avenue.

'Not at all.' His tone was equally correct. 'You would find it difficult to get past the stage door-keeper without being able to speak Russian.'

'I should like to learn some, but I don't suppose I shall be here long enough. Is it very difficult?'

'Not once you have mastered the Cyrillic alphabet.'

The subject lasted them for a few more minutes and then silence fell. As they reached the Nevski Prospect and turned into it, they both began to speak simultaneously and both halted with a laugh. Somehow it seemed to break the ice and they began to talk more naturally.

'It was most unfortunate that you were involved in that train crash,' Gerald said sympathetically. 'It must have been a very alarming experience.'

'Yes, it was, but we were very lucky really. Although the coach toppled over we only got a few bruises and an odd scratch or two. Some people must have been much more seriously hurt than that.'

'How in the world did you get out?' he exclaimed, looking down at her with his brown eyes alight with interest.

Letty hesitated, reluctant to mention the man she had hoped to pluck right out of her memory—and now here she was, after only a few hours in St Petersburg, being forced to think about him again.

'Oh—er—someone came with a ladder,' she explained, optimistically expecting that would suffice.

Mr Sheldon was apparently a practical man. He immediately exclaimed, 'Ladders are not usually left lying about for anyone to find, particularly at very small country stations. Did you have a very long wait?'

'N-no. The man came quite quickly. I expect we were just fortunate.'

It seemed that he could not leave the subject alone for he went on to ask her if they had had to spend the night at the station. And this time Letty's ingenuity was unequal to the challenge.

'Count Nicholas Namorov was on the train,' she admitted reluctantly, 'and Mrs Kemp knew him slightly. He invited us to sleep at the house of his great-grandmother, which was not very far away.'

'Really?' She had plainly astonished him. 'The Namorovs are a very old Russian family,' he went on, 'and they own a lot of land around Petersburg and down on the Crimea. They used to be tremendously wealthy but I don't think they've got quite so much money now.'

'You seem to know a lot about them. Are they customers of the bank?'

'Yes, and Mr Kemp would not approve of my talking about them, but I have only told you what is known to everybody.'

'Yes, I suppose so.' She paused and then, perversely, felt a strange urge to go on discussing the subject she had most wished to avoid. 'Are the Namorovs a big family?'

'If you mean the present generation, there are two sons and two daughters and they have, of course, dozens of cousins. Nicholas is the eldest and the other son about three years younger. Paul is his name, I think. I don't know much about the daughters, but the males of the family are generally considered rather wild. Not that there's anything unusual in that. The same could be said of most of the Tsar's relatives. So different from the royal family.'

Letty had heard all about them from Mrs Kemp. How beautifully brought up the four Grand Duchesses were, and how sad it was that the little boy who was the heir had such poor health. Not wishing for a repetition, she changed the subject.

'Are we nearly there, Mr Sheldon? Mr Kemp told me it's not far to the Mariensky Theatre.'

'No distance at all. It's just round the next corner.'

Letty's heartbeats quickened as her excitement mounted. The moment to which all her energy had been directed for the last three weeks was almost upon her. She had looked forward to it so much that now she was terrified something would go wrong. Marina might not be at the theatre. It was possible that she had practised all the morning and was now at home resting before the evening performance.

But if that were the case, surely the theatre would have her address?

It was ridiculous to torment herself with what *might* happen. Marina would have had her letter, she reminded herself, and—if she was not there in person—would have left a message for her.

'There it is,' said Gerald, pointing ahead.

Letty saw a massive brick building with huge posters advertising the programme for tonight—she assumed—and giving the names of the dancers. But owing to her inability to read the Cyrillic alphabet she could not even tell if Marina Varaskaya was among them.

'Allow me.' Her escort was making his way round to a side door and she followed him nervously.

Their way was immediately barred by a burly doorman, just as she had been warned. He began to argue furiously, apparently in a tremendous rage, and Gerald answered him back with equal vigour. For a moment there was stalemate, and then something was slipped into a willing hand, and the situation changed completely. The man retreated into his own little sanctum and Gerald turned round with a smile.

'This way, Miss Mayfield.'

Once more she followed him, this time along a narrow dingy corridor and then up a flight of uncarpeted stairs. As they mounted higher the sound of a piano being thumped with very marked rhythm came to their ears. There was a strange smell compounded of many different odours, but mostly greasepaint and gas.

And then, suddenly it seemed, they were looking into a large room lined with mirrors and practice bars, dazzlingly lit after the darkness of the stairs. Ballet dancers of both sexes were exercising in corners and, in the middle of the room, a man and a girl performed intricate steps in front of a small group of dancers. They were all very strangely dressed and, though Letty had seen ballet in London, she found this close-up sight of the male figure embarrassing.

But there was no time to worry about that, because a bearded man who seemed to be directing them was glaring at the intruders as though he would like to have them thrown out bodily. Luckily the pianist was pounding on and the choreographer turned back to the dancers, apparently deciding to ignore them.

Relieved, Letty began to look around for Marina. She saw a girl in a far corner being tossed up into the air by a tall young man as though she had weighed no more than thistledown, and for a moment she looked very like Marina. There was the same fair hair—unusual in a ballerina—neatly folded round her head, the long neck and flat figure, the slim but powerful legs. But it was not her sister—the face was quite different.

Mr Sheldon was talking to a man wearing ordinary clothes who had appeared from nowhere, and he now turned to Letty.

'This fellow says Marina Varaskaya is not here just now, Miss Mayfield. However, he tells me there is a letter in the office and he is going off to get it.'

Letty could have cried with disappointment, in spite of having told herself this might happen, but she hung on to her self-control. Marina had left a letter for her and no doubt that would give an address where she could be contacted. It was frustrating and she wasn't at all sure whether she ought to impose on Mr Sheldon's time any longer, but that could be sorted out when she knew a little more.

The man came back very quickly, but at the sight of the letter he was holding out triumphantly Letty felt as though an icy hand had clutched at her heart.

It was her own letter, the one she had written in faraway Ely, announcing her coming visit. It had reached the theatre safely but, for some reason beyond her comprehension, had never been delivered to the intended recipient. *Why?*

## CHAPTER FIVE

FOR a moment Letty felt sick with shock. The nondescript face of the man who had brought the letter swam before her eyes, and if she had seen him again the next day she would not have recognised him.

'I don't understand!' Her cry of anguish rang through the big rehearsal room and all the dancers stared at her. One by one they stopped what they were doing, even those in the centre under the eye of the choreographer, and came crowding round. He flung up his hands and shouted at them in French and Russian but they took no notice.

Letty turned impetuously to the nearest one, the girl who had reminded her of her sister, and addressed her in French. 'Please, can you help me? I am Marina Varaskaya's sister, and I wrote this letter in answer to one I had about three weeks ago asking me to visit her. Why has she not received it?'

The girl's lashes instantly dropped to veil her eyes. She said primly, 'I regret, *mademoiselle*, I am unable to be of assistance. We do not know where Marina Varaskaya is.'

'But surely *somebody* must know?'

The only answer was a shrug and the girl melted away into the crowd. Her place close to Letty was taken by a tall male dancer with black hair hanging over his forehead and a wide, passionate mouth.

'I am Yuri Ivanovitch, *Mademoiselle*. Even I, who am her friend, do not know Marina's whereabouts. One day she is here practising with the utmost dedication because she is to dance Odile/Odette in *Swan Lake*, and then she is gone.'

Gerald Sheldon now entered the conversation, speaking rather laboured French. 'She must have lived somewhere. Surely the theatre has her address?'

'But naturally! It is the first place where we have looked for her but the apartment is empty and the landlady says the tenancy was abruptly terminated.'

'Her clothes and other possessions—have they also disappeared?'

He flung out his hands in a dramatic gesture. 'All—all are gone. It is a great mystery.'

Despairingly, Letty looked round at the circle of faces, beautiful girls, all remarkably alike, and willowy yet powerful young men. They stared back at her, their faces strangely expressionless. Were they deliberately hiding something? Did they know more than they intended to admit?

The choreographer was shouting at them again and almost stamping in rage. Suddenly obedient, they abandoned Letty and flung themselves back into their work. Close to tears, she was about to turn away when she became aware that Yuri Ivanovitch still lingered.

*'Mademoiselle,'* he spoke in a half-whisper, his voice urgent, 'give me your address. It may be that I shall one day have news.'

For the first time Letty realised she didn't know either the name of the avenue or the number of the house. As she hesitated, Gerald quickly came to her rescue. He said something in Russian and Yuri repeated it after him; then he, too, melted away.

There seemed no point in lingering any longer, nevertheless Letty was reluctant to leave. Here, at least, in this alien world she had a link with Marina, even though an invisible barrier seemed to have been erected across it. When she returned to the world outside the Mariensky Theatre she would have nothing, for at that moment of total despair she could not believe she would ever hear any more from the male dancer who said he was Marina's friend.

They did not speak as they went down the dark stairs and out into the bright sunlight. So great was Letty's distress that it hardly seemed possible that life outside the theatre was continuing just the same as when they left it. Horse-drawn trams were still rattling down the Nevski Prospect, and open carriages and cabs, which the Russians called droshkys, were weaving their way in and out of the traffic together with the occasional motor car. Well-dressed ladies were staring into the Fabergé shop where beautiful gold and silver articles and marvellously decorated eggs were displayed. At any other time Letty would have liked to join them, but at the moment she felt far too depressed.

'Cheer up, Miss Mayfield,' Gerald encouraged her. 'Marina Varaskaya is well-known in Petersburg. I don't think——' He broke off in astonishment as a tall young man suddenly appeared in front of them and swept off his hat, revealing dark waving hair.

Nicholas Namorov bowed as elegantly before Letty as if she had been a grand duchess. 'Miss Mayfield! This is indeed an unexpected pleasure.'

In actual fact, although his first glimpse of her that afternoon had been completely unexpected, the present meeting had been carefully planned. He had been extremely surprised—and also somewhat perturbed—to see her vanishing into the stage door of the Mariensky Theatre. He had therefore positioned himself in a suitable spot for accosting her and had spent ten whole minutes impatiently waiting for her to reappear. He had felt like a shop assistant waiting for his young lady and had not cared for it at all.

Somehow Letty managed to pull herself together. 'Good afternoon, Count,' she said coldly. 'If you will excuse me, I——'

'Forgive me, Miss Mayfield, but you look somewhat pale. Are you feeling unwell?' He studied her face with extraordinary intentness.

She wanted to shout back at him, Of course I'm looking pale—I've just had a terrible shock. Instead, she cast an anguished glance at Gerald, but he was standing stolidly in the background and making no attempt to intervene. Before she could think how to answer, the Count went on speaking.

'Have you a carriage waiting in the vicinity?' he enquired.

'Certainly not! We walked here from Mr Kemp's house. It is no great distance.'

'Nevertheless, I do not think you are feeling fit enough to return on foot. I will summon a droshky and see you safely back to where you are staying.'

Letty's pale cheeks were suffused with colour at the effrontery of it. 'I assure you, Count, that it is quite unnecessary——'

'You must permit me to be the judge of that,' he said calmly. 'I have two sisters and am familiar with the fragility of ladies, and I am quite sure it would be better for you to drive back.' He made a lordly gesture and a droshky appeared beside them. 'If you will be kind enough to give me your address——'

Letty had a terrible feeling of being trapped. Why in the world did Gerald make no attempt to rescue her from this impossible situation?

'I don't know my address,' she snapped. 'I have not yet had time to learn it.'

The Count appeared to notice her escort for the first time. 'Perhaps you could supply it?'

Gerald hesitated, glanced at her dubiously and then, to her fury, gave the required information. She looked round wildly, trying to think of some means of escape without creating a scene, but her ingenuity was unequal to the task. With a horrible sensation of helplessness, she found herself being handed ceremoniously into the droshky.

'It is a beautiful afternoon for shopping,' Nicholas observed, seating himself beside her. 'How did you find our Petersburg shops? Some of them are considered very good.'

'I—I have not been shopping.'

'Indeed?' He raised his eyebrows. 'Then what have you been doing to make yourself so exhausted?'

Her eyes flashed at the impertinence of the question. 'I really don't know what right you imagine you have to quiz me like this. How I spend my time is no concern of yours whatsoever.'

To her surprise he made no reply. If she could have read his thoughts she would have been still more astonished. Her visit to the Mariensky Theatre appeared to him now to have been the sole reason for the afternoon's expedition and he could only regard it with the deepest foreboding.

The short drive was over. Hoping desperately that Mrs Kemp was not looking out of the window—most unlikely—Letty said an extremely curt, 'Thank you', and hurried indoors. She found her hostess in the drawing-room and poured out the story of Marina's disappearance.

'Your sister writes to you saying she would like to see you,' Mrs Kemp exclaimed, 'and then vanishes! It really is an amazing thing to happen.'

It did not seem to occur to her that there might be a sinister explanation and for that Letty was grateful. The idea was only just beginning to nibble at the corners of her mind and she did not want it encouraged.

Later that endless day she had to go through the whole thing again when Mr Kemp returned from the bank. She could see he was astonished and perturbed, though he pretended to make light of Marina's disappearance.

'I am sure there is a good explanation for your sister's strange behaviour, or one that seems good to her. People with the artistic temperament can't be judged in the same way as sensible folks like you and me, Miss Letty. And you must remember that, not having received your letter, she had no knowledge of your intended visit——'

'She begged me to come.'

He raised a podgy hand adorned with a ruby-studded signet ring. 'Allow me to finish. Personally I have no doubt the letter was written while suffering from an attack of homesickness, and soon forgotten. You should not worry your pretty head too much about it.'

Letty closed her mouth firmly and said no more, but on her way upstairs at bedtime she chanced to overhear a comment which Mr Kemp intended only for his wife's ear.

'To my mind it's perfectly obvious the girl has run off with a lover. I do not suppose the moral standards of ballerinas are any higher than those of chorus girls on the musical comedy stage.'

'I hardly think we can suggest that to her sister,' Mrs Kemp demurred.

'No, no, Edith, of course not. All we can do is try to give Letty as good a time here as possible, so that she does not dwell too much on her disappointment.'

Letty boiled with indignation as she continued on her way upstairs. Ballerinas were *not* like chorus girls, or Marina would never have been allowed to take up the profession, and she would certainly not desert her career for the sake of an illicit love affair. Or would she?

Letty knew so little about her sister's inner thoughts. Her letters home had been scrappy and filled with ballet news. There had been practically nothing about her private life and never any suggestion of a love affair. And yet that might mean absolutely nothing, for Marina wouldn't dream of mentioning anything of the sort when writing to her parents.

Worn out with emotional strain, Letty undressed quickly and slipped between the cool linen sheets. How different this bed was from the one she had occupied last night! *Was* it only last night? It seemed a hundred years ago. For a moment the arrogant, amused face of Nicholas Namorov floated before her eyes and she experienced a recurrence of the intense dislike she had felt for him when he'd invaded her room. It faded quickly, for she was too tired for emotion of any sort, and in any case she would probably never see the hateful man again, so there was no point in letting herself get worked up about him.

She saw him the very next day.

Greatly refreshed after a good night's sleep, Letty was feeling much more inclined towards optimism when she went downstairs in the morning. Mr Kemp had already left for the bank, but his wife was still at the breakfast table and she seemed greatly relieved to find her guest in a more cheerful frame of mind.

'I suggest we take a drive this morning, Letty, since the weather is favourable. It will give me great pleasure to show you St Petersburg.'

'I shall enjoy that very much,' Letty said politely, and with more sincerity than she would have thought possible yesterday.

'My husband is using the motor,' Mrs Kemp went on, 'but the carriage is available for my use and in some ways I prefer it. I think it is warm enough today to have the hood down, and certainly we shall see more that way.'

As they sat side by side in the comfortable vehicle, Letty's spirits rose still further. She was wearing her newest hat, a pretty natural-coloured straw with a bunch of velvet pansies in the front, the sun was shining, and all around she saw magnificent houses, huge churches and other important-looking buildings, all coloured in delicate shades of green, pink and cream.

'Many of them are eighteenth-century,' Mrs Kemp told her, 'and still appear as designed by the Italian architect. They are quite a feature of Petersburg.' She paused to pull up the fur rug as a cool breeze met them. 'I have told Fyodor to drive us down to the river. There is much of interest to see along the Neva.'

In the distance, the golden spire of the Admiralty, which she remembered seeing yesterday, gleamed against the sky. As they neared the waterfront an immense palace came into view, stretching almost as far as Letty could see, and with a vast courtyard in front of it, guarded by tall iron gates.

'The Tsar's Winter Palace,' said Mrs Kemp. 'Not that he ever uses it, except for a few state occasions. He and his family live out at Tsarkoe Selo, a few miles away, which they much prefer. It is said there are a thousand rooms in this palace and a hundred staircases. I do not know if it is true.'

'It certainly looks big enough,' Letty commented. 'Have you ever been inside?'

'Once, to some function or other. It is incredibly magnificent and the grand staircase is the most ornate I ever remember seeing anywhere.'

They had reached the River Neva and the carriage was halted to allow Letty to admire the view. Opposite there were several small islands, reached by graceful bridges, and the water in between sparkled in the sunshine, causing Letty to screw up her eyes.

'It seems unbelievable that only a few weeks ago men had to be employed to break up the ice.' Mrs Kemp paused to put up her parasol. 'The seasons change quickly in Russia, going from one extreme to the other. In no time at all it will be too hot for comfort, and the sun will scarcely set at all.'

'It seems to be a country of extremes,' Letty ventured. 'Rich and poor, aristocrat and peasant——' She broke off as the sound of church bells playing a solemn tune drifted across the water. 'What is that?'

'It comes from the Cathedral of St Peter and St Paul, over on one of the islands. It contains the tombs of the Tsars. On the same island there is a dreadful political prison where people who have offended the Tsar get shut up and are forbidden to speak.'

'He sounds an absolute monster.'

'I would not describe him as that.' Mrs Kemp lowered her voice even though they were speaking English. 'It is probably the system which is at fault rather than the man. The present Tsar has many virtues, but they are more those of a family man rather than a ruler, or so my husband tells me.'

Letty would have liked to ask more questions, but the carriage was moving on now and there was so much to claim her attention. The perfectly matched chestnut horses paced slowly along the riverside, allowing plenty of time for staring about, and eventually coming to another halt near an enclosed patch of grass which contained the huge bronze statue of a man on a leaping horse.

'That is the man who was responsible for all this.' Mrs Kemp waved her hand vaguely towards the city. 'Peter the Great himself. But don't ask me anything about him, dear, because I know very little—except that he was not at all a nice man in spite of being so clever.'

Letty sat looking at the statue and thought how wonderfully the sculptor had captured the feeling of power. For a moment she was oblivious of her surroundings as she reflected on the brilliance of the engineering project which had created this wonderful city on the muddy delta of the Neva. And in the eighteenth century too!

She was recalled to her surroundings by the realisation that a carriage coming towards them had been obliged to stop quite close while an area of confusion was sorted out by the coachmen involved, there being a great deal of traffic about at the time. Automatically Letty abandoned her study of Peter the Great and glanced sideways at the vehicle halted beside them.

She found herself looking straight into the smiling eyes of Nicholas Namorov.

He swept off his hat and bowed. 'Miss Letty Mayfield, I do declare! I hope you are quite recovered from your shocking weariness? You certainly look in splendid form today.'

He was on her side of the carriage and scarcely more than three or four yards separated them. Opposite him two extremely attractive girls, very smartly dressed, were staring at her in not unfriendly astonishment, as if wondering how their escort could possibly be acquainted with her.

Letty could feel the hot colour dyeing her cheeks as she bowed her head in acknowledgement of his greeting. She said frigidly, 'I am quite recovered, thank you, Count.'

On the other side of her Mrs Kemp now became aware of his presence and leaned forward to bow. Sitting with his hat in his hand, his dark hair gleaming silkily in the sunshine, the Count returned her greeting with great correctness. At that moment his carriage moved forward and the incident was over. It was like a casual meeting between acquaintances driving in Hyde Park.

'How extraordinary that we should meet him,' Letty exclaimed, adding in her own mind, 'of all people!'

'Not so very. One is always meeting people in St Petersburg——' Mrs Kemp broke off to order their coachman to drive on also. 'I expect the Count was escorting his two sisters somewhere. We are quite likely to meet them all again in a few days' time, for my husband was telling me we are invited to an evening function at the Grand Duchess Anna's house.'

'But surely I'm not included?' Letty asked.

'Oh, yes, indeed you are, my dear. That is, anyone who happened to be staying with us would automatically be included.' She paused and then added delicately, 'I'm afraid I omitted to tell you to bring a ballgown with you, so it is my fault if you have nothing suitable and I shall certainly make it my business to remedy the matter. We have excellent shops in——'

'It's very kind of you.' Unconsciously Letty lifted her head proudly. 'But as it happens I brought a suitable dress with me, just in case it was needed.'

Her mother had insisted on it, she remembered, and sent a tiny message of gratitude winging across the two thousand miles of land and sea which separated her from Ely. They had gone to Cambridge for it, an expedition which Letty had found exciting and Charlotte totally exhausting. She had even had to be revived with smelling salts in the shop, but her health had not prevented her from looking at the various gowns with a Frenchwoman's eye and unerringly choosing the one most becoming.

'Will it be a very splendid party?' Letty asked. 'A grand duchess is a sort of princess, isn't she?'

'Much the same, but I never think it sounds quite so important. The Grand Duchess Anna is a cousin of the Tsar and a somewhat eccentric lady. Her house is magnificent, but the servants are not as well-trained as, in my opinion, they should be. Not that they are in the least like those two maids at Liev,' she added hastily. 'It would be difficult to find any servants less well-trained than they were.'

What would she think if she knew the whole story? Letty repressed a wry smile and marvelled to find herself capable of finding humour in such a situation. She would certainly not have done so yesterday! Puzzling over the change, she decided that her experience at Liev had been overshadowed by the distress caused by Marina's disappearance. She would never forgive the Count for the light-hearted way he had viewed the matter, but his attitude no longer seemed quite so monstrous. Even the thought that she might meet him again at the party, though certainly not welcome, was not unbearable.

In other words, Letty summed up triumphantly, Count Nicholas Namorov had become quite unimportant.

It was therefore rather surprising that, staring at herself in the mirror on the evening of the party, she should experience a sudden hope that the Count might find her appearance pleasing. Eventually she decided it was because she—an English girl from a prim and most unfashionable little town—did not wish to feel herself in any way inferior to the grand Russian ladies among whom she was about to be plunged. She was using the Count as a sort of barometer and if *he* thought she looked nice, then she would at least pass muster among the other guests.

It was an elaborate and somewhat laboured explanation, but it satisfied Letty, and she gave one last critical glance at herself before easing on her long white gloves. The stiff taffeta—in a delicate shade of pale green, which her mother called eau de Nil—had a swathed bodice embroidered in a rose design with tiny seed pearls. It was very tight at the waist, making her look even more slender than she really was, and swirled out below her hips into a very full skirt with a tiny train. The pearl roses were repeated all over it, giving a shimmering effect which was misleadingly ethereal. Excitement, combined with nervousness, had made her look pale and she would have liked to borrow a little of her mother's rouge, so frowned upon in Ely.

It was time to go downstairs. Letty tied a white silk scarf loosely over her bright hair and picked up her cloak. Mr Kemp was in the hall, exuding an air of impatience which vanished when he saw her. His white bow-tie, white waistcoat and smart tail coat did nothing to improve his portly appearance, but he looked exceedingly prosperous. His wife, who had followed Letty to the hall, was in maroon brocade, with an elegant black feather fan and a great deal of jewellery. For a moment Letty's confidence wavered. She had no real jewellery at all, only a plain gold chain round her neck with a heart-shaped locket containing miniatures of her parents. They would all think she looked indecently bare.

But her hosts' obviously sincere admiration and pleasure in her youthful good looks did much to restore her, though she had another attack of nerves when the limousine joined the queue of cars and carriages waiting to deposit their occupants outside the large house where the party was to be held. So many people, and all strangers. Would she have to spend the entire evening under Mrs Kemp's motherly wing, with no one else to talk to and no fun at all?

Having left their cloaks in a huge downstairs room sparkling with mirrors, and with nearly as many maids as there were guests, they joined another queue to mount the grand staircase. As she went slowly up, Letty allowed her fascinated eyes to wander over the glittering scene. In the hall below there was a marble floor, marble-topped tables and colonnades round the walls as though it had been a temple. Above her head chandeliers twinkled with light and, higher still, she gazed in awe at a magnificent painted ceiling glowing with colour.

They were being announced in French by an imposing person in white satin knee breeches and a powdered wig.

'Madame Kemp, Mademoiselle Letty Mayfield, Monsieur Kemp.'

A hand clad in white kid touched Letty's briefly as she curtsied, aware of the uninterested scrutiny of two black eyes in an ageing and much made-up face. The Grand Duchess Anna was in white satin, with a tall pearl choker hiding her wrinkled neck and a diamond tiara perched on a mass of rusty-red hair.

The first floor seemed to consist of state rooms all opening out of each other. In one of them a string orchestra played light music, in another long tables were laid with an array of food and wine, and in the other rooms people circulated and talked to their friends.

'We had better have supper first,' Mr Kemp decreed, 'while there is still sufficient room to eat in moderate comfort.'

Letty was too excited to be hungry and would have liked to find a quiet corner where she could watch everyone else. She trailed behind the Kemps and another banker and his wife who seemed to be friends. The choice of food was bewildering and some of it was unfamiliar to her, so she loaded her plate with as little as possible and looked round for her companions, only to find they had moved on more quickly and been swallowed up by a crowd of people. Now was her chance to retire to a corner and hope to be unnoticed for a short time while she adjusted to surroundings which were outside anything she had ever experienced before.

A footman with a silver tray of wine-glasses found her there almost at once. He was a tall youth, rather younger than the others, and he stumbled over his French. Letty smiled at him, wondering if he felt as out of place as she did. Not that she wasn't enjoying so much magnificence, but it took a bit of getting used to. She accepted a glass of wine and barely had time to notice that it had been filled a little too full when the boy stepped aside to allow someone to pass and the edge of his tray just touched Letty's arm. A few drops of wine slopped over and fell on the edge of her dress. Fortunately it was white wine and did not show much, but she gave an exclamation of distress and the young footman burst into embarrassed apologies in a muddle of Russian and French.

It had not really been his fault and she told him so, conjuring up a smile and sending him on his way, after which she sat down on a handy chair and took stock of the damage, if any. Feeling sure no one had noticed the incident, she surreptitiously began to rub the slight damp patch with her handkerchief.

But she was wrong about no one having noticed.

'I should leave it alone, Miss Letty,' advised a familiar voice. 'Anyone looking at you will merely observe the beauty of your gown and be unaware of a faint wine mark on the hem.'

Nicholas Namorov, elegant in evening dress with the sash of some order making a streak of bright blue across his stiff shirt-front, was bowing before her. 'It would be much better to forget all about it,' he continued, 'and the easiest way to do that would be to come and dance with me.' Obviously quite certain that the invitation would be accepted, he held out his arm.

Letty ignored it. 'Thank you, Count,' she said coolly. 'I don't dance.'

'I find that hard to believe.'

'Really?' She raised her eyebrows. 'It happens to be the——' She had been going to say 'the truth' but honesty suddenly prevailed. 'Very nearly true,' she substituted. 'The only dances I was allowed to go to at home were those run by the Tennis Club. Rather different from here, I assure you.'

'I cannot believe that the steps performed at the Tennis Club differ much from those we dance in Petersburg.' He was still holding his arm out, arrogantly sure his wishes would prevail and taking no account whatever of the fact that she had been about to eat her supper.

Letty would have dearly liked to disappoint him, but to her chagrin a treacherous inner self seemed to be urging her to accept. Still hesitating, she found she had risen to her feet. As though mesmerised she took his arm, her gloved hand lying lightly upon it.

But not so lightly that she was unaware of the firm flesh beneath the fine black cloth, and a tiny tremor passed up her own arm and found its way to her heart.

# CHAPTER SIX

AT FIRST they were correctness itself. Letty could scarcely feel the delicate touch of the Count's hand on her back; her hand on his shoulder was light as a butterfly's wing. Dancing at arm's length, they circled the room sedately.

She had little of Marina's talent, but love of the dance was in her blood and she was naturally graceful. Skilfully led by her partner, she found her own performance raised to a higher level than she would have believed possible. It was very different from the vigorous romping at the Tennis Club.

Conversation was equally correct. The Count began by asking if she had enjoyed her drive around St Petersburg.

'Immensely! I wouldn't have believed such a beautiful city could exist so far north.' In her enthusiasm, Letty glanced up at him and, finding his eyes on her face, hurriedly resumed her study of his diamond-studded shirt front.

'It's sometimes called the Venice of the North, but I don't myself see a great deal of resemblance. Are you familiar with that city, Miss Mayfield?'

She shook her head. 'But my parents were there on their honeymoon and I have heard them speak of it.'

'My young brother is there now and has announced his intention of making a long stay. He fancies himself artistic and is studying painting, but I doubt if anything will come of it.'

Detecting a slight note of bitterness in his voice, Letty cautiously looked up from beneath her lashes, but his expression told her nothing. 'You have two very pretty sisters,' she remarked.

'Clara and Sonia. I would have introduced them the other day if the carriage had not moved on at that moment. They are a lively pair and at times cause me a certain amount of anxiety. It will be a relief to get them married.' Forestalling the question which she was on the verge of asking, he went on, 'My father is much involved with managing our estates and my mother is dead.'

At that moment they were involved in a slight collision with another couple. It was entirely the fault of a short fat man who was dancing exuberantly with a much taller lady. In executing a fancy twirl he managed to bump his partner into Letty.

It was impossible to be annoyed with him for he recognised his fault and burst into profuse apologies in fluent French. She smiled and answered equally fluently in the same tongue.

'You speak French?' the Count exclaimed.

'Oh, yes.' Letty could not help savouring his surprise. 'My mother is French and it's a second language to me.'

There was a long pause and she found his eyes searching her face with what she considered a most unnecessary intentness, but in a moment his light-hearted manner had returned and he exclaimed, 'Then why the devil have I had to work my brain to its limits in order to talk to you in English?'

Her lips twitched. 'If I remember rightly, you perceived I was English the moment you saw me and naturally used that tongue. I don't see I can be blamed for not telling you I am bilingual.'

The dark eyebrows rose fractionally but all he said was, 'We will speak French in future.'

'Very well,' Letty agreed demurely. 'I would not like to think I was forcing your brain to work harder than you would wish.'

Her eyes were dancing as she met his indignant stare, but almost at once his expression changed again. 'This room is becoming extremely crowded,' he said abruptly. 'Let us find somewhere else.'

It was obviously useless to protest, even if Letty had wanted to, and she found herself being steered expertly out of the crowd and into a smaller room lit only by candles in silver sconces on the walls. After the brilliance of the salon they had left it was not immediately apparent that other couples had sought the same refuge, and not for the purpose of dancing.

When Letty did notice them her already rapid heartbeats quickened still further and she felt her whole body stiffen in his grasp. Her tension instantly conveyed itself to her partner and his grip loosened. The music could still be heard, though the throbbing strings were muffled by distance, and they revolved sedately and in silence in the small space available.

Suddenly Nicholas said carelessly, 'We were in the middle of a conversation when that oaf bumped into us. I believe I was about to ask whether you have any brothers or sisters.'

Startled, Letty glanced up into his face and found it unusually serious. Speaking a little breathlessly, she told him about Edward and his scientific experiments and then came to a full stop. Marina's mysterious disappearance was never out of her mind, though sometimes she could keep it in the background, as on this occasion.

And as she hesitated an idea leapt into her mind and clamoured to be put into words. Count Namorov was a sophisticated member of Petersburg society. Very likely he patronised the Imperial Russian Ballet and was familiar with the dancers. Was it possible that he might have information about Marina which was unknown to people like the Kemps who admitted their total lack of interest in anything more cultural than musical comedy?

At that moment Nicholas gave her an opening by asking with careful casualness, 'You do not mention sisters. Have you none?'

'I—I have an older sister, but she doesn't live at home.' Still hesitating, she waited with hammering pulses to see if he would continue his interrogation.

Nicholas also seemed strangely doubtful about the wisdom of proceeding but he did so eventually. 'I presume this older sister is married?'

'Oh, no—she is a dancer—a ballerina——' She broke off, startled by the expression on his face. 'Why are you looking like that? Do you know her?'

It was as though a hidden hand had massaged away every trace of the consternation which he had momentarily been unable to control. 'How can I possibly answer that when I don't know the lady's professional name?' he said smoothly.

'That's easily remedied!' Now that she had taken the plunge Letty was desperate to pour it all out. 'She calls herself Marina Varaskaya—Marina is her real name, but not the other, of course. She is a very good dancer and sometimes plays lead, but a few weeks ago she wrote to me and invited me to visit her. We all thought she was unwell and I persuaded my parents to let me journey to St Petersburg with Mrs Kemp. But—but when I got to the theatre my sister was not there and no one seemed to know her whereabouts and—and I'm so dreadfully worried.' There was a quiver in her voice and her eyes were bright with unshed tears.

He was so long replying that Letty grew frightened. Perhaps he knew something dreadful about Marina and did not want to tell her.

'*Do* you know her?' she repeated anxiously.

'I have seen her dance. She is, as you say, very good.'

She waited for him to elaborate but he appeared to have no intention of saying any more. His arm had tightened a little round her waist, but otherwise he appeared unmoved by her story and passionate appeal.

And suddenly Letty was furiously angry. She snatched her hand from his clasp and removed the other from his shoulder. Standing there in the middle of the floor, she faced him with rage in her eyes and scorn in her voice.

'I believe you *do* know something about Marina and for some reason you don't intend to tell me! I just don't know how you can stand there and behave so callously when I am nearly torn to shreds with worry.'

Her onslaught seemed to startle him and he allowed a brief softness to appear in his eyes. 'You must believe me when I say I am unable to help you in this matter,' he insisted. 'I realise how distressing it must be for you and I give you my promise that I will endeavour to obtain information for you should this be possible.'

The speech was so elaborate and so formally worded that it left her feeling bewildered and desolate. Bitter disappointment welled up in her and her head drooped. She was astounded when he suddenly bent his own so that his lips were close to her ear where a red-gold tendril curled provocatively.

'A party is no place for such a solemn conversation as we have just had. Do you not agree?' Without waiting for an answer, he went calmly on. 'If I venture to tell you that you are looking very lovely this evening, will you accept the compliment as being sincere and well meant—which it is—and try to forget your troubles for a while?'

She stole a peep at his face, so close to her own. His head was still bent and at that moment he moved it slightly. She felt a hard masculine cheek touch her soft skin with a delicate pressure. She was drawn closer, and closer still, and she knew she ought to protest, yet felt no urge to do so. Her anger had died like a smothered fire and a completely different and unfamiliar emotion had taken its place. With a sigh she did as she had been told and banished all unhappy thoughts. Closing her eyes, she relaxed and allowed herself to drift on a wave of emotion as insubstantial as mist.

The Count moved his head again and his mouth lightly brushed her cheek. In a trance she offered no resistance and did not know how fortunate she was that he ventured no further, that his lips had merely tasted the sweetness of her rose-petal skin and not devoured it.

Suddenly the magic began to fade and the well-brought-up girl disguised as a glamorous creature in pale green taffeta resumed charge. Letty made a small sound of protest and pulled away from him so as to leave a more decorous distance between them.

'I will take you back to Mrs Kemp in a moment,' he said, smiling, 'but first I want to ask you something.'

Her heart missed a beat. 'What is it?'

'Don't look so frightened! It is a very small thing. Now that we are friends, I would like your permission to call you Letty in future, and you must use my name which, in case you have forgotten, is Nicholas. If you will allow this, I will promise to be formal when the occasion calls for it.'

'But—but we may not meet again.'

'We will meet,' he said calmly.

There was no answer to that and Letty accepted his decree in silence, uneasily conscious that it accorded only too well with the wishes of her own heart.

As they approached the largest of the state-rooms, where most of the non-dancing, non-card-playing guests were congregated, they became aware that something had caused a ripple of excitement to pass through the elaborately dressed throng. Most people had stopped talking to each other, and some of them—nearly all ladies—were pressing forward and craning their necks to see over each other's shoulders. Others had ostentatiously turned their backs, and most of these were men.

'Whatever is happening?' Letty exclaimed as they paused in the doorway.

Nicholas was a tall man and had no difficulty in seeing over the bobbing heads adorned with feathers and sparkling tiaras, right out to the gallery which led to the stairs.

'It seems there is a late arrival,' he said shortly.

'It must be somebody important to cause such a stir.' Letty stood on tiptoe. 'Is it someone from the Imperial family? One of the Tsar's daughters perhaps?'

'The Imperial family does not attend parties and, in any case, the Grand Duchesses are not yet old enough to be out in society. This—person who has just arrived is not a member of any of the great Russian families. He is a peasant, and a thorough-going scoundrel, and yet he has become the most influential man in all St Petersburg.'

She gazed at him in wonder, none of it making any sense to her, but clearly he felt very strongly about this new guest and she longed to hear more. 'What is his name?' she asked.

'Rasputin, but some people call him Father Grigori. He is a monk who is a disgrace to his habit, lecherous, foul-mouthed and frequently drunk.'

Letty was not entirely sure what lecherous meant, but she had no difficulty with the other adjectives. 'If he is such a terrible person,' she said, 'how is it he can come here to a grand house like this, and why do so many people seem pleased to see him?'

Nicholas lowered his voice. 'By some means—thought by many to be supernatural power—he has wormed his way into the closely guarded palace at Tsarkoe Selo and endeared himself to the Empress. It seems that he has a strange influence over the health of her only son, the young Tsarevitch Alexis, who, poor child, has a strange bleeding disease. Rasputin is always sent for when the boy has one of his attacks and Her Imperial Majesty believes firmly in his power to effect a cure. It is said she practically worships the ground the disgusting fellow walks on.'

At that moment the crowd in front of them swayed to one side, and Letty found herself looking straight through the gap towards the man about whom she had been absorbing such amazing information. He came walking slowly towards her, smiling left and right like royalty and sometimes touching a bowed head with a hand which, even from a distance, looked far from clean.

His monk's habit was not clean either and his sandalled feet were ingrained with dirt, but though she was aware of these unsavoury details it was his face which caught her attention—and in particular his eyes. Very pale blue—almost colourless—and deep-set, they glowed with some mystic power so that she found her own gaze held and her feet rooted to the spot.

Vaguely she became aware of a hand on her arm and that she was being drawn away, back among those who had not pressed forward to welcome Rasputin. Those amazing eyes no longer held her prisoner and the so-called monk became simply a revolting creature from some other world.

'Just for a moment, Letty,' the Count murmured, 'you looked quite mesmerised. Surely *you* did not feel the power of that man?'

'I certainly felt something.' She tried to laugh. 'But I hope it was only disgust! However can these grand ladies bear to associate with anyone like that?'

'Personally I find it entirely inexplicable.'

He had answered her impatiently and she felt the subject of Rasputin had ceased to interest him. He was looking about him and she guessed he was searching for Mrs Kemp. He would then hand her over to her chaperon and the wonderful, magical evening would be over. She sighed, a small, forlorn sound which nobody heard, and sensed inside herself a gradual withdrawal from the glittering scene around. She didn't belong here; she was only pretending to be part of this crowd of Russian aristocrats and foreign businessmen and their wives. It had been wonderful while it lasted, but she must put it behind her now and remember she was not in St Petersburg to enjoy herself, but to uncover the mystery surrounding Marina.

She was very silent in the car going home, which scarcely mattered since Mr and Mrs Kemp were expressing themselves forcibly on the subject of Rasputin. All they needed was an audience, and Letty was very willing to supply that and make small sounds of agreement from time to time. She went straight up to bed when they reached the house and, undressing slowly in the warm, comfortable room, made no attempt to stem the tide of depression which washed over her.

She could not put off the letter to her parents much longer, nor could she continue to impose on the kindness of her hosts. In fact, she was uneasily aware she had no right to be there at all, since it was in order to see her sister that she had come. To stay on indefinitely, waiting for news which might never come, would be imposing on the generosity of the Kemps to an intolerable degree. All her hopes had been pinned on Yuri Ivanovitch, the male dancer, but no word had come from him. As for Nicholas Namorov, her suspicion that he might know something about Marina was rapidly fading.

The soft feather pillow soaked up the tears she could not help shedding, but did nothing to cool her burning cheeks. Tossing and turning, she found sleep elusive, but the surrender to grief had brought its own release, and eventually she drifted into deep slumber.

Strangely, it was not her sister who occupied her last thoughts but the memory of how she had felt when Nicholas had kissed her in the ante-room.

She slept late and was barely awake when the maid brought her hot water for washing. The girl seemed excited, her broad peasant face rosy with the effort to make herself understood. Having a natural gift for languages, Letty had already learnt a few words of Russian, but they were no use to her now. She tried a little simple English but only received an emphatic shake of the head. There was nothing for it but to wait until Mrs Kemp could translate.

Not that it mattered. Almost certainly the girl had been trying to tell her something mundane concerning her personal laundry or whether she would like breakfast in her room. She had a vague memory of her hostess saying something about it.

Letty preferred eating at a table and she dressed quickly. Downstairs, she turned towards the morning-room where breakfast was usually served, but the first thing she noticed when she opened the door was that the big round table had not been laid. She should have stayed upstairs after all.

As she hesitated in the doorway, her hand still on the knob, she realised that the room was not empty. A tall lean young man in a conventional suit had risen from an armchair in the corner and at first she stared at him without recognition.

'You have forgotten me, *mademoiselle*?' He smiled, showing white teeth in his dark face. 'I am Yuri Ivanovitch.'

How *could* she have forgotten? Letty plunged into a hasty explanation. 'You look so——' she had been going to say 'ordinary' but hurriedly changed it to '—different.'

'I was in my practice clothes when we met at the theatre, and I am on my way to rehearsal now, but I could not let another moment pass without telling you the wonderful news.' He broke off to fumble in his pocket.

Letty's eyes widened and she stepped forward eagerly. 'Do you mean that—that you have news of Marina?'

He nodded vigorously. 'Indeed, yes, *mademoiselle*. I have received a letter and I have brought it for you to read.'

Her hand was trembling as she held it out. 'I hope it's not in Russian?' she said nervously.

'In French. You will have no difficulty.'

The writing was undoubtedly Marina's and it was a great deal better written than the agitated note Letty had received in Ely. This letter had been written without haste and probably after much thought. It began by begging Yuri not to mention to anyone that he had heard from her. It was because of their friendship that she was writing, since she knew he would be worried. There was absolutely no need for him to feel concerned about her—this was heavily underlined—as she was well and safe, and hoped before long to return to the ballet company.

Letty's eyes flew to the head of the single sheet. There was no address. 'But we still don't know where she is! In a way, the mystery is as great as ever.'

'Not so, *mademoiselle*. Surely it is good that we know she is safe?'

'Yes, yes, of course. I'm sorry—I should have thanked you at once for letting me see the letter, and certainly it's good news. It's just that—well, I can't help feeling disappointed as well as relieved.'

'I understand and I share your feeling. I think we shall have to be patient—maybe very patient indeed.' He took back the precious letter and put it carefully away in an inner pocket. 'You will excuse me now, please? I must not be late for rehearsal.'

She smiled. 'Certainly you must not, or that man who was shouting at the dancers when I visited the theatre will be very angry. Aren't you all afraid of him?'

He shrugged. 'Sometimes, but he is a very good choreographer. I think perhaps we are more afraid of the director who is in charge of the whole Imperial Russian

Ballet. He has the power to dismiss us at a moment's notice.'

As they were crossing the hall a sudden thought struck Letty. 'Do you think he will dismiss my sister? That would break her heart.'

The manservant permanently on duty at the double doors had sprung to his feet and was opening them, but Yuri paused for a moment.

'It is my belief,' he said in a low voice, 'that the director knows the truth about Marina. She would not write so confidently that she means to return to the ballet if she had merely absented herself without telling anyone at all. Do you not agree?'

'Yes, I think you may be right, but I still think it strange she did not confide in her family. I can't help feeling a little hurt.'

'It depends, does it not, on the reason for her leaving? It may be something she does not wish you to know. After all, she was not aware you were coming to visit her.'

'That's true. I suppose she invited me on an impulse and either forgot or didn't expect anything would come of it.' Letty looked up into the dark unfathomable eyes. 'You seem to be a great friend of my sister. Have you any idea at all why she is behaving in this extraordinary way?'

Yuri hesitated just a little too long, and it appeared to her searching eyes as though a shutter came down on his face. 'None at all, *mademoiselle*,' he said firmly, and ran down the steps.

Letty gave the doorman a mechanical smile, which seemed to surprise him, and went thoughtfully back to the morning-room. She had almost forgotten about breakfast and the appearance of a maid with a laden tray was a pleasant surprise. As she ate, she tried to think what she should tell her parents. It would undoubtedly be the most difficult letter she had ever had to write, since she would have to reconcile two opposing lines of approach. She shrank from deceiving them, and at the same time did not want to worry them.

There were writing materials at a small desk by the window, and when she had eaten she settled down to her unwelcome task. After some delay while she chose a nib which suited her, and several false starts, she at last began her letter. The pen was well-chewed before she got it done, if not exactly to her liking, at least as well worded as she could manage.

> You will be surprised to learn that I have not yet seen Marina. She is away from St Petersburg on vacation and did not get my letter before she left, so she does not know I am here. Mr and Mrs Kemp are being so kind and are most anxious I should stay for as long as possible, and naturally I want to be here when Marina gets back after travelling all this way to see her. St Petersburg is a beautiful city and I am so much enjoying myself, so I hope you will not mind if I prolong my visit.

When she had finished she read it over, hoping what she had said about Marina would turn out to be the truth, and also that her hosts would be willing to allow her to remain for longer than had been anticipated. She had no reason to doubt it, for both had frequently said how much they enjoyed having her.

Mrs Kemp did not appear until nearly lunchtime and she listened in astonishment to Letty's account of Yuri's visit. It was plain she considered Marina's behaviour both mysterious and inconsiderate, though she was too polite to say so. Without having to make the first approach Letty found herself being warmly pressed to stay on as long as she liked.

Her gratitude was so genuine that it was easy to express fervent thanks, and even to fling her arms round Edith Kemp's stout form and give her a quick hug. It was less easy to thank her husband because she was beginning to feel she must be on her guard with him. It was instinct rather than anything else, since his obvious admiration of her youthful attractiveness never went any further than a fatherly pat on the hand or paying her compliments with lumbering gallantry.

'There is one thing I would like to do while I am here, Mr Kemp,' she said as soon as she got a chance to break in on his fulsome remarks about how delightful it was to have such a charming young lady in the house.

'And what is that, my dear?' he enquired.

'I want to learn Russian. At least——' she corrected herself '—I would like to learn as much as possible of the language in the time available.'

'Good gracious! What an extraordinary ambition for a pretty girl! Surely you could find a more suitable way of spending your time?'

'I don't know about that.' She smiled, anxious to keep him in a good mood. 'But I would certainly find it useful to know a little Russian. It is very frustrating to go out in St Petersburg and not be able to read any of the public notices, or even to say "thank you" in a shop, or anything at all.'

'You would have to learn that terrible Cyrillic alphabet first,' Mrs Kemp warned.

'Yes, I know, but I don't mind. I would consider it a challenge.'

They both looked at her dubiously, as though wondering why she should be interested in anything so unfeminine as a challenge, but to her relief neither of them asked. She would not have found it easy to explain.

'Mr Sheldon speaks extremely good Russian,' she went on, 'and he told me he had an excellent teacher. I was wondering if it would be possible for me to go to the same man.'

Mrs Kemp looked at her husband. 'Do you know who it was, Albert?'

'I haven't the faintest idea, but I suppose I could find out. Turning to Letty, he continued, 'Of course it would depend on where the fellow lives. If it were near here, there would be no problem, but it would be out of the question for you to go gallivanting about St Petersburg by yourself if he lived at a distance.'

'I could take a droshky,' she said eagerly, and some imp of wickedness prompted her to add, 'or a tram. I would love to ride on a tram.'

'Quite impossible!' he snapped.

In spite of his disapproval, Mr Kemp did what he could for her. At the dinner table that evening he announced that Gerald Sheldon would call for her on Saturday afternoon and would escort her to see his language professor who lived, most fortunately, over a bookshop in the Nevski Prospect.

Letty thanked him prettily. 'It's very kind of you to make these arrangements for me, and kind, too, of Mr Sheldon to give up his time.'

'I'm quite sure the young man enjoys it and I know I can safely entrust you to his care. Sheldon is one of the most dependable men on my staff. You could not be in better hands.'

'I'm sure your dear parents would approve,' Mrs Kemp put in.

Looking up from the peach she was peeling just in time to catch her host and hostess exchanging a meaningful look, Letty received a distinct jolt. Was it possible they had matchmaking in mind? Socially, a young man with good prospects in an English bank abroad would be very suitable for a Canon's daughter and might even be considered a 'catch'.

Thinking about it, Letty decided she liked him well enough in a lukewarm sort of way. He had been interesting to talk to, but she could not envisage falling in love with him.

Her mother had once said in her hearing that it did not matter much how a girl felt about her husband-to-be at the time of their wedding—provided she did not actively dislike him—because love would come later. Just why it should do that, Letty could not understand, though she guessed it had something to do with the secrets of the marriage bed. How would she feel if Gerald Sheldon became the man who had the right to reveal those secrets to her?

Blushing furiously, she bowed her head over her dessert. Unbidden, into her mind there had come a fleeting memory of another, much darker head actually lying beside her in the great bed at Liev.

## CHAPTER SEVEN

NICHOLAS was not in the habit of sleeping badly. Normally he worked hard—when the occasion demanded it—and played hard, and allowed very little to worry him. Consequently he was extremely annoyed on the night after the party to be beseiged by a number of tiresome problems which denied him his proper rest. He rose in the morning unrefreshed and not in the best of tempers, only to be further disturbed by a message to say that one of his ships had been slightly damaged at Grimsby and would therefore dock at St Petersburg several days late.

There was no need for him to deal with the ensuing complications himself—he had a capable manager—but he enjoyed surprising his aristocratic friends by his interest in business matters. Besides, it gave him an excellent excuse for putting off a task which he viewed with extreme disquiet.

Several days later he knew he could no longer delay making the journey to Liev, the reason for which was irritating the back of his mind, like the grit in an oyster which eventually results in a pearl. Except that this particular irritation was most unlikely to turn into anything so attractive. In fact, the only bright spot in the whole wretched affair was the opportunity to try out his new Hispano-Suiza on a twenty-mile run.

It awaited him outside the front door, a two-seater sports model, bright yellow and splendidly polished by a groom so that it shone in the sunlight. Wearing a short leather coat, a peaked cap turned back to front and goggles, Nicholas ran a loving hand lightly over the bodywork just as he might have caressed the body of a woman, and waited for his man to swing the starting handle.

After several attempts the engine fired and the journey began. Once clear of the city, Nicholas increased the speed so that the wind whistled past his head and a glorious exhilaration took possession of him.

The proximity of Liev forced him to remember the reason for his visit. Without doubt the interview would be difficult, but he supposed some solution to the problem would be found.

Passing the drive leading to the great house, he swung his motor car down a narrow grassy track leading through the woods and, eventually to the clearing where the dacha was hidden.

The door was flung open before he reached it—no doubt she had heard the chug-chug of his approach—and the tall fair girl Nicholas had visited on the night of the accident came on to the veranda. This time her pale blonde hair was wound into a roll at the nape of her neck, and although her clothes were simple she looked as out of place in rural surroundings as a swan in a duck pond.

'Nicholas—how lovely to see you!' She stood on tiptoe and kissed him affectionately. 'I was feeling so dreadfully depressed and now you have come to cheer me up. Come in.'

She had given him an opening and he seized it immediately.

'I am afraid I do not bring very cheering news, Marina.' Seeing her large blue eyes dilate in alarm, he hurried on. 'Your sister is here in Petersburg. She has come to see you.'

'Letty? Oh, *no*!' Horrified, she backed towards the table and clutched its edge.

'She says you invited her, that you wrote a letter which made your family think you were unwell and saying you longed to see her. She had the opportunity of travelling to Russia with highly respectable people and was allowed to come. She was most distressed to find you had disappeared in somewhat mysterious circumstances.'

'Oh dear—this is terrible! She would be horribly worried, naturally.' Marina collapsed into a chair. 'I do remember writing that letter but I didn't know at the time what had happened to me. I just felt ill and depressed, and when I discovered the awful truth I forgot all about my invitation. Anyway, I never imagined Letty would be able to come.' She sat silent for a moment, twisting her long thin hands together. 'However did you meet my sister, Nicholas? I would not have expected your paths to cross.'

Relieved that the news was broken, he sat down also and stretched out his long legs. 'Our paths have crossed to a remarkable degree. You remember I brought two English passengers to spend the night at Liev after the train crash? They were your sister and her chaperon but I did not, of course, know that at the time.'

'Letty was so near and I never knew?' she exclaimed.

'It was better that you remained in ignorance.'

'Yes, indeed! How did you discover the relationship?'

'I was a little uneasy right from the beginning. There is a certain likeness, and I knew you had a sister called Letty, but I was unaware of your real name which is, of course, hers.' He went on to give her an account of the party.

'What did you say when she asked if you could help her to find me?' she asked fearfully.

'I said it was unlikely I could help.' Seeing her still anxious, he added, 'You may rest assured I gave nothing away.'

Marina jumped to her feet and went to stare out of the window. 'Oh, Nicholas, what am I going to do?' she moaned.

He folded his arms and addressed her backview. 'I have given the matter a great deal of thought and it seems to me there is no insuperable difficulty. As soon as the arrangements are made and you have recovered from the—er—operation, you can write to Letty saying you have been ill, but you hope to see her soon.'

'I sent a short note to Yuri Ivanovitch telling him I would be back at the theatre before long. I knew he was to be trusted.'

'There you are then—you can write a similar letter to your sister.'

Confident that she would agree, he waited for her reply. It had not been as bad as he expected and would soon be over. Then they could have a convivial lunch together, after which he would drive back to the city. He was not even apprehensive when Marina left the window and returned to her chair by the table, but it was a little worrying to see her rest her head on her hand and appear unable to meet his gaze.

'It is not as simple as you think,' she whispered.

'Why is that?' Suddenly alerted to danger, Nicholas spat out his question like the crack of a whip.

'Since I wrote to Yuri I have done a great deal of thinking and—and I have changed my mind. I no longer wish for an abortion.'

'Changed your mind? In heaven's name—*why*?' he flung at her.

She made an effort to pull herself together and get her thoughts into some sort of order. 'I'm not sure exactly, but I think the way I was brought up had a great deal to do with it. We were all taught it is wicked to take life in any way. As I sat here day after day I kept remembering going to Cathedral services with Letty when we were small children, and how much we admired our father in his canonicals. He would be utterly appalled if he knew I intended to—to get rid of a baby.'

'He would be appalled that you allowed yourself to become pregnant,' Nicholas pointed out harshly.

'I don't need to be reminded of that!' Marina raised her head and looked at him appealingly. 'I'm sure your Russian Orthodox Church disapproves just as much of abortion. It would not have been easy to arrange.'

'Everything is possible where there is sufficient money,' he said cynically. 'Will you not change your mind again, Marina? It would be so much more sensible.' When she shook her head violently, he shrugged and continued in a businesslike tone, 'Then perhaps you will be good enough to tell me what you propose to do?'

'I shall stay here until the baby is born and then return to Petersburg and resume my career.'

His black eyebrows shot up but all he said was, 'And the child?'

'I—I think I may keep it, if I am brave enough to flout public opinion.'

It was impossible not to admire her courage and, in the midst of his exasperation, Nicholas permitted himself a curt nod of commendation. 'What about your sister?' he demanded then. 'You will either have to tell her the truth——'

'No! Letty has had a sheltered upbringing and knows nothing about the real world. The shock would be too great.'

'So you intend to allow her to continue to worry about your disappearance?'

Marina wrung her hands. 'I don't want that, either.'

'Then what do you suggest?' There was no other alternative and he knew it, but he restrained his impatience briefly while she, with a visible effort, struggled to think of one.

Eventually she said, 'You will have to give me more time to consider it. Until a little while ago I had no idea that Letty was in Russia and I can't possibly think what should be done when my mind is in such a state of turmoil.'

'Very well,' he agreed reluctantly, 'but kindly speed up your thought processes as much as possible so that some decision may be reached without too much delay.'

He stayed to lunch as he had planned but it was certainly not a convivial meal. Marina was silent and ate very little, but Nicholas—made hungry by so much fresh air—enjoyed the simple fare provided by Varya, the peasant girl who looked after the dacha. He left soon after, but not before he had made another appeal to Marina to tell her sister the truth.

'How old is Letty?' he asked abruptly.

She wrinkled her brow in thought. 'Let me see—she must be twenty now. Dear heaven—she had a birthday recently and I did not remember it!'

'You had other things on your mind.' Nicholas stood in the doorway, massive in his lined leather coat. 'She is not a child, Marina, though I suspect she is remarkably innocent. However, I think you should shatter her innocence by confiding in her. I believe she would survive the shock.'

'How can you possibly say that?' Her voice rose hysterically. 'You know nothing about young girls——'

'Perhaps your present worries have wiped from your mind the fact that I have two sisters?' he interrupted sarcastically, adding with a wicked twinkle, 'In addition, I am not uninformed about the female sex in general.'

She ignored that. 'Clara and Sonia are quite different from Letty,' she insisted. 'You can have no conception of the narrowness of life in a cathedral city. Letty would be so horrified that she would refuse to have anything more to do with me and, in addition, she would certainly consider it her duty to tell our parents.'

'I think you misjudge her.' Into his mind there flashed the memory of that shocking scene in the bedroom at his great-grandmother's house. Letty had not seemed so much embarrassed then as furiously angry.

'Believe me, Nicholas, I know what I am talking about,' Marina declared and, as he turned away with a shrug, she called after him, 'That's my last word on the subject.'

'It's not mine,' he retorted, but she had already closed the door.

Putting all his frustration and annoyance into the task, he swung the starting handle with such vigour that the engine fired at once. Driving back to the city, he found Marina's obstinacy occupying far too large a proportion of his thoughts, with the result that he was obliged to come to a decision. He would in the near future endeavour to see more of Letty with the intention of getting to know her better. He might even put out a few cautious feelers and discover her reaction. If the results were satisfactory he would make another attempt to break her sister's resolution.

Just before he reached St Petersburg, it occurred to him to wonder why he should be taking all this trouble. Not finding an answer, he dismissed the question from his mind.

Luck was on his side. Within a few days he had an unexpected meeting with Letty.

Although the month was now May, it was a day typical of April, with sunshine and showers alternating. Driving along by the river, Nicholas was caught in a heavy downpour and was glad he had had the forethought to put the hood up before starting out. Long silver rods lashed the surface of the Neva and swept along the road like a solid steel curtain. People were hurrying for shelter and among them he spotted a girl with no umbrella running faster than anyone. She was clinging to her hat with one hand and holding up her skirts with the other, displaying a really shocking amount of bedraggled lace.

Letty was making for an archway about twenty yards ahead. She had nearly reached it when she thought she heard a shout. Still continuing to run, she turned her head and was astonished to see, keeping pace with her along the road and making a loud chugging sound, a motor car of such a brilliant yellow that it seemed to light up the dreary scene.

Unconsciously she slowed down a little and the vehicle stopped. Someone leaned across and opened the nearer door, which was so low it hardly seemed like a door at all.

'I'm afraid you are getting exceedingly wet.' Nicholas peered out from beneath the hood. 'Jump in quickly and I will drive you to wherever you are going in such a hurry.'

Letty scarcely hesitated, though she knew she ought to refuse with dignity and continue splashing on her way. Well-brought-up young ladies did not ride unchaperoned in motor cars with young men, unless they happened to be chauffeurs. With a breathless gasp of thanks, she scrambled in, showing even more petticoat, and settled herself in the passenger's seat.

'I would be obliged if you would let me into the secret of your destination,' he said impatiently. 'The engine does not care for idling and will probably stop soon. I have no wish to get out into the rain to restart it.'

'I'm sorry.' Letty pulled herself together hastily. 'My immediate destination was that archway farther along, where I hoped to shelter, but I should really, of course, be hurrying back to Mrs Kemp's.'

'And that is?'

She gave the address in Russian with so much fluency that Nicholas glanced at her in surprise. 'I've been taking lessons,' she explained. 'In fact, I was on my way back from one when I got caught in the rain.'

'Your teacher lives by the Neva?'

'N-no—his apartment is over a bookshop in the Nevski Prospect.' She laughed and confessed she had been out for the first time by herself since leaving Ely. 'I am supposed to take a droshky to and from my lesson, but this morning Mrs Kemp wished to visit her dressmaker and so gave me a lift. She said she would not be home until lunchtime and I'm afraid I decided to walk back—and I was making a short detour when the rain caught me.'

'Most reprehensible behaviour,' Nicholas said solemnly. 'Do you often flout convention in this manner?'

There was a slight pause before she answered and Nicholas held his breath. The question had been a serious one, but he had not wanted her to realise that.

'I'm flouting convention now,' she said eventually. 'I should not be riding in your motor car. Mrs Kemp would be very shocked—and so would my mother.'

'You have been strictly brought up?'

'Naturally!'

Although his eyes were on the road, Nicholas sensed she was looking at him indignantly and cursed his clumsiness. If he wanted to discover whether there was any hope that she would be able to accept Marina's condition, he would have to do better than that.

'This is a beautiful motor car,' Letty said politely, changing the subject.

'It is also extremely fast—fifty miles an hour! Can you imagine it?'

'Indeed I cannot!' she gasped.

'I should greatly like to demonstrate its powers, but that is impossible in Petersburg. One day, if you can escape from Mrs Kemp, I will take you for a short run into the country.'

'That would be wonderful,' she said wistfully, 'but I don't think——'

'It may have escaped your notice,' he interrupted, 'that I do not accept defeat easily.'

It had not escaped her notice at all but she ignored the remark. Glancing through the celluloid side-curtains, she noted that the rain had nearly stopped, and said hastily, 'Please let me get out here, Count. It would be better if I approached the house on foot.'

'Nicholas.'

'I beg your pardon?'

'We agreed at the Grand Duchess Anna's party to be less formal in future.'

Letty did not remember agreeing to anything of the sort but she let it pass, since the car had stopped as requested. Getting out, she thanked him briefly and set off at a great pace.

There was a letter from her father lying on the hall table and she took it upstairs with her. As soon as she had changed into dry clothing, she opened it with a fast-beating heart. Would he order her immediately back to England?

To her great relief her parents seemed to have taken Marina's absence from the city 'on vacation' remarkably calmly. The Canon wrote:

> It is most unfortunate she did not receive your letter before she left, but now you have made the journey it would be a pity not to remain until your sister's return, providing your kind hosts have no objection. We miss you here, but your mother has your French grandmother staying with her and the two of them chatter away in French from morning till night, so I do not think she is lonely.

Letty read the letter through a second time and then put it away in her handkerchief sachet. Faint sounds of voices were drifting up from the hall and she guessed both Mr and Mrs Kemp had returned. It was time to go down to lunch.

The gong had not yet sounded and she found them in the drawing-room. When they had greeted her, she told them about her father's letter. 'He would like me to stay until Marina returns,' she finished, 'but he is not at all sure I should impose on your kindness——'

'It is a very great pleasure for myself and my wife to have you here, my dear,' Mr Kemp assured her ponderously. 'You must stay just as long as you like.'

Letty thanked him prettily and, as the gong sounded at that moment, was rewarded by being offered a ceremonious arm to conduct her into luncheon. As she walked beside him a strong smell of the bay rum he used on his hair was wafted towards her and she repressed a shudder. There was no doubt that his attentions were becoming increasingly distasteful to her. She hated having her cheek pinched or her bare arm patted with plump fingers and, whenever possible, avoided being alone with him.

Greatly daring, she continued to walk home from her lessons whenever the weather permitted it. As the late Russian spring became early summer, she thought longingly of the trip into the country which Nicholas had suggested. It seemed as impossible as ever and no doubt he had by now accepted the fact, in spite of his proud boast, 'I do not accept defeat easily.'

Owing to her natural talent for languages, her knowledge of Russian increased at a speed which astonished Professor Dernitsa, her tutor. His pleasure in her prowess gave her great satisfaction but, apart from that, the nagging worry about Marina prevented any true happiness. She had said in her letter to Yuri that she would return 'before long', yet there had been no further news of her and several weeks had passed. The more Letty thought about it, the more incomprehensible it seemed.

Another cause of distress during the long light evenings was her host's increasingly disturbing display of affection. He simply could not keep his hands off her and appeared oblivious to her embarrassment. She did not so much mind having an errant curl tweaked but she hated the feel of his hands on her bare flesh.

He meant no harm—she was sure of that. Or was she? Sometimes when she was unavoidably alone with him she was just a little frightened, and then she would tell herself not to be silly. After all, he quite often patted her in front of his wife, who clearly saw no reason for anyone to object. He was only being fatherly.

But there was nothing fatherly about his behaviour the night he came home after an all-male dinner.

Mrs Kemp had gone to bed early with a bad attack of indigestion. After enquiring if there was anything she could do, and being told that hot water and bicarbonate of soda would probably put her right, Letty settled in the drawing-room with one of her Russian books. She had not meant to stay up late, but time had, for once, slipped away.

She smelt the brandy as soon as Mr Kemp opened the door, and observed his wavering progress towards a chair with some alarm. She forced herself to listen to a long-winded story, the point of which quite escaped her, and then rose to her feet. 'Well, goodnight, Mr Kemp,' she said rapidly. 'I'm so glad you had such a good evening.'

'Not over yet, m'dear.'

The words, slurred though they were, reached her clearly as she retreated. She had no idea what he meant— perhaps the consumption of more brandy?—but she fled nevertheless, racing up the stairs, along the gallery and into her room. Breathless, she leaned against the door. If only there were a key she could turn, but although the door had a lock—a huge elaborate brass affair— there was no means of putting it into operation.

It was some minutes before Letty dared to begin undressing, and first she cautiously opened the door and peeped out. But the house was still and quiet, with the silence broken only by the distant ticking of a clock. With hands that trembled slightly, she began to undo the twenty-three pairs of hooks and eyes which fastened the bodice of her blue muslin dress. Carefully she stepped out of it and hung it over a chair. Then she removed her lace-trimmed petticoat and stood before the mirror in her chemise and under-petticoat.

Suddenly she froze. Over her reflected shoulder she could see the door opening slowly and silently.

Stifling a scream, she spun round, her hand over her mouth and her eyes dilating in shock and horror. He was there, actually in the privacy of her room, his hot eyes devouring her bare shoulders and arms—the man whose affection for her was supposed to be fatherly.

'Don't be alarmed, m'dear—I don't mean any harm.' His speech was more slurred than ever. 'Only just want to look—you're so pretty.' He drew nearer and she shrank back against the dressing-table, her hands trying to cover her naked flesh. 'Such lovely white skin—never saw so much of it before.' He stretched out his sweaty hand and caressed her shoulder.

His touch galvanised Letty into action. She was still frightened, but now she was angry as well. With a swift vigorous movement, she flung out her hands and caught Albert Kemp full in the chest. He reeled backwards, almost lost his balance and grabbed a chair to steady himself.

'I wonder what your wife would think of you!' Letty flung at him furiously. 'You're so drunk you've lost all sense of decency. Will you kindly get out of my room *at once*!'

To her embarrassment, his eyes filled with maudlin tears. 'You won't tell Edith?' he begged. 'She doesn't know how I feel about you—she would never understand——'

Letty drew herself up and looked down at him where he still clung to the back of a chair. 'I don't know whether

I shall tell her or not, but if I don't it will be for her sake rather than yours. And now will you *please* go?' Fully as dignified in her underwear as she would have been in her ballgown, she swept across the room and held the door wide.

As he shambled past her she thought she heard a mumbled apology but she ignored it. She certainly had no intention of forgiving him no matter how sorry he was. Not ever.

But, when she had closed the door and dragged a heavy chair in front of it, all her fury abruptly left her and she burst into tears. It had been horrible—utterly horrible and degrading—and it had left her feeling unclean. Sobbing convulsively, she dipped a face flannel into cold water and rubbed it fiercely over the shoulder his fingers had touched. Then she tore off her remaining clothes, all the time watching the door feverishly, and plunged into her nightgown which, thankfully, covered every bit of her except face and hands.

But it was a very long time before she slept.

In the morning the problems which had kept her awake were still there and the only thing she had decided was that she could not possibly tell Mrs Kemp about her husband's behaviour.

She lingered in her room as long as possible, determined not to go downstairs until she could be sure Mr Kemp had left for the bank. When she eventually descended she found Mrs Kemp just finishing breakfast and was obliged to pretend she had overslept.

'What a thing it is to be young!' Her hostess smiled indulgently.

'Do you feel better this morning?' Letty asked.

'Oh, yes, thank you. Unfortunately indigestion is one of the many troubles which middle age seems to bring and which we women have to endure. However, it will certainly be no concern of yours for a very long time yet. What would you like to do today, dear?'

They discussed it at length, in spite of the fact that there was really nothing to discuss at all. Letty would do whatever Mrs Kemp decreed, since she had no Russian lesson that day.

And suddenly she wanted to rebel. This was not what she had come to St Petersburg for, this empty frittering away of time. If only Marina had not gone away so mysteriously they could have had such fun together. Surely, surely she would be back soon?

Another week passed, an uncomfortable one for Letty, since she had at all times to avoid being alone with Mr Kemp. After one day of bad temper on his part, due as much to over-indulgence in brandy as to his humiliating experience in her bedroom, he had returned to his former coyly flirtatious attitude. But whereas before she had merely disliked the touch of his caressing hand, she now found she positively loathed it.

She was in this unhappy state of mind, longing to escape from the Kemps' house and yet determined to see Marina, when Yuri brought her another letter.

Letty seized it eagerly and began to read. This one was longer than the first, but gave no more information except the disquieting news that Marina's vacation—she was now using the same word that her sister had chosen to describe her disappearance—would last for some months. But she would definitely return to the ballet company eventually and in the meantime she begged Yuri not to forget her.

'I don't understand any of it.' Letty looked up piteously into his grave face. 'Do you, Yuri?'

Was it her imagination or did his dark eyes suddenly become blank, just as they had done before? Was it possible he understood—or guessed—more than he was prepared to say? Almost immediately Letty dismissed the idea as nonsense. He wouldn't take all this trouble to share his meagre knowledge with her if he were not as confused as she was.

'It is indeed most puzzling, *mademoiselle*,' he said sadly. They were both silent for a moment and then he went on, 'Will you remain in Petersburg in the hope of eventually seeing Marina, or must you return to England?'

Letty was asking herself the same question and could only give him a non-committal reply. She was still asking it when she sat down to write to her parents. It was another letter which had to be very carefully worded as she walked the now familiar tightrope between outright deception and the truth, which would inevitably greatly distress them. Eventually she settled for telling them that Marina would be away longer than she had expected and letting them make what they could of it.

Her heart was heavy as she sealed the envelope. Without a doubt when the Canon wrote again he would order her home.

# CHAPTER EIGHT

LETTY saw the yellow car as soon as she opened the outer door to Professor Dernitsa's apartment. It stood by the kerb, a brilliant splash of colour which attracted all eyes. People were pausing to stare at it and several young men stood transfixed, lost in wonder and envy.

The hood was down and the driver was fully visible. He was sitting with folded arms, looking straight ahead and ignoring the interest his vehicle was causing. As Letty stepped out on to the pavement she heard a muttered comment from one of the youths, 'Cursed aristocrat!' and it was spoken with such venom that her blood momentarily chilled in spite of the heat of the summer's day.

And then she forgot all about it as Nicholas saw her and swung a leg over the low door to climb out and hurry round to the other side. He swept off his cap and opened the passenger's door, standing holding it like a chauffeur, the sun burning down on to his bare head and discovering golden lights among the thick dark hair. Immediately Letty remembered his suggestion that he should take her for a drive.

Did he expect her to go with him now? He was certainly making it very plain that he wished her to get in, but she couldn't possibly go off with him into the country. Of course she couldn't! Or could she? Would it be such a crime if she agreed to go for a short drive? A *very* short one?

Her feet carried her across the pavement and brought her to a halt by his side. For a moment his grey eyes were alive and dancing, and then, with a wooden expression, he whipped out a light fawn coat from somewhere in the car and held it out for her to put on. Mesmerised, she slipped her arms into it and folded it round her, protecting her cream linen skirt and delicate embroidered blouse from contamination by dust.

'*Mademoiselle* would do well to tie her hat on,' Nicholas advised, handing her a bright green chiffon scarf as she got into the car.

Letty burst out laughing. 'You could always get a position as a chauffeur if you should ever need to earn your living!'

'There are worse jobs.'

When he had swung the starting handle and got the engine going, he leapt in and began to give his full attention to threading a way among the droshkys and private carriages. A cloud of black smoke from the exhaust caused elegant ladies to wrinkle their noses in disgust, and a slight increase in speed so much alarmed the plodding horse drawing a tram that it shied like a thoroughbred.

'It will be better when we leave the traffic behind us,' Nicholas said. 'How much time have you got, Letty?'

'None at all!' She laughed again. 'You had no right to assume I would agree to go for a drive. You know quite well I ought to go straight back after my lesson.'

'But you have not done so, and consequently we have a little time, even if it is stolen. You remember I promised to take you out into the country and show you how fast my motor car could go?'

Of course she remembered. She had thought about it constantly and longed for it to happen, while at the same time feeling sure it was impossible.

'You would like that we drive through the woods?' he asked.

Letty flung caution to the wind which was streaming past, making her glad her hat was firmly tied on. 'I should love it,' she said simply.

They did not speak again until they had passed the last of the houses. A rough country road stretched before them, white with dust, and with trees crowding closely on both sides. Apart from a farm cart in the distance, there was no traffic.

Nicholas seemed to have forgotten his wish to demonstrate the car's speed and was driving more slowly. 'You were surprised that I knew where to find you?' he asked.

'Very surprised.'

'I remembered your professor lived over a bookshop on the Nevski Prospect and the rest was easy.' He braked sharply to allow a squawking moorhen to escape sudden death. 'It is too long since we met.'

'It's only two or three weeks since you rescued me from the rain,' she protested, hoping he would not guess it had seemed ages.

'That was a mere five minutes, with no real opportunity for conversation.' He paused briefly and when he continued his voice had changed slightly. 'Now we have more time, I would be interested to know how much longer you can stay in Petersburg. I am aware you are a guest of the Kemps, but whether it is for the summer, or perhaps only six weeks—this I do not know.'

As he waited for her answer, his mind reverted to the letter he had had that morning from her sister. He had hoped it would contain Marina's permission to divulge her whereabouts to Letty, but apparently she remained adamant. Nevertheless, she appeared anxious for news and had begged him to find out, if he could, whether there was any chance Letty could stay until after the baby was born, by which time she could emerge from her retreat and arrange a meeting. 'I should love to see my sister,' she had finished pathetically.

Since the infant was not due until December, it appeared to Nicholas to be highly unlikely the two would ever meet.

Letty sighed and emerged from her own wandering thoughts. 'I know no more than you,' she said sadly.

'Why is that?'

She hesitated and then said impulsively, 'Do you remember why I came to Russia? I told you at the party.'

'Certainly I remember.' He spoke quietly with his eyes on the road. 'It was to see your sister, the ballerina Marina Varaskaya.'

'But I've been here weeks and still I have not seen her!' she burst out. 'Oh, Nicholas, I'm so dreadfully worried.'

He said something softly under his breath. It sounded like a curse, but she scarcely noticed it.

'I feel so afraid she is really ill,' Letty went rushing on. 'She wrote twice to a friend of hers at the theatre—someone called Yuri Ivanovitch, whom I met when I went there to look for her. He was kind enough to show me the letters. The first one said she would be back soon, but in the second, which came the other day, she told him she would be away much longer than she had at first intended. There was no address on either letter so we are unable to write to her.'

'It is certainly very mysterious, but at least you know she is not so ill she cannot write letters. In my opinion, she has been ordered a long rest from dancing.'

'But why the mystery? Why does she not simply say so?'

'No doubt she has her reasons.'

Letty felt she wanted to scream. Obviously Marina had her reasons, *but what were they*? As she struggled for control she found, to her dismay, that her pent-up emotions were about to manifest themselves in a different form. Tears filled her eyes and flooded down her cheeks; she gulped, groped for a handkerchief which she failed to find, and was reduced to turning her head away and hoping the flow would remain unnoticed.

The small sounds she made were lost in the chug-chug of the car, but her averted head and prolonged silence caught Nicholas's attention. He saw a glistening splash land on her gloved hand and, with an exclamation, brought his vehicle to a halt.

'Letty—you must not cry! You will see Marina again one day, I feel sure——'

'I can't believe I ever will,' she sobbed. 'I've tried to remain hopeful all this time but—but——' Desperate for comfort, she turned and raised her swimming eyes to his face. 'Oh, Nicholas, what am I to do?'

She looked so pitiful, and yet still so lovely, that he did the only thing possible and gathered her tenderly into his arms, holding her closely until the sobbing ceased and her breathing held only an occasional quiver.

Then he kissed her.

As she felt the firm pressure of his lips, Letty's first reaction was astonishment. No man had kissed her on the mouth before, though one impertinent young man at the tennis club had tried it when they were both hunting for a lost ball. She had smacked his face and felt utterly revolted.

She did not feel revolted now, but it would have been hard for her to say exactly what her emotions were since they were so unfamiliar. Certainly the sensation was enjoyable and at first she made no attempt to resist. But as the kiss was prolonged her well-trained conscience began to assert itself. Enjoyable things, she had discovered early in life, had an unpleasant habit of turning out to be wrong, and being kissed by a man to whom she was not even engaged, let alone married, was certainly among them.

'Please——' She raised both hands and pushed them against him. 'Please, Nicholas, let me go——'

Neither of them had noticed the slow approach of the farm cart, but both became suddenly aware that it had stopped in front of them, unable to pass because the car was blocking the narrow road. Left to its own devices, the engine of the Hispano-Suiza had stopped, and Nicholas leapt out to restart it. At the end of some vigorous swinging, interspersed with hearty swearing, it roared into life, sending a cloud of black smoke from the exhaust. The terrified farm horse immediately attempted to copy the one pulling the tram in the Nevski Prospect and the driver, who had been scowling at the yellow monster, now had to haul on the reins with all his strength.

Somehow dodging the flying hoofs, Nicholas jumped in again and drove on to the grass. Ignoring the countryman's shaken fist, he turned again to Letty.

'Have you really no notion of how long you can stay with the Kemps?'

She shook her head. 'They appear to like having someone young in the house, and even my parents seem to think it is all right for me to remain until Marina comes back.'

'That may be quite a long time,' he said half to himself.

Letty looked at him sharply but his expression told her nothing. She remembered her earlier suspicion that he might know something about Marina's absence but it seemed so impossible that she dismissed it from her mind and concentrated on answering his next question.

'What about your own feelings, Letty? Do you enjoy life with the Kemps?'

'Very much.' Her red lips closed with a snap and she knew at once that she had been too emphatic and he did not believe her.

Until then they had been speaking in French, but Nicholas now broke into English. '"The lady doth protest too much, methinks." That was said by your William Shakespeare, I believe. Am I not right?'

The excellent education upon which Letty's father had insisted enabled her to answer at once. 'Yes, it is from *Hamlet*, but I don't understand why you used it.'

'Liar!' he said calmly.

'I beg your pardon?'

'You protested so vigorously that your life with the Kemps is a happy one that I did not believe you, and I wish to know the reason. You will tell me, please.'

Letty hesitated no longer. 'You're right in thinking I am not entirely happy. Mrs Kemp is almost too kind, and in a way Mr Kemp is too but——' her cheeks were hot and she faltered '—he seems to find me rather too—too attractive and he is inclined to—to take liberties.'

Nicholas muttered something furiously, using an expression which even Letty's fluent French had not encountered. He swung the car again to the side of the road and stopped beneath the spreading branches of a beech tree. The engine gave a convulsive splutter and stopped too, but he ignored it.

Turning to Letty he put his arm along the back of the seat. 'He has made himself truly offensive, this fat little banker?'

'Only when he was drunk and he came to my room, but I managed to get rid of him.'

His eyes blazed with anger, and then for a moment the rage was replaced by amusement. 'Kemp is not the first man who, having imbibed too much brandy, has invaded your room since you came to Russia. You seem to be singularly unfortunate in such matters.'

Letty felt as though the scarlet in her cheeks was now dyeing her whole body, but she ignored her embarrassment. 'The fact that it has happened *twice* does not say much for your country!' she flung at him furiously.

'My country is ill-governed, decadent and, I sometimes think, on the verge of revolution, but it is not to blame for what happened to you. The first occasion was due entirely to error and my intentions were never anything less than honourable—in spite of my being greatly tempted.' Again his amusement showed briefly. 'The second occasion was due to your personal charm, but that is no excuse for Kemp. The man is not fit to have an attractive young lady staying in his house.'

'The real reason for his behaviour was the fact that he had been to a dinner at which only gentlemen were present,' Letty protested.

'So you are defending him now and trying to blame it all on the function he had been attending? You think men are beasts when in the company of their own sex?'

Letty knew little about the behaviour of men when on their own but she said defiantly, 'I think it very likely.'

She was not pleased when Nicholas burst out laughing, but he sobered almost immediately and returned to the subject they had been discussing. 'It seems to me, Letty, that you have at the moment only two alternatives. You can remain with the Kemps and be forever on your guard, which would be tedious, to say the least, or you can return to England without seeing your sister.'

'Oh, no! I don't want to do that either.'

'That is good. I, too, do not wish you to leave Petersburg.'

He had spoken quietly and with apparent sincerity, and Letty stole a glance at his face from beneath her lashes. Did he mean he wanted to get to know her better? Or was he merely finding it intriguing to indulge in verbal fencing with an English girl?

'What we must do,' he continued thoughtfully, 'is find some other means of prolonging your stay.'

'Some other means? I don't understand.' She waited a moment but he continued to frown into space without sharing his thoughts with her.

As the silence continued, she suddenly became aware of a small insistent prodding at the back of her mind, and with an exclamation of alarm she snatched at her watch. It was long past the time when she should have returned from her lesson and Mrs Kemp would be seriously worried. She should never have allowed Nicholas to persuade her to drive with him!

And then she remembered that he had made no attempt at persuasion. She had got into the motor quite shamelessly of her own free will, and the scolding which undoubtedly lay in wait for her when she got back would be richly deserved.

She said urgently, 'Nicholas, we must go—it's terribly late——'

He came out of his reverie, but showed no sign of haste. 'One more minute will make no difference and it would be a pity to leave without repeating that extremely enjoyable experience we shared a short while ago.'

She stared at him, her eyes dilating, but before she could protest he had seized her in his arms with a force he had not shown before, when his intention had been to comfort. Then, his mouth had been firm, but also gentle, but now it was fiercely demanding and full of longing and a passion which Letty did not understand even though it was echoed in her own body.

He released her so abruptly that she fell back in the corner, gasping for breath and with racing pulses. Dabbing at her lips with a handkerchief, she scarcely noticed when he restarted the engine and drove off down the road at a terrifying speed. With difficulty he found a place where he could turn round and they began a rapid journey back to the city, still in total silence.

It seemed to take hours and Letty was in a panic by the time the first houses appeared. Neither of them spoke until she was getting out at a discreet distance from the Kemps' house.

'I shall see you again soon, Letty, and it may be that I shall have a solution to your problem. Until then, *au revoir*.'

She had no idea how he could possibly solve it and was far too agitated to try and guess. During the drive back she had tried hard to think of an excuse for her lateness, but the only idea which presented itself involved more deception.

For a moment she was tempted to tell the truth. What would happen if she were to say frankly, 'I went for a drive with Nicholas Namorov and he kissed me? Would she be sent straight back to England in disgrace? Such a fate was too awful to contemplate. She would cause immense distress to her kind hostess, whom she genuinely liked, and to her parents whom she loved. Besides, she would lose all chance of eventually seeing Marina.

Mrs Kemp came out of the drawing-room as she entered the hall and Letty plunged straight into her fabrication.

'I'm so sorry to be late, but I've been having an extra lesson. The pupil who should have followed me sent a message to say he was ill and so I stayed on for another period. I do hope you were not too terribly worried.'

'Well, of course I was worried, dear.' Mrs Kemp pressed a hand to her well-corseted chest. 'It has made me feel quite ill.'

Letty said again, 'I really *am* sorry and I know it was very thoughtless of me to be so late—but I do so much enjoy my lessons and Professor Dernitsa is such a charming old man.'

'He really *is* an old man?' Mrs Kemp demanded with sudden suspicion.

'Oh, yes! He has quite a long white beard.'

'Well, I suppose I must forgive you this time, but you must promise never to let it happen again. You had better go upstairs now and tidy yourself for luncheon. Is it windy outside today, dear? You really look most dishevelled and your hair appears to be in danger of falling down at any moment.'

Letty fled up the stairs and reached the privacy of her room with relief. Pulling off her hat and looking at herself in the mirror she saw that Mrs Kemp was right about her hair, and also that it was not the only clue as to how she had spent the last half-hour. There were stars in her eyes and her cheeks were unnaturally pink. She had been very lucky indeed to have her story accepted.

It could only be because Mrs Kemp believed her to be trustworthy—and she wasn't. She was deceitful and a liar, and she drove unchaperoned with a young aristocrat in a fast car, a man about whom she knew almost nothing. Except that the sight of him sent her head spinning and turned her heart upside down.

Lunch was a silent meal. Mrs Kemp was pale and ate very little, but even Letty's guilty conscience could not make her believe it was due to the worry she had caused. Her diffident enquiry resulted in the information that her hostess feared she had caught a 'stomach chill'.

'I think it was probably caused by not wearing a coat when we went out in the carriage yesterday. The wind by the river was very fresh and I remember feeling chilly.' Mrs Kemp folded her stiffly starched napkin and slipped it into its silver ring. 'I am going to lie down now, Letty. You can amuse yourself this afternoon by studying your Russian.'

There had been a trace of acid in that last sentence and Letty knew she was not entirely forgiven. It served her right, she thought bitterly, not at all enjoying her present low opinion of herself.

She spent the afternoon in her own room, working hard until it was time to change for dinner, and going downstairs at the last possible moment. It was an unpleasant surprise to find Mr Kemp alone in the drawing-room. He was sipping a whisky and soda and looking pleased with himself, which she did not consider at all suitable when his wife was apparently not feeling well enough to come down.

'Just an—er—stomach upset, Letty,' he explained. 'I expect she will be fully recovered tomorrow.'

'She wasn't feeling well at lunchtime and seemed to think she had an internal chill.' Letty sat down as far from him as possible.

'Very likely, very likely. Ladies are delicate creatures—not nearly as robust as we men—though I must say you look the picture of health, my dear.'

'I am seldom ill.' Letty picked up a copy of *Punch* sent out from England and began to turn the pages without seeing much of what was printed thereon. The empty evening stretched before her and she viewed it with foreboding.

She was nervous when they left the dining-room after a long session and would have liked to shut herself in her room on some pretext or other. Unfortunately the lack of a key made it inadvisable.

To begin with she tried to get Mr Kemp to tell her some more about the history of St Petersburg, a subject on which he was well informed, but she met with little encouragement. Albert wanted to talk about *her*. He asked numerous questions about her life at home, whether she had 'a young man' and how strict her father was with her, and she answered him with brevity and careful politeness.

When he got up to pour himself another whisky and soda she returned to her copy of *Punch* and for a few minutes actually did manage to lose herself in an article which was both interesting and amusing.

Mr Kemp had just reseated himself when the door opened and one of the female servants entered, a middle-aged woman called Masha whose special duty it was to look after her mistress's clothes and other personal matters. She said something in Russian and, while Letty was gratified to find she understood it, she was alarmed at the news the maid had brought.

Mr Kemp did not seem particularly worried. He drained his glass and rose to his feet in a leisurely way. 'My wife is complaining that her abdominal pain is getting worse, but I don't suppose it's anything more than severe indigestion due to her chill. However, she seems to have got it into her head she wants a doctor.'

'Is there an English one in St Petersburg?'

'Oh, yes—more than one. Our own man is a splendid fellow and I suppose I had better send for him. Can't have Edith feeling herself neglected or some such nonsense.'

When he had left the room to telephone, Letty called to Masha, who was following him out, and asked in careful Russian if she might visit the invalid.

*'Da,'* the woman agreed at once, seeming pleased at the suggestion, and they went upstairs together while Mr Kemp bellowed into the telephone in a small cupboard-like room off the hall.

Mrs Kemp lay on her side in the big double bed ornamented with brass knobs and draped with side-curtains of red brocade. Even to Letty's inexperienced eyes she looked really ill. Her skin was colourless and clammy, and she obviously did not care that her hair straggled untidily across the pillow, showing unmistakable signs of grey at the roots.

'Kind of you to come, dear,' she said faintly.

'Is the pain very bad?' Letty asked, feeling totally inadequate.

'Like a knife—I'm sure it can't be just a chill. Do you think it's something I've eaten?'

'I should think it might be, but the doctor will give you some medicine to make you feel better. Mr Kemp is telephoning for him now.'

'I hope he won't be long. I—I don't think I can stand much more of this.'

'I'm so sorry.' Letty touched the glistening forehead with gentle fingers. 'I do wish there was something I could do.'

'Sit beside me and talk for a little while. I might not answer but it will help to listen to your fresh young English voice.

So Letty sat down on the bedside chair and wondered what to talk about. Instinctively choosing a subject which was typically English, she began to describe life in the small cathedral city she knew so well. It was very unexciting, but she managed to instil a little humour into it and had the satisfaction of seeing a wan and fleeting smile on the ashen face of her listener. Just as she was beginning to search for fresh ideas, Masha came in and announced Dr McEwan.

He was taller than Mr Kemp, but about the same age and nearly as portly. He had a very Scottish look with sparse ginger hair and a neat ginger beard streaked with grey. He saluted Letty with a courtly bow and then transferred his attention to his patient. Thankful that he had come so quickly, she slipped out of the room and went to her own to wait.

It seemed a long time before Dr McEwan went downstairs again, and he talked for some while to Mr Kemp in the drawing-room before leaving the house. As soon as he had gone, Letty went along the gallery to tap on the door of the sick-room. Mrs Kemp was lying much as before, but with her eyes closed, and at first Letty wondered whether to creep away again. As she hesitated the invalid stirred.

'Oh, there you are, dear.' She winced as the pain tightened its grip.

'Didn't the doctor give you anything to make you feel better?'

'I think he said he would send something round from his surgery. But I hardly listened.' She suddenly opened her eyes wide and there was fear lurking in the shadowy depths. 'Oh, Letty—he gave me such a terrible shock! He says I've got appendicitis and I must have an operation—tomorrow!'

Letty was horrified. Operations were completely outside her experience, but she had a clear memory of King Edward's having appendicitis soon after he came to the throne and his coronation having to be postponed. She had been ten at the time, old enough to understand how near to death he had been, and to take part in the prayers for his recovery being said in the Cathedral. There had been tremendous rejoicing when the surgeons had successfully removed the royal appendix and declared His Majesty out of danger.

'It will be wonderful to get rid of that horrible pain,' she said gently. 'Just think—perhaps by this time tomorrow it will have gone. Won't that be worth all the fuss and bother of an operation?'

But Mrs Kemp could not see beyond the ordeal which awaited her the next day.

'I felt sure it was only something I'd eaten,' she moaned, 'or perhaps Masha had laced me too tightly and given me extra bad indigestion. I never for one moment dreamt it was appendicitis. Oh, Letty, I do so dread the operation—they say the chloroform, or whatever they give you, makes you feel terrible.'

It was a relief when Masha came in with a dose of something which had just arrived from the surgery, and Letty was able to escape. She hesitated outside the door, wondering whether to risk going downstairs again to find out a few more details, but decided against it. Tomorrow would be soon enough to discover what effect this totally unexpected development would have on her own future.

# CHAPTER NINE

LETTY slept uneasily and every time she opened her eyes, there was daylight creeping round the edges of the heavy curtains across her window. She knew about the 'white nights' of St Petersburg, when the sun did not set until midnight and bounced up again within an hour, but she had not been kept awake before by the lack of darkness and she knew it must be due to her disturbed state of mind. Eventually—earlier than her normal time—she was jerked wide awake by a strange bumping sound accompanied by men's voices.

She slipped out of bed and, pulling her négligé round her, went to the door and opened it a crack. To her astonishment she saw two men labouring up the stairs with a large table of plain scrubbed wood, just like the one in the kitchen at home. Masha was there, looking pale and heavy-eyed, as though she had been up all night. She cried out as the men banged their burden against the wall and burst into a torrent of angry Russian quite incomprehensible to Letty. Fortunately the top of the stairs was reached without any further damage being done, and the men set off with the heavy table along the corridor leading to Mrs Kemp's room.

There was a group of servants peeping round a corner, and among them Tika, the girl who usually brought Letty's hot water. Imperiously, Letty beckoned her and, when the girl approached, began to question her as best she could.

Tika's eyes widened and she made a dramatic gesture, pointing to her stomach and imitating the thrust of a knife, at the same time repeating one word emphatically. Immediately Letty grasped the significance of the kitchen table. Mrs Kemp was going to have her operation at home.

And why not? Well-off people frequently did, though others had to brave the horrors of hospital. It would certainly be much less alarming for the patient to remain in her own bedroom.

Later, as Letty was going downstairs in search of breakfast, the front doors opened to admit two stout women in navy blue capes and with small plain bonnets that tied under the chin. Each carried a large basket covered with a white cloth. There was something very English about them, and when Letty said 'Good morning', she was not surprised to be answered in her own tongue. There was a strong smell of disinfectant hanging round them and it was easy to guess that they were nurses.

By the time a closed carriage brought Dr McEwan and a tall, thin man who was presumably the surgeon, the hospital odour had permeated the whole house. They were conducted upstairs by a subdued Mr Kemp, who then announced his intention of going to the bank as usual.

'No point in hanging about here, Letty. There's nothing I can do, nor you either.'

'How long will the operation take?' she ventured.

'Don't ask me. I'm only the patient's husband and I'm not told anything.'

His limousine was waiting for him and he went off with an air of relief. Wandering restlessly from morning-room to drawing-room, her dislike of the smell of disinfectant increasing rapidly, Letty wondered what to do with her day. Unfortunately she had no Russian lesson that morning and there would not even be an afternoon drive to look forward to. As she contemplated the empty hours which must somehow be made to pass, temptation assailed her.

She could not possibly have a better opportunity for going out by herself.

There was much that could be argued in favour of it. Mr Kemp himself had said there was nothing she could do here. In fact, the only thing against it was that Mrs Kemp certainly would not have approved, and to deceive her when she was ill seemed much worse than when she was in normal health.

Letty went slowly upstairs, glanced fearfully along the corridor at Mrs Kemp's closed door, and then somehow found herself in her own room taking off the simple cotton house-dress she was wearing. With care, she selected a pretty pale yellow gown in sprigged muslin and crowned it with a wide-brimmed hat trimmed with green silk rosettes. She added a cream, bottle-green lined parasol which Mrs Kemp had insisted on her borrowing now the sun was so hot, and went sedately down to the hall. As the doorman sprang to perform his task, she was guiltily aware of a simmering excitement, and then she was outside—free of that horrible disinfectant with its sinister associations. Free, too, of any need to worry about the time, so long as she was back for luncheon. The morning was hers and she could do what she liked with it.

Where should she go?

There was no difficulty about finding an answer. It would be cooler by the river and she had never had an opportunity to wander far on foot along the waterfront. As she set out in that direction, she was reminded of the day when she had been caught in heavy rain and Nicholas had rescued her.

It was so different this morning. The Neva sparkled like a billion diamonds, and the carillon of St Peter and St Paul, softened by distance and water, rang out like fairy chimes. Letty found herself humming the tune as she strolled along, watching the boats, the people and carriages crossing the bridges, and the visiting foreigners staring at the statue of Peter the Great. Watching, too, for a bright yellow motor car.

Eventually she reached a more workaday part of the waterfront, where commercial boats were moored by the quay, and rough-looking men were busy loading and unloading cargo. They stared at the elegant young lady and made remarks to each other in a variety of languages. Embarrassed, Letty decided to turn back, but she did not want to make it too obvious the men had driven her away, and so she sauntered on for another few yards.

It was then that she saw Nicholas, though at first she had difficulty in deciding it really was him. A tall man, informally dressed in a light summer suit, his dark head bare and his eyes screwed up against the dazzling light, was standing by a gangway with some sort of document in his hand. He seemed to be checking items on a list and appeared totally absorbed, so much so that she hesitated to approach him and say 'good morning'. This commercially minded Nicholas was someone she had not met before and she felt very unsure of her welcome.

At that moment one of the sailors loading cargo under his direction noticed her and called out something, adding a raucous laugh which added to her confusion.

Nicholas turned his head and saw her.

'Letty!' He came striding towards her. 'What the devil are you doing here?'

'I've been exploring the waterfront.' The disapproval in his voice caused her to tilt her chin defiantly, and her eyes seemed to reflect the green of her parasol lining as she met his accusing grey stare.

'It was most unwise of you to venture as far as this,' he said sharply.

'I had just come to that conclusion myself. In fact, I was about to turn back.'

'So I should hope. These seamen are no respecters of well-brought-up young ladies. How is it you are able to be out by yourself after all you have told me about it not being allowed?'

'Mrs Kemp is ill.' She added a few details and then continued, 'I know it was wrong, but I felt I just *had* to escape from the house.'

He grinned suddenly, his teeth very white in his tanned face. 'I suppose I had better stop scolding you and make sure you are safely escorted from this dangerous place.'

Letty's heart leapt, but all she said was, 'But aren't you too busy?'

'Certainly I am, but there are more important things in life than supervising cargo. If you begin to walk slowly back I will join you in a moment.'

He was with her very quickly and she gave voice to her curiosity by commenting on the work she had interrupted. 'I had no idea you were involved with anything more than the managing of estates.'

'My father attends to that. He does not care for trade, so when his brother died and left him a small shipping line he handed it over to me. My vessels sail regularly to your country, plying between Petersburg and Grimsby, carrying all manner of cargoes. The work interests me and it is not at all arduous, so that I am only busy spasmodically. An Englishman would doubtless consider it a hobby.'

Letty was fascinated by this sidelight on someone she had hitherto thought of as an idle aristocrat, dangerously attractive, but without the sterling qualities admired in England. But before she could question him further, he changed the subject.

'I wanted to see you, Letty, and was wondering how it could be accomplished. I had no wish to approach the formidable Mrs Kemp and demand an interview with you.'

They had reached Peter the Great and Nicholas slipped his hand under her arm and steered her towards a seat which was shaded by the drooping branches of a small tree. She offered no resistance and turned eagerly towards him as they sat down.

'I can't imagine what you have to say. Please don't keep me in suspense!'

'I shall be brief because of the necessity of returning to my duties. I believe you no longer wish to stay with the Kemps, but would like to remain in Petersburg. Am I right?'

'Quite right, but how in the world——'

'If you don't interrupt you will shortly hear how it can be done. I have a friend who is anxious to obtain the services of a young English lady to give her little boy, aged four, his first lessons.' Seeing her about to burst into impetuous speech, he held up an imperious hand. 'I am sure you do not want to take employment as a governess on a regular basis, but this would be a temporary post. The—er—family may be moving to England before long and it would be an advantage to the child to be able to speak a little English.'

He took her bare hand—she had forgotten to put on gloves before starting her adventure—and held it in a firm clasp. It seemed to Letty that a tremor passed right up her arm, but she tried to ignore her physical sensations and concentrate on what Nicholas had been saying. It was quite true that being a governess did not appeal to her, but it would be a wonderful opportunity to leave her present hosts who, in any case, surely would not want her there under the new circumstances. Well...Mr Kemp might, of course, but that would provide another reason for escaping.

'I think you would find Countess Natalia Brassova very less restrictive than Mrs Kemp,' Nicholas went on. 'She is young and a most charming lady, but she has had a somewhat unhappy life and that makes her sympathetic towards others.'

Until then Letty had been too surprised at the suggestion to wonder exactly what relationship Nicholas had with the attractive young Countess. Now the possibility that he was romantically interested hit her with full force and she recoiled under the blow.

There was no time to ask herself why it should be a blow—even if she had wanted to—because he was speaking again.

'I know you cannot possibly make up your mind immediately, but at least let me take you to see Natalia. This afternoon would suit me very well. Would it be convenient for you?'

Letty suspected he had added that last sentence as an afterthought dictated by good manners, and she had a not altogether unpleasant sensation of being blown off her feet by the strong wind of his personality.

'I will meet you at the Admiralty at three o'clock,' he went on, 'and we can drive to Natalia's house. Please do as I ask, Letty. It is important to me.'

She agreed without further delay and then watched him stride away. As she began to walk slowly in the opposite direction, her mind was busy with questions. Did he mean her own continued stay in St Petersburg was important, or was the convenience of the Countess Brassova his main object? If so, that must surely indicate that *she* was important to him.

Strolling back beside the sparkling river, she saw nothing of the scenes which had interested her on the outward walk because another problem had occurred to her. If she was offered and accepted the post of temporary governess, what would her parents' reaction be? Thinking it over, she came to the conclusion that they would probably agree about the necessity to leave the Kemps now that her chaperon was ill. Her father might even be glad she had found some work to do while she waited for Marina to return from her 'vacation'.

Back at the house, she entered with some trepidation. The odour of disinfectant seemed stronger than ever, and mixed with it was a strange smell which reminded her vaguely of the incense in St Isaac's Cathedral. Everywhere seemed very quiet and as she went upstairs she wondered how to obtain news of Mrs Kemp.

She was fortunate to discover Masha hovering in the gallery above the hall and she noticed at once that the Russian woman looked put out. Before Letty could form a question, she burst into a tirade which was difficult to follow, but it seemed she was outraged because the nurses would not allow her in her mistress's room.

'The operation is over?' Letty enquired, using the word she had learnt from Tika that morning, and, on being told it was, she went along to Mrs Kemp's room and tapped on the door.

After a short pause it was opened a little way and one of the nurses appeared and glared at her. She was now enveloped in an immense white apron which covered her from neck to feet, except for her navy blue sleeves. She had quite a well-grown moustache, Letty noticed, and tried not to show her repulsion.

Somehow she produced a friendly smile which was not returned, and made her request for information as politely as she could.

'The patient is sleeping,' she was told in a grudging tone.

'But the operation was successful?'

'Naturally, but the patient must have absolute quiet to enable her to make a good recovery. No visitors, on doctor's orders.' And the door was firmly closed.

Letty relayed the information to Masha as best she could and went to her room where she sat for some time thinking about the arrangement Nicholas had made. It was a good thing he had suggested this afternoon. Tomorrow Mrs Kemp might wish to see her, if she was feeling up to it and the dragons allowed her in.

She ate a solitary lunch and then went out into the scorching heat of early afternoon. Somehow her mind seemed to have made itself up without much help from its owner, and she was now almost sure she would accept the post of temporary governess if it were offered to her. She told Nicholas so as soon as she got into the car and was rewarded with a smile of commendation which turned her foolish heart upside down.

It seemed to be a very long way, most of it through the beautiful tree-lined avenues which made the city so attractive. At last, after what seemed miles of sunshine and shade, they drew up before a large house standing well back from the road. It was not as grand as the Kemps', but elegant enough with its wrought-iron balconies and windows draped with frilled muslin.

'I telephoned to say we were coming,' Nicholas said as they followed a maid across the hall.

She showed them into a large drawing-room overcrowded with little tables loaded with ornaments and photographs in silver frames, and numerous gilt-legged chairs upholstered in pink satin. The Countess Natalia Brassova rose to meet them, a slender woman with a mass of mid-brown hair and huge limpid eyes which looked as though they might have forgotten how to smile. 'Nicholas, my dear!' She returned his kiss of greeting with eager warmth. 'How very kind of you to bring Mademoiselle Mayfield to see me.'

Her lips were smiling as she held out her hand to Letty. 'So you are the young English girl whom Nicholas thinks would make an excellent governess for my little Nikki. Please sit down and let us talk.'

'You will get to know each other better without a male listener,' Nicholas said abruptly. 'I will go up to the nursery and see my friend Nikki.'

'He will play a boisterous game with him, and Nikki will get overheated and untidy, but he will love it,' the Countess said indulgently when he had left them.

She began to talk about the position, giving details of the work involved. It did not sound as though the governess's duties would be arduous, since the little boy already had a French nurse and was too young for proper lessons. Her main task would be to encourage him to learn a little English.

'Well, now, Mademoiselle Mayfield,' she asked, 'what do you think? Would you like to come here for a while and help to look after Nikki?'

Letty scarcely hesitated. 'I would like it very much, Countess, if you think I am suitable.'

'I have no doubts about that. Nicholas Namorov assured me you had the makings of an excellent governess.'

It was only with difficulty that Letty repressed her indignant exclamation. It sounded so appallingly dull! Did he really view her like that?

'Now we must talk of important things like salary and free time,' the Countess went on.

Until then the fact that she would actually be paid for teaching Nikki had not occurred to Letty, which she now realised was absurd. It would be a new experience to earn money and she found the prospect exciting. Exciting, too, was the information that she would have a great deal of free time—most afternoons and alternate evenings.

When she had accepted the conditions with enthusiasm, she waited expectantly for the Countess to send for her little son in order that they might be introduced. But instead Natalia sat silent for a moment, a brooding expression on her face.

Suddenly she looked up. 'There is something I must tell you, and, indeed, I should have done so earlier. I am divorced, and it may well be you do not approve of divorce.'

Letty was considerably startled. Divorce was outside her experience and it certainly did not happen in the Cathedral Close at Ely. Before she could think of a suitable reply, the Countess went on speaking.

'I fear that is not all. I now wish to marry again which, in the opinion of many people, makes the situation a great deal worse. If you have any moral objection to my—er—circumstances, I should be glad if you would say so frankly here and now.'

For a moment Letty could not think what to say. This must be the real reason for Nicholas's retreating upstairs. He would know all about it, of course, and would not wish to subject his friend to the embarrassment of someone else being present when she confessed to the new governess.

Brushing that aside temporarily, she concentrated on what her parents would think. They would certainly be horrified if she should take up residence in such a household! Yet she felt instinctively that her prospective employer was not at all a wicked woman, and maybe her unfortunate past had not been her fault. Surely she would not look so sad if she had not been more sinned against than sinning?

As Letty debated the matter, temptation wriggled into her mind just as the serpent had invaded Eden. There was no need to tell her parents anything about her employer except that she liked her very much—which was still true.

'Well, Mademoiselle Mayfield?' the Countess prodded gently.

Letty smiled into the mournful dark eyes. 'I don't think the situation in this house is any concern of mine, and I have no wish to withdraw my acceptance of the position of governess.'

Countess Brassova sprang to her feet with the agility of a schoolgirl and crossed the room to the bell pull. 'I am delighted to hear it, and now I will send for my little son, and you must take tea with us.'

Nikki was brought in by his French nurse. A lively looking little boy with shoulder-length golden curls and his mother's dark brown eyes, he was dressed in a miniature version of an English sailor's uniform, and carried a cap with 'HMS Warspite' embroidered on the band. Behind them came Nicholas, and Letty could not help noticing that his eyes went immediately to Natalia and she gave a little nod.

The tea party was a happy one with conversation in a mixture of languages, but afterwards when Nicholas was driving Letty back her mood changed. 'I think you should have warned me about the divorce,' she said reproachfully.

He turned his head sharply and studied her face but she kept her eyes on the road ahead. 'I wanted you to meet Natalia first. I knew you would like her.' He paused to change gear noisily. 'Were you very shocked?'

'I was certainly surprised. As for being shocked——' she hesitated '—I felt that I ought to be but, at the same time, it seemed none of my business. My parents, of course, would be greatly shocked.'

'Will you tell them?'

'No.'

He said no more, but she sensed his satisfaction and felt she had taken yet another step on the downward path.

Back at the house she put everything else out of her mind and concentrated on preparations for moving. There was much to be done, since she meant to leave the next day, but most important of all were the two letters she had to write. One was to Mrs Kemp, to be read when she felt up to it. This was a letter of explanation and thanks, and presented no problem since she was genuinely very grateful for the opportunity she had been given to spend some time in St Petersburg.

Alternately chewing the end of her pen and joining up the black blobs on the blotting paper into interesting shapes, Letty tried to compose a suitable letter to her parents announcing her change of address. She had already made up her mind there was no need to mention the divorce, as it would only worry them. She would concentrate on the impropriety of remaining where she was, with Mr Kemp her sole companion, and she would also emphasise that she intended to work as a governess only for a short time, 'that is, of course, until Marina gets back to St Petersburg.'

The letter was finished at last and the next duty was to break the news of her impending departure to Mr Kemp.

She waited until dinner was over and he was settled comfortably in the drawing-room, busying himself with the selection of a cigar. Although his wife's sudden serious illness had been a shock, there was no doubt he was recovering rapidly.

'How fortunate I am, Letty, to have your charming company in my loneliness,' he murmured sentimentally.

Inadvertently he had given her an opening and she snatched at it eagerly. 'If you give the matter a little more thought, Mr Kemp, I'm sure you will realise I can't possibly stay here now. Your wife is likely to be in bed for some time and, apart from any other considerations, I don't wish to be a burden on the household——'

'What's all this nonsense?' In the act of cutting the end of his cigar, he glared at her. 'The household is swarming with servants who don't have enough to do and it's ridiculous to speak of yourself as a burden.'

'With respect,' she pointed out, 'an invalid and two nurses are bound to make a difference, even in a big house like this. But it's not only that. I'm quite sure my parents wouldn't think it at all suitable for me to remain here under present circumstances.'

Mr Kemp's eyebrows and beard seemed positively to bristle. 'Utter damned nonsense—begging your pardon!' he exploded. 'I've got grown-up children of my own.'

His age and respectable position in society had not prevented him from offending her on many occasions, apart from that awful night when he came to her room, but Letty could not bring herself to mention the revulsion he had aroused by his patting and stroking. Instead, she decided to confront him with an established fact—that she was leaving tomorrow.

For a moment he was too astounded to speak and then he burst out, 'Where the devil are you going?'

'I have been fortunate to obtain a temporary position as governess to a little boy. It was pure chance that it happened just at the right moment.'

Holding her breath, she waited for him to demand to be told who had mentioned the matter to her, but fortunately he immediately wanted to know the name of her employer.

'The Countess Natalia Brassova. I had an interview with her this afternoon and I like her so much——' She broke off, startled by the expression on his face.

'That woman! You cannot possibly go there, Letty. She is divorced.'

'I know,' she said calmly. 'The Countess was quite frank about it, but——'

'Did she tell you she's been divorced *twice*?'

Letty gasped and the look on her face immediately gave away the fact that she had not known about the second divorce. For a moment she could not think what to say, but Mr Kemp's triumphant and rather unpleasant smile caused her to rally quickly.

'I'm sure it is perfectly possible to make two mistakes in marriage, and I don't see why a lady should be condemned because she has been unfortunate in that respect. As I told you, Mr Kemp, I liked her very much indeed and I have every intention of keeping to the arrangement I made.' She rose hastily to her feet. 'And now, if you will excuse me, I have a great deal to do. Goodnight.'

## CHAPTER TEN

'You have actually introduced my little sister into the household of—of that woman!' Marina exclaimed passionately. 'Shame on you, Nicholas!'

There was a dangerous glint in his grey eyes but he kept his temper. 'Natalia is a friend of mine,' he said coldly. 'I do not care to hear her referred to as "that woman". As for Letty, you seem to forget she is an adult.'

'She is under twenty-one.'

'It makes no difference. I believe she has grown up a lot since coming to Russia.'

'But she is still innocent. I simply can't imagine what made you recommend a divorced woman as an employer. It is outrageous!'

'I have explained to you that your sister could not remain where she was. I saw a means of helping both Natalia and Letty.'

'But how did you come into it?' she demanded.

Nicholas raised his eyebrows at her probing. 'A chance meeting. Have you finished your inquisition?'

'No, I have not!' She broke off and shrugged. 'But I suppose it is useless.'

'I am glad you realise that.' His tone still lacked its normal warmth. 'I am now going to put to you the question I ask every time I come to Liev. Have you changed your mind about telling Letty the truth? The continuing mystery is causing her a great deal of pain and I feel she may now be sufficiently mature to accept the situation. She was not unduly shocked when she heard about Natalia's divorce. In fact, she said it was none of her business.'

Marina shook her head vehemently. 'My misfortune is quite different and would, in a way, be very much her business, since we are sisters. I can't do it, Nicholas.'

They were on the veranda at the dacha, Marina in a rocking-chair and Nicholas leaning against the rail. Her reply did not surprise him, though he was always hopeful. Letty's large greenish eyes, full of distress, swam before his inner vision. To which sister did he owe the most loyalty?

The answer was plain enough. He owed none to Letty at all.

To hell with logic! He had always believed feelings to be of greater importance.

He abandoned his lounging position and looked straight at Marina. 'I give you due warning that I am no longer prepared to keep the secret of your whereabouts, should the occasion arise when I feel it must be revealed. I shall not tell Letty about your pregnancy—it would hardly be suitable for me to do so—but I shall explain where you can be found.'

She stared at him incredulously and struggled to her feet. 'Never, never did I think you would let me down like this, Nicholas! I thought I could trust you above all people.' Her voice shook but whether with tears or rage he could not tell. 'I think you had better go now, since we appear to have nothing else to say to each other.'

Nicholas returned to the city with less than his usual pleasure in driving. Although he felt sure he had done the right thing, he could not be entirely comfortable about letting down someone who had already been so grievously let down and was now paying for it in full.

As he threaded his way through the crowded streets of St Petersburg, he thought he caught a glimpse of Letty with a little boy, but, as she appeared to be escorted by a rough-looking man in workman's clothes, he managed to convince himself he had been mistaken.

In actual fact, he was perfectly correct and Letty and Nikki were indeed in the company of a man who looked like an artisan. She had been taking the child for a Sunday afternoon walk when a voice she vaguely recognised called her name.

'Miss Mayfield! This is a great surprise!'

Letty stopped and looked round, holding Nikki's hand tightly in case he should try to run away and hide. In spite of looking like an angel, he was a mischievous little boy.

At first she could see no one whom she knew. The Sunday crowds streamed by, enjoying the sunshine and a whole day off work. They were all strangers, or so she thought until she noticed a broad-shouldered young man standing still and smiling at her. He held a peaked cap in his hand and his bare head was the colour of beech leaves in autumn.

It surely had to be Gerald Sheldon—but why was he wearing the shapeless blouse of a workman, with loose breeches tucked into the tops of high boots?

'Mr Sheldon!' she exclaimed in astonishment. 'I didn't recognise you looking like that. You are usually much more formally dressed.'

'I am not a bank clerk today and so there is no need for me to look like one.'

'Oh, I see.' Letty's tone made it clear that in actual fact she saw nothing. 'Is it perhaps more comfortable to dress that way?'

'Certainly it is, but that's not my reason.' He came nearer and lowered his voice. 'If you will allow me to walk along with you for a short distance, we shall come to some gardens where it will be easier to talk, and the little boy can run about without being in danger of getting under the hoofs of a horse.'

Consumed with curiosity, but outwardly composed, Letty inclined her head and they walked on for a few moments in silence.

'I think we both have some explaining to do,' Gerald suggested eventually. 'I must admit I'm somewhat surprised to find you out with a small boy, apparently in charge of him——'

'I *am* in charge.' She laughed at his bewilderment. 'In fact, I am Nikki's governess. I have taken a temporary post.'

'So you have left the Kemps?'

'Yes—a week ago.' Letty paused, and Nikki, bored with the grown-up English conversation, asked plaintively how much longer he would have to wait before he could run about and play. 'It will be very soon,' she assured him, and then returned her attention to Gerald. 'You will have heard about Mrs Kemp's illness?'

'Oh, yes, we all know at the bank.'

'Have you any recent information? It is a day or two since I enquired.' Countess Brassova had told her to use the telephone to make her enquiry, and Letty had been so nervous of the instrument that her hands had trembled. And then, when the ordeal was over, she had only learnt that Mrs Kemp was 'comfortable.'

'I think she is progressing quite well,' Gerald said. 'But it takes a long time to recover from a serious operation like that. No doubt she will be an invalid for some time.' He paused and then asked diffidently, 'Was it because of her illness that you left?'

'Yes, of course. I'm sure you will understand that it was impossible for me to remain there with only her husband for company. My parents would have considered it most unsuitable.'

'I understand,' he said quietly. 'How did you manage to obtain this post just at the right moment?'

'I was very lucky. Someone—that is——' She floundered, strangely unwilling to mention the part Nicholas had played in the affair, and then, because there seemed no reason to keep it a secret, she brought out his name with unnecessary force. 'Count Nicholas Namorov is a—

friend of my employer and he suggested I should apply for the post.'

She could see he was both surprised and puzzled, but too polite to enquire further into the role Nicholas had played. They did not speak again until they had reached the gardens and found a seat, and then he asked diffidently who was the child's mother.

'The Countess Brassova.' She glanced at him from beneath her lashes to see what his reaction would be, and at once noticed his unconcealed surprise. 'And—and I know all about her being divorced and I don't care one little bit because I like her very much.'

'I'm glad to hear it,' he said drily. 'Sometimes people who have risen in society are not at all likeable. She was not born a Countess, you know. She acquired the title from one of her husbands.'

'You are speaking as though she has had half a dozen,' Letty exclaimed angrily.

'I did not intend to give that impression. I merely wondered if you knew she is the daughter of a lawyer and not an aristocrat. I think none the worse of her for that,' he added hastily. 'Far from it, in fact.'

'You surprise me, after the way you have been talking about her.' Letty paused and reined in her temper. She did not want to quarrel with Gerald whom she genuinely liked. 'Since you are so well-informed,' she went on coolly, 'perhaps you also know the Countess is planning to marry again?'

'It is rumoured in the city, and the Tsar is said to be greatly incensed.'

Letty was on the brink of asking him what it had to do with the Tsar when he abruptly changed the subject. 'Now it's my turn to hand out information. You were wondering why I have chosen to dress like a working man and the answer is perfectly simple. I wish to pass myself off as one in order to attend a meeting. If I looked like a bank clerk I should probably be thrown out.' He paused and then added gravely, 'You see, Miss Mayfield, the meeting I am going to this evening is one organised by an underground revolutionary movement.'

'Revolutionary!' Letty looked at him in amazement. 'I don't know much about it, but I would have thought an Englishman would keep well away from anything like that. Whatever would Mr Kemp say? He thinks you are a model of respectability.'

Gerald laughed aloud. 'That is what I intend him to think. I'm glad I have been so successful.' Abruptly he was serious again. 'The people who are organising these meetings have every reason for their revolutionary views. They are overworked and underpaid, with practically no civic rights, and their Tsar is a distant being who believes himself to be appointed by God. Think about it, Letty, and use your eyes and ears when you are going about St Petersburg, and you will see what I mean.'

She was silent as she turned over his words in her mind. She had been in Russia long enough to be vaguely aware that the poorer people lived very hard lives, though she knew nothing about civic rights. It might be interesting to find out a bit more. And suddenly an outrageous idea popped up into her mind and clamoured for attention.

At that moment Nikki came running up and asked her to play with him. 'I'm neglecting my duties.' She smiled at the child and threw the ball for him to run after. 'What you have been saying is extremely interesting, Mr Sheldon——'

'Couldn't you call me Gerald?' he interrupted.

'Oh—er—yes, I suppose so—Gerald. What I was going to say was that I would like to come to one of these meetings some day. I have plenty of free time.'

He raised his eyebrows and looked her up and down. 'You would need to change that very pretty gown for something less elegant and expensive. I doubt if you have anything suitable.'

'I expect I could find something.' She stood up and held out her hand. 'Will you take me to a meeting if it can be fitted in with my time off and I promise to be suitably dressed?'

'It would all be in Russian,' he warned her.

'I have progressed considerably in my studies. No doubt I should be able to understand a lot of it.'

There was a pause and then he said quietly. 'Very well. I will do my best to arrange it.' As she was smiling her thanks and moving away, he called after her. 'Have you any news of your sister?'

'None. I've thought about it until my mind is so confused I can hardly think at all. Yuri Ivanovitch had two letters but neither gave an address.' A sudden inspiration struck her. 'Mr Sheldon—Gerald—you seem to be very knowledgeable about what goes on in St Petersburg; couldn't you make a few discreet enquiries? You might just possibly pick up a clue.'

He hesitated, his face strangely blank, and then assured her that he would do what he could, but she was not to count on his being successful. Since Letty had long ago ceased to count on anything where Marina was concerned, she accepted the warning with equanimity.

She had much to think about as she played with Nikki in the gardens, though she took care the child was unaware of her abstraction. Was it really possible that there might one day be a revolution in Russia? Even Nicholas, she remembered, had said something about it and had actually sounded as though he might be, to a certain extent, on the side of the workers.

What were her own views on the matter? Walking slowly home with Nikki trailing beside her, tired after his energetic play, Letty could be sure of only one thing. The mere thought of revolution was terrifying. She could vividly recall lessons on the French Revolution. People had had their heads cut off then, often for no better reason than the fact that they were aristocrats. That had all happened more than a hundred years ago and it was inconceivable that anything similar should take place in Russia. All the same, she must have been crazy to ask Gerald Sheldon to take her to a revolutionary meeting!

It was all thrust out of her mind by the sight which met her eyes as they turned the corner near the house. Outside the tall wrought-iron gates there stood a bright yellow motor car.

Her heart was pounding as they entered the hall, though she knew it was unlikely she would see Nicholas. He was a drawing-room visitor who, no doubt, rarely went up to the nurseries. There was certainly no reason for anything to change just because Nikki now had an English governess whom the Count had casually kissed.

But when they reached the second floor they found Marcelle awaiting them impatiently.

'You are to go downstairs for tea. It is Madame's birthday and she has a visitor. Please to tidy yourself and I will put Nikki into his velvet suit.'

'Why did nobody tell me about the birthday?' Letty demanded. 'I would have made sure Nikki had a present ready.'

'Perhaps things are different in this outlandish country.' Marcelle's shoulders rose in a very French shrug. 'Hurry now, if you please, *mademoiselle*. You have been a long time out walking.'

Five minutes later they went downstairs again, the little boy enchanting in dark red velvet with a wide lace collar, and Letty looking, she feared, rather too much like a governess, in a white shirt blouse and plain blue linen skirt.

The big drawing-room was cool, with windows shaded against the sun and tall ferns in brass pots filling the fireplace. Letty was surprised to see the Countess's favourite chair decorated with wreaths of white daisies and assumed it must be a Russian custom. On a round table, that was covered with a lace cloth, there was a towering birthday cake which made Nikki cry out in excitement.

Natalia was not sitting in her chair. Instead she and Nicholas stood close together at the far end of the room, apparently deep in conversation. At the sight of them, obviously intimate and at home with each other, Letty's spirits, which had risen alarmingly, took a steep downward dive. Although she had been living in the house for a week, she still did not know the name of the man whom the Countess proposed to marry. No doubt Marcelle could have told her, but some strange reluctance prevented Letty from asking.

Now she felt almost certain it must be Nicholas.

Consequently she greeted him with careful casualness and kept her eyes veiled lest he should read too much in them. As they ate pieces of the rich cake and drank tea out of small transparent porcelain cups, the conversation was mostly centred on Nikki, but afterwards the Countess produced a picture-book and settled with her child on one of the sofas, and consequently Nicholas and Letty were thrown into each other's company.

'You are happy here?' he asked in a low voice.

'Oh, yes, indeed.' She was still avoiding his eyes and the only sign of her inner turmoil was her busy fingers, which plucked at a piece of cotton which had escaped from the seam of her skirt. 'I already love the little boy and I am more than satisfied with my working conditions. I get a wonderful amount of free time.'

'What do you do with it?' But before she could tell him, he checked her. 'No, wait—I can guess. You go out on foot and explore the city.' Smiling, he contrived to capture her elusive gaze and hold it.

'Quite right. I am becoming most knowledgeable.' She paused, but he made no comment and so she rushed on, saying the first thing which came into her head, because there must on no account be silence between them. 'The only difficulty is that, though I am often free in the evening, I don't care to venture out by myself then, even though it is daylight until so late.'

'Very wise,' he agreed solemnly, his eyes scanning the lovely curve of her figure beneath the tightly fitting blouse.

The hot colour was dyeing her cheeks, partly because of the look on his face, but also because she now realised she must have sounded as though she were begging for an escort.

'I am quite happy staying in my room,' she assured him hastily. 'I work hard at learning Russian and am progressing extremely well.'

'But I think you would not wish to remain here and study if a suitable invitation were offered to you?'

A suitable invitation? Did he mean another ride in his motor? Letty was not at all sure such a suggestion could be described as suitable, but she was eager to hear what he had in mind.

It turned out to be something so surprising she could not have imagined it if she had tried for weeks.

'Tomorrow evening,' Nicholas told her, 'there is an event out at Tsarskoe Selo which I think would interest you——'

'You mean at the Tsar's summer palace?'

'In the grounds. I have promised to escort my two sisters to it and we would all be glad if you would come, too. It is an exhibition tennis match, Letty, before the Tsar and Tsarina, and no doubt all the family, since they are rarely separated. Your English champion Alice Ryan will be there, with other international players. You would like to go?'

Letty's eyes were shining and she forgot her previous awkwardness. 'Oh, Nicholas, I should love it! I have always wanted to see the Imperial Family——'

'It is not they who will be on exhibition, but the tennis players.'

She laughed and gave his hand a small playful slap. 'I shall enjoy watching *everybody*, and tomorrow is one of my free evenings so there will be no difficulty there. Is the Countess going as well?'

He did not answer for a moment and she sensed a slight reserve in him. 'Natalia leads a very quiet life and does not attend court functions,' he said eventually.

It was because she was divorced, Letty realised, and was angry with herself for asking a stupid question. She glanced across at the sofa where the Countess sat with Nikki, the brown head and the golden one very close together. She was so sweet and gentle, she deserved more from life than two unhappy marriages and royal disapproval.

Perhaps, before so very long, she would be happy again. But not, please God, with Nicholas Namorov. But even as she despatched the tiny impulsive prayer, Letty felt almost sure it would not be answered.

The following evening she spent a great deal of time surveying her wardrobe and trying to decide what to wear. At first she assumed they would be travelling in the yellow car, and then she remembered Clara and Sonia would be present so they would use one of the Namorov carriages.

A tennis match at court was right outside her experience and she decided it would be best to dress as for any other grand outdoor function, such as a garden-party. Accordingly, she donned a smart outfit in her favourite pale green, a lovely dress trimmed with ruched ribbon in a darker shade, and on her piled-up red-gold hair she perched a small hat of natural straw turned up in front with a huge bunch of silk violets.

'How sensible of you not to wear a large hat,' approved the Countess. 'There will be no fear of your spoiling other people's view. I should take a scarf, dear, in case it turns cooler later.'

So Letty draped a wide cream lace scarf round her shoulders and went to wait impatiently in the hall for Nicholas to arrive.

'You look very elegant,' he said with a smile. 'Not in the least like a governess.'

In the carriage, his two sisters greeted her enthusiastically and, she thought, with a certain amount of curiosity. Sonia was dark like her brother, with grey eyes full of laughter, and she wore pink. Clara had brown curls and clear hazel eyes and was dressed in yellow.

'Do you play tennis, Miss Mayfield?' Sonia asked, and before Letty could answer Clara broke in.

'We have a court at our dacha on the Gulf of Finland but we don't use it much. There's so much else to do when we're there and tennis is such a hot game.'

'The Liev dacha has one too,' Sonia reminded her, 'But we haven't been there for *ages* and I expect it's all overgrown now.'

At the mention of Liev, Letty found herself stealing a glance at Nicholas before she could control her eyes. She had expected to catch a glimpse of a wicked twinkle, but he was looking unusually sombre and apparently staring at nothing.

'I wouldn't like to play tennis in Russia,' she said, 'but in England, where the summer is cooler, I thoroughly enjoy it.'

'The four Grand Duchesses—I mean the Tsar's daughters—are all good players.' Sonia took up the conversational lead. 'Not that any of us have actually seen them play—they are kept far too much in the background for that.'

There was a great deal of traffic on the road to Tsarskoe Selo, mostly carriages, with a few cars impatiently trying to overtake the horses and upsetting them badly. She had been told it was an hour's journey by fast car and the carriage must have taken longer than that, though the time passed quickly.

Eventually they passed through wide open gates, carelessly guarded by a few soldiers, and into a large beautiful park which appeared to contain a sort of village composed of many different sorts of houses, some very grand, others quite small, but nevertheless elegant. There were green lawns, numerous lakes with fountains playing, and great beds of brilliantly coloured flowers so well watered that they had survived the summer heat. It was a lovely place, and Letty was not surprised the Tsar liked it so much better than his huge, gloomy palace in the city.

Serious tennis had not yet begun and most of the spectators were strolling about, but a few players were hitting balls back and forth on the half a dozen courts. The men wore spotless white flannels and white silk shirts with various club ties, and the ladies were in white also, their tightly belted skirts almost touching the ground and their blouses severe with high boned collars. Perched on each neatly coiled pile of hair there was a pert straw boater tilted so as to give a little shade to the eyes.

Nicholas found four vacant seats with a good view of the court where it seemed likely the most important matches would be played, since there was a roped-off enclosure containing much grander chairs than those provided for the guests.

'Is that where the royal family will sit?' Letty asked.

'Probably.' He did not sound very interested. 'I chose this court because it is where the English lady, Miss Alice Ryan, is to play. I thought you would enjoy seeing one of your countrywomen.'

'That was kind of you.'

Unwisely she looked up into his face as they paused before sitting down and found her eyes examining the lean line of his jaw, his firm chin and sensitive mouth, and those diamond-bright eyes which so faithfully reflected the mood within. Suddenly a strange tremor started deep down inside her body, so strong that she trembled with the force of it and was overwhelmed with fear.

Fear of what? Was it the strength of her own feelings for this man about whom she actually knew so little?

Although no announcement had been made, people were now settling down round the various courts and looking expectant. At some unseen signal, everyone stood up, and Letty, hastily following suit, found she had an excellent view of the Tsar's party which was now making an entrance.

It was very formal, their Imperial Majesties coming first, and looking as stiff as animated wooden figures. The Tsar, slim and bearded and much resembling his cousin, the Duke of York, who would be England's next king, had his wife beside him, her gloved hand resting on his arm. The Tsarina was coldly beautiful, her face like a mask, and quite simply dressed in mauve moiré silk. They were followed by their precious only son, the Tsarevitch Alexis, in a sailor suit. The four Grand Duchesses came in two by two, alike in plain dark dresses in some spotted material which were ornamented with huge white buttons arranged in groups of three. Anastasia and Marie's dresses ended at the ankle, but Tatiana and Olga wore theirs full length. All of them had huge ugly hats like mushrooms, adorned with a simple ribbon.

Letty studied them with interest. The girls looked happy, obviously eager to see the tennis, but their parents were bowing stiffly right and left in acknowledgement of the ripple of applause, without a flicker of a smile on their rigid faces.

Various courtiers followed them into the enclosure, and among them was a tall man with a black beard who seemed more important than the others, and actually sat in the front row, next to the Grand Duchess Olga. For some reason Letty's curiosity was aroused and she asked who he was.

'The Grand Duke Michael,' Nicholas said. 'Younger brother of the Tsar.' He lowered his voice. 'If anything happened to the Tsarevitch—I think you know he is frequently ill—the Grand Duke would be his brother's heir.'

'So that's why he is sitting with the family.'

'Yes, but I'm a little surprised to see it, all the same. After all, he's not much in favour just now.'

His voice had been full of meaning but Letty had no idea what he intended to convey. Consequently she demanded an explanation.

'You don't know?' he asked in astonishment.

'Would I be asking if—'

'No, no, of course not,' Nicholas broke in hastily. 'It's just that your ignorance seems rather surprising, considering your present abode.' He leaned closer, his shoulder pressing against hers and his voice so low that she could only just hear it, specially as her hearing was affected by the delicious hammering of her pulses due to his nearness. 'The Grand Duke wishes to marry outside the ranks of royalty and the Tsar does not approve. And when I tell you that the lady in question has been twice divorced, making the situation about twenty times worse, no doubt you will be able to supply her name for yourself.'

Letty had no difficulty at all, but what did cause her trouble was the necessity to hide from Nicholas her own sudden radiance. She tried to tell herself she was glad the Grand Duke Michael was in love with the Countess because it was all so romantic, and she hoped it would all turn out right for them in spite of the Tsar's opposition. But deep down in her heart she was only too well aware of an even greater gladness because Natalia was not going to marry Nicholas.

Fortunately the tennis match to be played in front of them was just beginning and she was spared having to make a reply which would not give away her delight.

After a while the four white-clad figures ceased to be invisible to her shining eyes and she began to take an interest in the match. She was much amused to discover that the players were being supplied with balls by a number of poker-faced footmen in powdered wigs who gravely handed them on silver salvers. Her sudden gurgle of suppressed laughter caused Nicholas to look at her.

'What's so funny?'

'Those footmen—I was just imagining them at the Ely Tennis Club!'

'They would certainly be out of place there, but I don't suppose anyone here—except yourself—finds them amusing.'

He had not sounded as though he thought them funny either and Letty wished she had kept her mirth to herself. Disappointed, she withdrew slightly within herself and tried hard to concentrate on the play.

Before long, a movement in the crowd caught her attention. People were looking towards the royal enclosure, where a latecomer had now appeared and room was being made for him between Alexis and Anastasia. Immediately all that she had heard about Rasputin's footing of familiarity with the Imperial Family flooded into her mind. Clearly sure of his welcome, the so-called monk had joined them with as much assurance as though he were a member of that family himself.

Letty shivered as she looked at him, this evil man who was either adored or hated by almost everyone in St Petersburg, and all the loathing she had felt for him at the Grand Duchess Anna's party came flooding back. How *could* people—mostly women—bear to flock around and fawn on him? Was there really any foundation for the notion that he had mystic powers? Even she, with all her dislike of the man, had felt something strangely compelling about his gaze when he had looked at her. Try as she might to take an intelligent interest in the tennis, her eyes kept coming back to that incongruous figure in the dirty monkish clothes, who seemed so much at home with the greatest in the land.

It was said he had saved the little heir's life more than once. That, no matter where he was, he *knew* when the child had an attack of the terrible bleeding and came at once to be with him. There must be *something* in it.

During the next hour Letty saw even less of the match than she had done at the beginning. At first the plan taking shape in her mind was just a germ of an idea, but slowly it grew and developed until it became something she actually intended to do, if possible.

She would need a lot of luck, and a great deal of courage too, and she couldn't be sure of having either. But somehow she meant to try and put her plan into action.

## CHAPTER ELEVEN

A SMALL part of Letty's mind registered the fact that Alice Ryan and her partner had won their match, but if anyone had asked her the score during the next she would have been unable to answer. Her eyes constantly strayed towards the royal enclosure where Rasputin lounged between the Tsar's two youngest children, his arm familiarly along the back of Alexis's chair.

'You're very quiet,' Nicholas murmured in her ear.

'I'm absorbed in the tennis.'

'Personally, I find it somewhat tedious, but I have not your British enthusiasm for sport. I shall be glad when it is over and we can resume our stroll round the grounds.'

'I didn't know you liked walking either,' Letty could not resist saying.

'It depends on the company.'

The tennis matches ended at last and the spectators left their seats, though few of them showed any urge to return to the hot city streets. Even the royal party did not immediately disappear into their palace. Accompanied by Rasputin, they moved slowly among the flower-beds, talking among themselves and ignoring everyone else.

Such an innocent occupation could not possibly interest the monk, Letty reasoned. Perhaps he would break away and look for diversion elsewhere. If he did that, it might not be too difficult to waylay him.

It was all wishful thinking, as she was well aware, but luck was on her side. As she half listened to Clara and Sonia, who were talking about fashion, her searching eyes caught a glimpse of movement in the Tsar's party, and suddenly Rasputin was no longer there. Fortunately she saw him again almost immediately, walking slowly and apparently aimlessly among the crowd.

Nicholas was talking to someone with his back half turned and Letty said quietly to Clara, 'Will you excuse me a moment? I caught my heel in the lace on my petticoat and I must find somewhere to examine the damage. I can't go about with it hanging down—it would be too embarrassing.'

'It looks all right,' Sonia put in.

But Clara raised no query. 'You had better retire to one of the grottoes. Look—there's one over there. Have you a safety pin if you need it?'

'I always keep one in my bag.' Letty was already hurrying away, desperate to escape before Nicholas turned round, and aiming for the spot where she had last seen Rasputin.

He had not travelled far and—miraculously—he was alone.

Until then Letty had been carried along by the strength of her determination. Now her courage began to falter. Rasputin, said by some to be the most evil man in Russia, was only a few yards ahead. She could see the filthy state of his clothes, his straggling, greasy and unwashed hair and beard. She fancied she could smell him. A sudden alarming thought added to her distress. She would have to speak to him in Russian, since it was certain he was too uneducated to understand French. Whatever was the Russian word for 'supernatural'?

At that point her courage almost deserted her, but she snatched at it with both hands and hung on grimly. Hastily assembling an opening sentence, she ran the last few yards and accosted the so-called monk.

'Please——' The words came tumbling out, sounding a great deal more confident than Letty felt. 'Please may I speak to you for a moment?'

He swung round in surprise, and when he saw the attractive young lady gazing up at him, her lovely greenish eyes full of appeal, his coarse features broke into an unpleasant smile.

'By all means, little sister, but we cannot talk here.' Glancing round, he noticed the ornate shell-decorated grotto which Clara had suggested for Letty's repair to her petticoat. 'Let us retire to that shelter and you shall tell me what is in your mind.'

She would have preferred to remain in the open air where the sour odour surrounding him was less offensive, but she dared not refuse. As they stepped into the grotto its dank mushroom smell was immediately overpowered by the smell Rasputin had brought with him, compounded of stale brandy, dirty garments and a body which rarely experienced soap and water.

'Sit down, little sister.' He indicated a rough rustic seat along the back wall.

Struggling to hide her revulsion, Letty did as he had instructed, leaving a gap between them which was not nearly as wide as she would have preferred. But she mustn't think about that now. By the most amazing luck she had her chance, and she must make full use of it. On the verge of speech, she remembered the name which his admirers used and decided to address him by it. He would like that.

'It is said that you have very special powers, Father Grigori, which enable you to see things which are hidden to ordinary people and thus you can help those who are ill or troubled in mind.'

'Surely a lovely young lady like yourself has no need of *that* sort of help?' he protested, his harsh voice sounding unnaturally loud in the confined space.

'Indeed, sir, I have great need.' Suddenly it all came pouring out with a fluency Letty had not known she was capable of. Now, at last, all those long hours spent poring over her Russian books were bearing fruit, and if her grammar was sometimes at fault he was probably too ignorant to notice.

'Oh, Father Grigori, I am so terribly worried about my sister.' Her voice trembled with emotion and she even momentarily forgot her loathing of him as she told her story. 'I came to St Petersburg specially to see her, but she left the city before I arrived and I don't know where she is. If there is any means by which you can help me find her, I beg you to use it, for I fear she may be ill.'

When she had finished Rasputin sat for a moment in silence, his head bowed. Suddenly he began a strange muttering which Letty at first found incomprehensible and then recognised as sentences from the Scriptures. Bewildered, but still hopeful, she sat very still, almost holding her breath.

The muttering ceased and he turned towards her. 'Look at me, little sister.'

Fearfully she raised her eyes to his. Hypnotic, abnormally large and strangely colourless, they held her gaze, and she could not have looked away if she had wanted to. His hands gesticulated in front of her face and she was aware of an odd floating sensation. Now his hands moved slowly to grasp her arms and she knew she was being drawn nearer though she could do nothing to avoid it.

Then, abruptly, she was seized in a grip of steel which there was no hope of breaking. An overpowering animal stench filled her nostrils and she felt as though she were swooning.

Perhaps Letty really did lose consciousness for a moment, for she did not realise someone had burst into the grotto until a shout of rage caused Rasputin to drop his arms and she was free. As she struggled to her feet, supporting her trembling limbs by a hand on the wall, she saw Nicholas's fist smash into the monk's dirty face, sending him reeling backwards with a cry of fury and pain.

Nicholas turned his attention to her. 'I don't know what you are doing here, Letty, but explanations can wait.' Seizing her arm with a grip fully equal to Rasputin's, he hurried her out of the grotto, looked round swiftly and then set off down a leafy avenue at such a pace she had to run to keep up.

'Nicholas—please——' she gasped. 'You're hurting me.'

'It's only what you deserve. I would never have believed you could be such a fool as to let that—that lecherous beast lure you into a place where you would be alone with him. Are you out of your mind? You know his reputation.'

'I wasn't thinking about that—well, not very much. I—I wanted to ask for his help.'

They had been moving so fast that the crowds were left behind and they were in a wooded glade where there was a seat facing a small lake on which ducks swam and quacked. Nicholas allowed his furious pace to ease and steered his captive towards this. Thankfully, Letty subsided on to it, still panting from exertion and shaking from head to foot.

She felt unclean and it seemed to her she still carried with her the odour of that terrible man. Although at first glance her pretty dress appeared miraculously unsoiled, her fastidious eyes could plainly see a stain on both sleeves where his hands had grasped her and she shuddered because she must carry the marks of her experience about with her for what remained of the evening.

'Now,' Nicholas was saying angrily, 'you will tell me why you imagined that—that devil could possibly be of assistance to you.' Leaning back, he folded his arms. 'I am waiting, so kindly get on with it at once before Clara and Sonia become alarmed at our absence.'

Letty drew a long quivering breath and began. 'A lot of people think Rasputin has supernatural powers. I had no idea whether it was true or not, but I thought there was just a chance he might be able to help me find my sister. I hated the idea of approaching such a dreadful man, and at the same time I felt there must be some good in him or the Tsarina would not think so highly of him. So, when I saw him walking by himself, I—I seized my opportunity.'

'And I suppose he suggested holding a private conversation in the grotto?'

'Well—yes,' she agreed reluctantly. 'I was thinking more of finding Marina than of any danger to myself.'

Nicholas ran his hand through his thick dark hair in a gesture of mingled distress and exasperation. 'Oh, Letty, how could you be so utterly crazy?'

She was beginning to recover a little from the ordeal. Tilting her chin defiantly, she said with a show of spirit, 'I have already told you I believed it to be worth the risk. I'm so desperate for news of Marina—and I don't mean just another vague letter to Yuri Ivanovitch, but *real* news—that I would do almost anything to obtain it.' She paused and heaved a sigh which seemed to rise from the deepest recesses of her heart. 'Unfortunately there appears to be nothing I can do.'

Nicholas was a long time replying, but Letty was so absorbed in her unhappy thoughts she scarcely noticed. When he did speak it took a few seconds for his words to penetrate.

'Maybe not, but there is something *I* can do.'

She stared at him blankly. '*What* did you say?'

'I said I could help you to find your sister.' He took a deep breath and plunged. 'It so happens I know where she is.'

'*You* know?' Letty still seemed bewildered. 'Do you mean you have recently discovered her whereabouts? Then why in the world didn't you tell me at once? You knew how worried I was——'

He held up his hand to stop the flow of words. 'I have known for—er—some time, but I did not consider the secret mine to divulge.'

Her eyes blazed green fire and she leapt to her feet. 'How dare you sit there and calmly admit it? I told you weeks ago all about Marina's disappearance yet you said nothing. It all sounds very fine saying you didn't consider the secret was yours to divulge but I thought we were supposed to be—friends. I—I don't think I can ever forgive you for not telling me.'

A spasm of pain crossed his face but she did not notice. 'I was faced with a difficult decision,' he said curtly. 'I had to choose between you and your sister. Owing to the—er—special circumstances, I felt obliged to keep Marina's secret.'

Letty gasped and sat down again as though her legs had given way. 'Then why have you admitted *now* that you know where she is?'

'Because of your asking that brute to help you. You must have been desperate to do that——'

'You have still told me nothing,' she broke in. 'I don't know what these special circumstances are or——'

'Marina must explain that herself.'

She turned to him impulsively and put her hand on his arm. 'I'm getting more and more confused with all this mystery. I do wish you would tell me the whole story.'

'There is no time now. Clara and Sonia will be wondering where we are. I left them talking to friends and said I would only be a few minutes. But you must not be afraid that your sister is ill, though she felt unwell for a time. There is a good reason for her long vacation but, as I have said, she must tell you about it when you meet.'

'But *where is she*?'

'Wait! I was about to say I will take you to visit Marina at the earliest opportunity.' Removing her hand from his arm, he stood up, drawing her up with him. 'There is no time to discuss the matter further now, but you have my promise. Surely you can trust me, Letty?'

Her eyes searched his face, finding in his steady gaze no sign of the wicked amusement which so often both intrigued and annoyed her. With all her heart she longed to trust him, yet it seemed to her that he had given her a tantalising glimpse of an end to the dark tunnel of mystery, while at the same time making the blackness even more dense.

None of it made any sense, but now—at least—there was hope.

'I shall have to trust you,' she said bleakly. 'I have no option.'

The reply did not please him, that was very plain. The dark, expressive eyebrows rose and she caught a flash of anger, but he said nothing and merely set off back up the avenue at a great pace.

When they reached the two girls they found them openly curious, and Clara's whispered question about the state of the lace on Letty's petticoat ended in a suppressed giggle.

'There was very little damage done,' Letty assured her, and left it to their brother to account for their absence if he thought it necessary.

But Nicholas made no attempt to do so. Instead, observing that the Tsar and Tsarina, taking their family with them, had disappeared, he suggested it was time to go home.

Later, saying goodnight to Letty outside Countess Brassova's house, he repeated his promise.

'It will be necessary to arrange for a whole day free. Leave it with me and I will fix it with the Countess.'

Until that evening, Letty would have taken that assurance as further proof of Nicholas's intimate relationship with Natalia. Now she knew better and, incidentally, found it easier to understand why the Tsar was so disapproving of the new marriage. Apart from the problem of the succession if Alexis died young, that stiff-necked Tsarina was probably horrified at the thought of having the daughter of a lawyer for a sister-in-law.

Up in her room, Letty dragged off the stained dress and relieved her feelings by kicking it into a corner. Then she had a thorough wash-down in cold water and, refreshed in mind and body, crept into bed. Instantly the further mystery surrounding Marina occupied her brain to the exclusion of everything else and it was a long time before she slept.

Several days went by without a word from Nicholas. Letty helped the time to pass by paying a visit to Mrs Kemp on one of her free afternoons. She found her former chaperon sitting in a chair in her room, clad in a vivid pink négligé trimmed with swansdown. She looked pale and had lost a great deal of weight, but she insisted she was making a good recovery.

'And how are you getting on, dear? Do you like being a governess?'

'Very much. Nikki is a very nice little boy——' unconsciously Letty allowed a note of defiance to creep into her voice '—and I find Countess Brassova most charming and so kind.'

'Nevertheless, it is a great pity you had to take a post with *her*,' Mrs Kemp said sharply. 'I cannot imagine what your dear parents would think it they knew the truth about your employer. I am assuming you have not told them?'

'I thought it better not to,' Letty admitted. 'The thing is, Mrs Kemp, the offer came just at the right moment. I am sure you'll agree it would not have been at all suitable for me to remain here while you were ill in bed.'

'H'm, perhaps not.' She paused and shifted her position with a heavy sigh, changing the subject as she did so. 'Have you any news of your sister?'

Letty had anticipated this question and, though she would have preferred to avoid it, she had her answer ready. 'Oh, yes.' she said brightly, 'and I'm going to see her soon. I'm looking forward to it so much.'

'I'm sure you must be.' Mrs Kemp looked at her curiously, obviously waiting for further information.

Letty could guess at the questions she wanted to ask as plainly as if they were written on the wall behind her. Why had Marina disappeared like that? Where was she hiding? She would think it most strange that the missing ballerina's own sister still did not know the answers. Letty thought it strange herself but she had schooled herself to be patient.

Fortunately at that moment the door opened and one of the nurses entered and brusquely ordered her to leave as 'my patient still tires very quickly'.

The visitor was so grateful for the interruption that she gave her a brilliant smile, kissed Mrs Kemp affectionately and left at once.

That evening the Countess sent for her and told her she could have the following day off to visit her sister. 'Count Namorov has made all the arrangements and will call for you at ten o'clock.' Natalia paused and then added with a shade of reproach, 'He has told me the whole story and I do wish you had confided in me when you first came. I might have been able to help you. Nicholas and I are very old friends.'

Letty longed to say, you must know a great deal more about it than I do, but she controlled herself. Instead she murmured, 'I'm sorry, Countess. I didn't think of it.'

That night she was too excited to sleep. The whole sequence of events concerning Marina—as far as she knew them—went through her mind over and over again, beginning with the arrival of the letter at Ely and ending with the intoxicating thought that in a few hours she would actually see her sister and hear the whole story.

She was tired and heavy-eyed in the morning, but the sight of the yellow Hispano-Suiza outside the gates, and the prospect of a long drive in it with Nicholas, was sufficient to send her spirits rocketing with the speed of mercury in a thermometer plunged into boiling water.

'How far is it?' she ventured to ask as they left the traffic of the city behind them.

'About thirty-five kilometres.' Nicholas changed gear with a great deal of noise and the car leapt forward down a long straight road which stretched as far as the eye could see.

'I wish I knew where we're going,' Letty said.

'You must allow me my little game. It is so very amusing to tease you and, in any case, our destination is in a way part of your sister's story.'

He was talking in riddles, no doubt deliberately, and Letty made up her mind not to encourage him by asking any more questions. Instead, she gave herself up to the joy of speeding through the flat countryside, birch woods and lakes and small villages all streaming past, with the occasional frightened horse and shaken fist the only signs of life.

'Russia seems an extraordinarily empty country,' she said thoughtfully. 'I noticed the same thing from the train.'

'It is vaster than anything you could possibly imagine.' Nicholas squeezed the bulb of the horn to clear a covey of partridges from the road. 'When I am in England I find the contrast almost too much.'

'You come to England often?'

'Several times a year. I go first to Grimsby in connection with my shipping line, and then to London to enjoy myself. Except for Paris, there is no better place for having a good time.'

Letty was silent as her imagination painted a picture of Nicholas in London, perfectly turned out in full evening dress, at the opera, perhaps, or the theatre, or dining at the Savoy. He would not be alone, that was a certainty.

She sighed and then thrust the picture from her as a cloud of black smoke in the distance caught her attention. They were obviously approaching a railway line and before long the road began to follow it only a few yards distant. Soon a tiny station came into view.

'That looks familiar.' She sat bolt upright and stared at it.

'One little station looks very like another,' Nicholas observed with a smile.

'I dare say, but I still think I've seen this one before.' She leaned forward and looked for the name board. 'Yes—I was right! It's where the accident happened. Liev.'

'Clever girl.' He swung the car away from the station and down a narrow road leading towards some woods. 'I presume you have also guessed we are approaching my great-grandmother's estate?'

For a moment Letty was too overwhelmed to speak as the memory of what had happened during that extraordinary night, now several months ago, washed over her and obliterated her astonishment because Nicholas had brought her back to Liev.

It was strange how her intense dislike for him had changed into—what? She was afraid even to say the word in her thoughts.

'Yes, of course I've guessed,' she said quickly. 'But—but I don't understand one single thing. Is my sister here, actually somewhere on the estate? Oh, if only I had known——'

'You did not know and it is pointless to think about it. Instead you should be happy because you are going to meet at last.'

'I *am* happy, but I can't help being nervous too. It must be five years since we saw each other and I don't know how much Marina may have changed.'

'You will soon find out,' Nicholas pointed out calmly, 'for we shall be there within a few minutes. Marina is staying at one of our summer cottages, a dacha deep in the woods, a charming little place we were all fond of when we were children.'

Questions jostled each other in Letty's mind until she felt it might burst. *Why* was her sister staying in a house owned by the Namorovs? And why didn't she want her friends in the Imperial Ballet Company to know?

They came to a clearing where the birch trees had withdrawn somewhat and left a wide grassy space. In the centre there was a pretty little house with the high steep roof to be seen in villages and a rustic veranda on three sides. An attractive and well-cared-for garden blazed with summer flowers.

Someone was sitting on the veranda and rocking slowly in a high-backed chair, a girl with fair hair knotted in the nape of her neck and wearing a dress of pale blue muslin.

'I'll leave you here and go and visit the old lady.' Nicholas leaned across and opened the door. 'I'm sure you won't want a third party witnessing the great reunion.'

He had sounded stiff and even a little awkward, Letty noticed with that part of her that registered everything to do with him. But she ignored his mood and got hastily out. She heard him say something about coming back in an hour but it scarcely penetrated her absorption. As she walked across the grass she felt utterly overwhelmed by the immensity of the occasion. Within the next few minutes all the perplexities of the past few months would be made plain. She would know—at last—the reason for her sister's mysterious behaviour.

As Nicholas drove away his cool and deliberately detached demeanour was replaced by an anxiety there was no longer any need to hide. Marina had been furious when he had broken the news to her of Letty's impending visit. She had accused him of ignoring her wishes and daring to put her sister first in his list of priorities, instead of sticking to what had been agreed between them.

He had made no attempt to deny the charge, but in giving her an account of Letty's appeal to Rasputin he had spared her nothing, with the result that he had the satisfaction of seeing her recoil in horror.

Perhaps now she had had time to adjust to the idea of meeting her sister, she would view it differently and not make her feel unwelcome. With all his heart he hoped that would be the case.

# CHAPTER TWELVE

THE girl on the veranda stopped her lazy rocking and got up slowly. She came to the rail and leaned on it with both hands, looking down. At the bottom of the steps Letty halted and for a long moment they stared at each other, strangely alike in their uncertainty and tension in spite of their different colouring.

It seemed to Letty that Marina was as unsure of her welcome as she was of her own, though she could not imagine why, since Nicholas had flatly refused to explain anything.

Swept by sudden emotion, she made the first move, bounding up the steps and, as her sister moved to meet her, flinging her arms round her in a fervent demonstration of long-denied affection. The embrace was reciprocated and they clung together with a warmth as full of tears as of joy.

After a while they drew back slightly and looked at each other. Letty saw a face that was familiar and yet different, much more rounded than she remembered it. The lean, hungry look of the typical ballerina had quite gone.

It was not only the face. The figure was rounded too, but at first the significance escaped her.

She burst out, 'You look wonderfully well—your long holiday must be doing you good. You've even put on quite a lot of weight.'

'I'm afraid I have,' Marina said quietly.

Startled by the look on her face, Letty was at first puzzled and then seized with a terrible suspicion. Was it possible she was being appallingly naïve?

'Oh, Marina——' Her voice shook and she could actually feel herself growing pale. 'Oh, *no*—not that!'

'If by *that* you mean am I pregnant, then you're right.' Marina tilted her head defiantly, but almost immediately softened. 'Poor Letty—are you dreadfully shocked? I hoped you would never know, but now you're here you'd better hear the whole story.'

The horror was so great that for a few minutes Letty felt physically sick. She sat down hurriedly on a nearby chair as into her mind there flashed the memory of a housemaid who had 'put on weight' and then vanished mysteriously from the household. Letty had been fifteen at the time and the incident had greatly puzzled her because Hannah had been a good worker and appeared to have committed no crime. Her mother refused to answer questions and the whispered explanation of a teenage kitchen-maid had left her still totally confused.

How *could* the girl be going to have a baby when she wasn't married? Where would she get it from?

Since then Letty had learnt that babies grew inside their mothers, started off by some strange process still wrapped in mystery, though it had not been Charlotte who provided the information but a more enlightened schoolfriend. She still did not know how it could happen when the mother-to-be had no husband.

And now Marina was going to have a baby, and she was not married either.

'You said you'd tell me the whole story,' she reminded her sister. 'I do wish you'd begin, because I've never felt so muddled in all my life.'

A squirrel ran down a neighbouring tree, raced across the clearing and vanished up another. Marina followed it with her eyes and seemed in no hurry to start. She leaned back in her chair, rocking rhythmically, as though the regular motion helped her to marshall her thoughts.

Eventually she began. 'Unfortunately I don't know how innocent you still are. I mean, how much do you understand about love and—and sex?'

'Sex?' Letty recoiled from that wicked word. So far the only person to use it in her hearing had been her well-informed schoolfriend, and even she had been slightly embarrassed by it. 'Not much,' she confessed. 'I suppose it's another name for love but only used when people are married.'

The violence of Marina's reply astonished her. 'It is *not* another name for love!' The chair rocked furiously. 'It is something quite different and should never be confused with the emotion people who are truly in love feel for each other. That is,' she corrected herself, 'you can have sex without love, but if you really love someone you want sex as well. It's only natural. Do you see what I mean?'

Letty was more confused than ever, but she refused to admit it. 'I wish you'd tell me about *yourself*,' she complained, 'instead of giving me a lesson. I want to know what's been happening to you all this time, and why you wrote to me inviting me to visit you and then disappeared.'

'Perhaps I'm trying to put off the evil moment,' Marina admitted. 'You're not going to like what I have to tell you, Letty, dear, but I can't help that. It's the truth and I imagine that's what you want.'

'Of course it is. I've waited long enough for it.' Letty was beginning to recover a little from the shock. Whatever Marina had to tell could not be worse than the awful realisation that she was pregnant. 'Start with the letter,' she commanded.

Her sister frowned, as though trying to remember she had ever written it. 'It seems so long ago and I don't like having to think about that terrible time, but I must have written to you before I knew what had happened to me. I was feeling unusually tired and rather ill as well, and I kept being sick. Can you imagine what it's like to suffer that sort of thing when you're a ballerina? You're supposed to be always in the peak of condition. I was so miserable and I had a longing for someone who belonged to me and that's when I sent the letter. Of course, I never for one moment thought you'd be allowed to come.'

Letty interrupted to explain about the great luck of meeting Mrs Kemp. 'I was so excited about it, but things began to go wrong before I ever got to St Petersburg. There was a railway accident and that was when I met Count Namorov. He was on the train too.'

'I know. He came to visit me that evening and told me about it. He also said he had brought two English people to spend the night at Liev, but I had no idea until later that they were you and your chaperon.'

So that was where Nicholas had vanished to prior to the shocking scene in the bedroom! Letty hastily averted her eyes from Marina's gaze and went on to describe her visit to the Mariensky Theatre with Gerald Sheldon. 'I was handed my own letter back and told you'd gone away. It was a most awful shock and a terrible disappointment too. Why did you vanish like that?'

'It was the only thing to do once I'd found out what was the matter with me. I told the director the truth and I hoped none of the others would ever find out. Perhaps that was silly of me, but I don't think I was quite in my right mind at the time. As for my letter to you, I forgot it completely. I'm sorry, Letty.' She leaned forward and put her slender boneless hand on her sister's arm. 'Please forgive me, and try to understand.'

Letty was not yet ready for promises of that sort. There was still so much that puzzled her. 'How does Yuri Ivanovitch fit into this?' she asked. Seeing the surprise on Marina's face, she added, 'He was kind enough to show me your two letters to him.'

'Dear Yuri.' The lovely passionate mouth curved into a tender smile. 'I am so fond of him and I knew he'd be worried because he believes himself to be in love with me.' Reading in Letty's eyes the question she hesitated to ask, she added, 'He's not the father of my baby. There has never been anything of that sort between us.'

Anything of that sort—what did she *mean*? Much as she longed to know, Letty found it impossible to frame a question which would produce the information she needed.

After a moment, Marina continued. 'I am now going to tell you something which may shock you. When I first discovered my pregnancy, I was in such a state that all I wanted was to get rid of the baby and return as quickly as possible to the ballet company.'

'Get rid of it?' Letty asked blankly.

'Have an abortion. I was in that state of mind when I wrote my first letter to Yuri saying I would be back soon. You remember?'

'I—I think so.' Letty's battered brain had just registered another shock and she was trying to cope with it. 'I've heard of people having miscarriages, Marina, but I didn't know you could—could cause one to happen. I suppose that's what you meant?'

'That's exactly what I meant.'

'It sounds very wicked to me. Whatever would Papa say if he knew?'

'He must never know and, anyway, I changed my mind.'

'Why did you do that?'

'There were several reasons, one being because it's so wicked, as you call it, but it's also very dangerous for the mother. I could easily have died.' She paused and then added wryly, 'Nicholas was extremely angry that I changed my mind. He had been trying to make arrangements for the abortion.'

It seemed to Letty as though an icy hand laid hold of her heart and squeezed it until she could scarcely breathe. Until then she had not given more than a passing thought to the father of Marina's child. There had been so much to assimilate, so much new and alarming knowledge to be stored away in her mind and looked at later. Having established that Yuri had nothing to do with it, she had been side-tracked by the mention of an abortion, but she was brought back with a jerk which was so agonising she literally flinched with the pain.

'You can't imagine how kind Nicholas was to me, Letty,' her sister went on. 'He took complete charge and arranged for me to come here to this quiet retreat where my child has developed physically within me and my mind has grown too and learnt to accept what has happened. At first I missed the ballet terribly and, of course, I shall be very glad to get back to it, but in a way I've enjoyed this peaceful summer in the woods.'

'When are you expecting your baby to be born?' Letty asked faintly.

'Early in December. Nicholas has made all the arrangements and booked a doctor to attend the birth and a nurse to come and look after the child and myself until I am fit again. After I return to Petersburg I shall employ a nanny.' She smiled brightly at Letty. 'So you see, we have got it all planned and I have nothing to worry about.'

We... The simple little word was like a knife thrust. Why should Nicholas be taking all this trouble? What reason could there possibly be except the obvious one? Knowing that she must somehow find the courage to discover the truth, Letty nevertheless took refuge in prevarication.

'Don't you think life will be difficult for you in the city with everybody knowing you have an illegitimate child? Won't people be shocked?'

Marina shrugged. 'Perhaps some of them will be, but I no longer care. I know I told you I wanted to keep it all a secret at the beginning, but that was when I was thinking about an abortion. After Nicholas whisked me away to the dacha, I began to change.' Her eyes had an inward look and she sat in silence for a moment while Letty waited unhappily, sensing there was more to come.

'Theatre people are expected to have different standards from ordinary folk,' she went on at last. 'It's called being Bohemian. And everybody knows the Tsar before his marriage had one of our most famous ballerinas for his mistress. Incidentally, she is still with the Company, but getting rather past it now, of course.'

Letty had hitherto regarded the Tsar as a model of virtue and it was another shock—though a mild one compared with the others she had received—to find he had not always been so. How very confusing it all was, and how much simpler things were in Ely where right was right and wrong was definitely wicked and not to be condoned under any circumstances.

'Have you thought what you are going to tell our parents?' she asked suddenly. 'They can't be kept in ignorance any longer.'

Marina started. 'Our parents? You're surely not suggesting they should be told the truth—that they are going to have a grandchild born out of wedlock?'

'Don't they have a right to know?'

'Certainly not! It would upset them both most dreadfully and Mama would probably have a heart attack.'

'But how are you going to explain disappearing like this? They know about it because I had to write and tell them, and you can't imagine how difficult it was to try and explain something I didn't understand myself.'

'Poor Letty—I do seem to have caused you a lot of worry and distress.' Marina's voice was warm with real sympathy. 'Incidentally, how *did* you account for my not being in Petersburg?'

'I said you were on vacation.'

'There you are, then—there's no need to mention the baby. I had been overworking and I was given a long leave of absence from the theatre. You can tell them we've had this meeting,' she added as an afterthought. 'That ought to satisfy them.'

Letty's rounded chin lifted defiantly. 'I am not going to tell them anything, Marina. *You* must be the one to write this time. I've done quite enough deceiving and now it's your turn.'

'But you would do it much better than I,' Marina coaxed. 'You know I've always hated writing letters.' Seeing that she was making no impression, she went on, 'After all, if you hadn't come to St Petersburg there would have been no problem because they wouldn't know I wasn't at the theatre.'

It was too much and Letty leapt to her feet. 'So it's all my fault, is it? *I* certainly wish I'd never come! I would have been spared a great deal if I had stayed at home and not taken any notice of the pathetic letter which you can now hardly remember writing.'

Marina was looking hurt. She said stiffly, 'There's no need to shout at me like that. I'll be the one to write home since you seem to feel so strongly about it, but I certainly shan't tell them the truth and I hope they'll never have to learn it.'

Suddenly Letty felt she had had enough. She had looked forward so much to this meeting, never dreaming of the distress it was going to cause her—though perhaps she would have suspected her sister might be pregnant if she had been more worldly wise—and now she was utterly devastated.

She sat down on the top step and put both hands over her face, longing for the relief of tears and yet not daring to give way in case she lost control completely. Marina must not be allowed to suspect she had another reason for her misery—it wasn't just the shame of having a sister who had 'got into trouble.'

Suddenly another question leapt into her mind, one she should have asked long ago if she had not been in such a state of confusion and shock.

'Marina——' She turned round and, kneeling on the hard wooden floor of the veranda, looked up into her sister's face. 'There's something I don't understand. Why isn't the father going to marry you?' To her surprise a look of anger and disgust flashed across Marina's face.

'I wouldn't marry him if he was the last man on earth!' She flung out her hands with a dramatic gesture, as though physically repulsing an unwanted suitor. 'Anyway, he's never shown the slightest sign of wanting to make an honest woman of me—he just couldn't get away fast enough.'

Letty felt as though she were groping her way through one of those terrible fogs they so often had in London. 'Peasoupers', they called them. She had experienced one once while staying with Aunt Eugenie and it was still a terrifying memory.

'I thought—that is——' She stopped and took a deep breath, clasping her hands together nervously. 'You gave me to believe that Nicholas Namorov was the father of your child. I know you didn't actually *say* so, but——'

'I most certainly did not say so.' Marina sighed and again her eyes had that inward look. 'I only wish it had been possible for me to make that statement,' she murmured, so softly that Letty hardly caught the words.

'You kept talking about him—you said he'd been kind to you and made all the arrangements——'

'So he did. Nicholas has a strong feeling of loyalty to the family. People think he's a rather lightweight character, but he's different underneath. I've got to know him very well during these months of waiting and——' her voice softened '—I admire him so much. If he'd been the one responsible for my unfortunate situation he would never have abandoned me and gone off to Venice to study art.'

'V-Venice?'

'Yes.' Marina went on talking rapidly, as if the subject was of no interest. 'It was Paul Namorov who seduced me, Letty—with my willing co-operation, I admit. He's the younger son and a great charmer, wildly good-looking and absolutely crazy about ballet. For a brief while I imagined myself in love with him, but before long I realised it was only physical attraction and by that time it was too late.' She broke off to study her sister's face. 'You remember what I said earlier about love and sex being two different things?'

Letty struggled to answer without giving away the intoxicated state of her feelings, now that she knew Nicholas had not been Marina's lover. 'Oh—er—yes, I think I remember, but I didn't really understand.'

'You're too inexperienced, of course, but you'll understand one day when you make the sort of marriage that will please the parents and settle down in Ely and produce a lot of legitimate grandchildren.'

'How do you know I want to do that?' Letty demanded, stung by the ordinariness of the programme outlined for her.

'Because you're the daughter who stayed at home when I escaped to the sophisticated life of the ballet world.'

'I didn't have a great talent like yours, but that does not mean I want to spend the rest of my life in Ely.'

Marina was not listening. Her mood had changed again. 'Letty, will you be able to stay in Petersburg until my baby is born? Childbirth is very—very frightening, and I'd like to have someone belonging to me to be there.'

Touched as she was by the appeal, Letty could not give the required assurance. 'I hope I shall be able to stay, but it depends on my employer.'

'Nicholas told me about your position as governess in Countess Brassova's household.' Marina looked amused.

'It's really funny to think of you—the daughter of a cathedral canon—working for someone with two divorces behind her.'

'I like her immensely. She's very nice and kind——'

'I don't doubt it, but that doesn't alter the situation. I suppose you realise why she's probably going to England? It's because her Grand Duke is insisting on marrying her and the Tsar is banishing them both.' She broke off suddenly to listen, her head on one side. 'What time did Nicholas say he was returning? I thought I heard the motor.'

'I hardly noticed,' Letty confessed. She strained her ears, but could hear nothing except the persistent calling of a wood pigeon, which certainly did not resemble the Hispano-Suiza's raucous note.

'I expect I was mistaken. I often imagine I hear it and then find I am wrong. It's probably because I enjoy his visits so much.'

'Does he come often?'

'Not as often as I would like.'

'You must find it very lonely here.'

'I did at first, but that's not really why I look forward so much to seeing Nicholas. It's because he's——' She paused as though searching for the right words, and then left the sentence unfinished.

But she could not hide the dreamy look in her eyes and Letty noted it with dismay. If Marina had fallen in love with Paul's brother and they eventually married, the baby would have a splendid home and his adopted father would also be a blood relation. Nothing could be more suitable and Letty knew she ought to be hoping most fervently that it would happen.

Unfortunately she found it utterly impossible to do any such thing, and she was overwhelmed with shame because of it.

'I'm not looking forward to the winter,' Marina was continuing. 'It will be horrible having to stay indoors all day in this little house. I'm not at all the sort of person who enjoys going out in the snow.'

An alarming thought struck Letty. 'I suppose there will be a lot of snow when winter comes. Are you likely to get cut off?'

'Cut off? Oh, no—not in Russia. Everybody goes about by sleigh in wintertime and the jingle of the bells makes such a pretty noise. It always reminds me of the snow scene in *Nutcracker*.'

They continued talking, descending gradually from the dramatic heights which they had occupied during the early part of their reunion. Letty felt emotionally drained and far from happy, but a strange kind of peace had taken possession of her. She knew it all now, and although she was deeply shocked by the reason for Marina's disappearance she knew she must learn to live with it.

When Nicholas came chugging into the clearing just before lunch, the two girls were indoors admiring the beautifully embroidered baby clothes which Marina had been working on during her exile. He was greeted enthusiastically by Marina, who flung her arms round his neck and kissed him with so much naturalness that Letty could only conclude it was her normal greeting. Certainly he appeared to return it with equal enthusiasm.

'Well, Letty?' he asked lightly when Marina had gone to the kitchen to see how the servant was getting on with lunch. 'You seem to have survived.'

'I can't pretend it was not a most dreadful shock. If only I had known earlier!' She sighed. 'Did you have much trouble getting my sister to agree to a meeting?'

'Experience had taught me not to attempt it.' He smiled ruefully. 'I merely issued an ultimatum.'

Marina's return to say lunch was about to be served saved Letty the necessity of replying. It was a cheerful meal, on the surface at least, and soon afterwards she and Nicholas left to begin the return journey.

'You'll come again soon?' Marina begged, looking from one to the other.

Which of them did she most want to see? The question popped up in Letty's mind, but she thrust it away unanswered.

'I can only come when I can arrange to have a whole day off,' she pointed out. 'It's not fair to ask for it too often.'

At first the drive was a silent one and then Nicholas said suddenly, 'I suppose you are feeling very bitter towards the whole Namorov family?'

Letty started and turned her head to look at him but he was staring straight ahead. 'Why should I do that? Certainly I don't have a high opinion of your brother——'

'That is understandable. I feel the same about him myself.'

'But I see no reason for condemning the whole family. I liked your sisters very much and——' She faltered to a stop, and then, sensing he was waiting for her to continue, managed to struggle on. 'I think you have been very kind to Marina and done your best to make amends.'

It sounded stilted and lacking in any real feeling. She was not surprised when he did not deign to answer. A wave of depression enveloped her and she was very conscious of an invisible barrier between them. At that moment it just did not seem possible that they could ever be relaxed and happy together again now that he had become—in a very irregular sort of way—her brother-in-law once removed.

By the time they reached the city, Letty's naturally volatile spirits were beginning to recover. She sat up straight and gave herself a good mental shake. Ordinary life was about to resume and she must not let anyone guess what a shattering day she had experienced.

'I'll come in with you and have a word with Natalia,' Nicholas said.

As they stepped into the hall, the doorman handed Letty a letter which had come by hand. The writing was unfamiliar and she tore it open quickly with a murmured apology. To her surprise it was from Gerald Sheldon, inviting her to accompany him to a revolutionary meeting a few days later. It seemed a hundred years since their conversation on the subject but she recalled it with an effort.

On an impulse she screwed the letter up into a ball. She now had absolutely no desire to go to such a meeting and could not imagine why she had ever imagined it might be interesting.

'That is not a very polite way to treat your correspondent,' Nicholas remarked.

'I meant no discourtesy.' She hesitated and then decided the simplest way of satisfying his scarcely veiled curiosity was to tell him the contents of her letter. 'But I don't think I shall bother to go,' she finished.

'This English bank clerk is a friend of yours?' he enquired.

'I suppose you could call him that. He was instrumental in arranging my Russian lessons.' No need to mention how she had first met Gerald, she decided. She had had enough of Marina's affairs for one day.

'Being a revolutionary does not consort well with banking.'

'I never said Mr Sheldon is a revolutionary!' Letty exclaimed in alarm. 'It's just that he is sympathetic towards the ideals they put forward and feels they have every right to be dissatisfied with the way ordinary people are treated in Russia.'

To her embarrassment, Nicholas began to clap his hands together softly. 'You should be standing on a soap box in your Hyde Park, Letty.'

'Don't be silly.' She was in no mood for teasing. 'I was only quoting what I have been told. Anyway, I have somehow received the impression that even you would admit there is room for improvement in such matters.'

'That is true.' He was serious again now. 'Repeat for me, if you please, the time and place of this meeting.'

'You're surely not thinking of going?'

'*Even I* must confess to a certain interest in these people who call themselves revolutionaries. It is more than likely they will one day actually bring about revolution in Russia if some of their more reasonable demands are not met.'

Letty felt she wanted to scream. The last thing she required at that moment was to stand there in the hall debating revolutionary ideas with Nicholas, or ideas of any sort for that matter. What she needed was to be taken in his arms and held there in a long comforting embrace, the way he had held Marina.

'I must go upstairs and say goodnight to Nikki.' She made a determined effort to break away. 'Thank you for everything, Nicholas. I shall always be grateful to you for finding my sister for me.'

With an angry gesture he flung her gratitude back into her face. 'Keep your thanks for a more suitable occasion. Since my family is responsible for your sister's unfortunate situation and the pain you have suffered today, I do not consider I have done anything more than was obligatory. I need no pretty speeches for that.'

She stared at him, not entirely certain of his meaning, and then, with a stifled sob, she fled upstairs to the nursery floor. It seemed like a haven of refuge.

## CHAPTER THIRTEEN

IT WAS several days before Letty made up her mind whether she intended to go to the meeting with Gerald. At first, when not actively occupied with Nikki, she thought constantly about Marina, going over and over their conversation, wondering whether the letter home had yet been written, or whether her sister was still putting it off, which seemed more than likely.

Eventually she reached the stage of finding out whether she would be free on the appointed evening and, when she discovered that she was, half hoping Marcelle would ask to change with her.

Absolutely nothing happened at the last minute to prevent her going and she began a hasty search through her wardrobe to find suitable clothes.

She had boasted to Gerald that it would be no problem but, in the event, she did not find it easy. Light summery clothes did not accord with secret underground meetings. At last she chose a plain dark skirt which would be much too hot, and a tailored blouse made of grey cotton. Most of her hats were too dressy, but she found a black straw with a moderate brim and cut off the bunch of sweet peas which adorned it. Now she really looked like a down-trodden, poverty-stricken governess, which she hoped would give the right effect. A lot of revolutionaries, she believed, were intellectuals rather than manual workers, so she ought to pass muster.

Gerald, waiting on a street corner, did not recognise her at first, and when he did he broke into a broad grin. 'Well done, Letty! Your own mother wouldn't know you.'

'My own mother would be horrified.'

As she joined him it occurred to Letty that she ought to tell him about Marina. After all, he was involved at the beginning and he deserved to be informed the search had ended.

Nothing would induce her to talk about the baby, though. Unmarried young ladies did not discuss coming babies with unmarried men, even when they were going to be born respectably. Gerald would have to be given the same story as the parents in faraway Ely.

'I have news for you,' she told him brightly as they walked along together. 'I now know where my sister is and, which is even more exciting, I have been to visit her.'

He looked down at her in surprise from beneath the peak of his pull-on cap. 'That's very interesting! Did that fellow at the theatre—Yuri something—get another letter?'

Too late Letty saw the pit into which she was about to fall. She definitely did not want to mention Nicholas's part in the story—yet how otherwise could she account for having discovered Marina's whereabouts? Annoyed because she had not thought to prepare herself properly, and at the same time anxious to avoid a series of lies, she decided to be vague.

'It was a stroke of luck really. One day when I was feeling particularly low because it seemed that I would never find out what had become of Marina, I happened to mention it to—someone, and that person actually knew where she was. Wasn't it an amazing coincidence?'

She could feel his curiosity as clearly as if it were something tangible, but she had banked on his being too good-mannered to question her regarding the identity of the person involved, and she had made no mistake.

Gerald absorbed the information in silence for a moment and then said carefully, 'It must have been a wonderful reunion.'

'Yes.'

The bare monosyllable hung in the air between them and Letty knew she must add something to it, if she did not want him to suspect the occasion had not been an ordinary meeting between two sisters who had not seen each other for years.

'We were quite right to think Marina was on a long vacation,' she continued. 'She had been overworking and was greatly in need of a prolonged rest. I think she hoped to keep her whereabouts a secret so that the holiday really was a complete rest.'

'Very wise of her.' He paused to check the name of the street they had turned into and Letty suddenly realised they had reached a poor neighbourhood she had never seen before. 'It was a great pity your sister left the theatre before she received your letter. If she had not done so you would have been spared a lot of worry.'

'It's no good crying over spilt milk, as my old nanny would have called it.'

'Mine too.' Gerald put his hand lightly on her elbow and steered her across the road. 'I think that's the place over there.'

Letty looked in surprise at a large dilapidated house, whereas she had expected a hall of some kind. There were plenty of people about, all very drably dressed, and she was glad that she and Gerald attracted no attention as they joined a steady stream—mostly made up of men—going round by the side of the house and down some worn stone steps which appeared to lead to a cellar.

'I think we should speak in Russian,' he said in a low voice. 'Can you manage that?'

'I'll do my best.'

Although some of the younger members of the audience, who looked like students, were talking together excitedly, there was not a great deal of conversation going on. Most people were serious and even grim, and it seemed clear they were present because they wanted to hear the speakers rather than to take part in debate.

The stone steps ended in a large low-ceilinged area with a very dirty and uneven floor. It was lit by evil-smelling paraffin lamps and furnished with rows of backless forms. There was a rough kitchen table at one end, with three chairs, but no platform of any sort.

They chose seats on the side farthest from the entrance and sat silently watching as people continued to pour in until there was standing room only, and the big cellar was packed with sweating humanity except for a small clear space round the table. Three men were now sitting there, Letty noticed suddenly, though she had not seen them arrive. Two were dressed like workmen but the third was different and looked like an intellectual. He was neat and even dapper in appearance, with a high, domed forehead, revealed by receding hair, and a well-trimmed moustache and small beard.

Someone was calling for silence and, craning her neck, Letty saw that one of the men at the table was apparently about to make a speech. Summoning all her powers of concentration, she strove to grasp its meaning. A lot of it eluded her, but the audience were absorbing it with relish, frequently showing their approval by shouting or applauding with hands or feet.

Then the clever-looking man stood up and began speaking, and right from the beginning it was obvious that he knew just how to hold an audience spellbound. There was a rapt silence, which was more significant than any amount of shouting and stamping, and when he had finished a storm of appreciation broke out.

'We're in luck tonight,' Gerald whispered. 'That was Lenin, one of their truly great leaders. I believe he's supposed to be exiled, but he creeps back from time to time.'

Letty had never heard of Lenin and remained unimpressed. She was beginning to wish she had not come. The hot, smoky atmosphere was stifling and she suspected that the ventilation of the cellar was totally inadequate. In addition, she had found it much more difficult than she had expected to understand the speeches. The Russian she had learnt had been intended for use in ordinary life, not for assimilating revolutionary principles.

'How long will this meeting last?' she murmured.

Gerald glanced at her, guessing at her discomfort. 'A long time, I'm afraid. Can you stick it out?'

'I—don't know.'

'I think we'd better leave after the next speech, before they throw the meeting open for discussion. That might go on for hours.'

It seemed to Letty that the speech itself lasted for hours, though it was no more than twenty minutes. She was so thankful when it ended that she started to rise from her hard wooden seat while the applause was still going on, earning black looks from their neighbours. She couldn't remember ever fainting, but she was horribly afraid she might do so as they wormed their way towards the door. It seemed to her she was surrounded by huge men with enormous black beards, wearing smelly working clothes, all of whom appeared to take pleasure in impeding her progress towards fresh air, or made it only too apparent they found her delicate-featured face and lovely colouring extremely attractive.

They had almost reached their objective when a shabbily dressed young man, who looked like a student, allowed Gerald through and then swiftly barred Letty's way.

'No exit permit without a kiss,' he leered.

He smelt of brandy and his body odour was nearly as repulsive as Rasputin's had been. As Letty recoiled he put out a dirty hand and dragged her nearer, breathing his brandy fumes into her face. Over his shoulder she could see Gerald struggling to get back to rescue her and being prevented by several other students, all of whom were eager for a fight. It was like a nightmare, with the flickering lamps casting giant shadows over the sea of unfriendly faces among which she felt herself trapped for ever.

Rescue came from a totally unexpected direction.

There was a sudden violent movement in the crowd pressing on Letty's back, an arm shot out and a fist crashed into her tormentor's face. It would have sent him flying if there had been room to fall; instead it gave him a bloody nose which immediately began streaming down on to his dingy shirt-front. The owner of the fist was laying about him with enthusiasm, hitting all those within reach regardless of whether they deserved it or not. Next, he seized Letty in a grip of iron, propelling her before him towards the bottom of the steps and cursing loudly as he did so.

Until then she had had no idea of his identity. She had simply assumed he was a member of the audience who for some reason had viewed a half-fainting young lady as in need of protection, instead of regarding her departure as an insult to the speakers, or—worse still— her femininity as some sort of challenge.

Now she *knew* who he was.

In the doorway, Gerald had succeeded in opening up a gap and Letty was squeezed through it and pushed up the steps by both men. As they regained ground level she drew in great gasping breaths of the cool evening air and immediately began to feel better, which was fortunate as a noisy argument down at the bottom of the steps suggested that some people were in favour of pursuit.

'I don't think we should hang about here, Count Namorov,' Gerald said urgently. He seized Letty by the arm and began to hurry her down the street.

'It goes against the grain to run away from those louts, but I agree entirely.'

Nicholas took her other arm and they raced her along at such a speed that at times she felt as though her feet scarcely touched the ground. Safely round a corner, they slackened somewhat and eventually stopped to get their bearings.

'How the devil did you know my name?' Nicholas demanded, looking at Gerald. 'I did not think we were acquainted.'

'I've seen you in the bank. Also I was with Letty at the Mariensky Theatre. My name's Sheldon.'

'Good God! I had forgotten the fellow who took Letty to this unsavoury place was a bank clerk.' His eyes travelled slowly over Gerald's workmanlike outfit. 'You make a very good artisan, if you don't mind my saying so.'

'On the contrary, I take it as a compliment.' Gerald smiled coolly. 'I'm afraid your own disguise, Count, is not entirely successful. That tweed suit suggests a sporting Englishman rather than a lower-class Russian. I rather think the youths you were doing battle with realised you were bogus.'

Nicholas shrugged. 'It hardly seems to matter now.' He turned to Letty. 'Have you abandoned your intention of fainting?'

'Oh, yes, I'm quite all right now, but I don't mind admitting I was dreadfully frightened at first when I got separated from Gerald. Then I heard your voice and I knew nothing terrible would happen to me and we would all get out safely somehow.'

She had spoken emotionally, overdoing her gratitude with the extravagant words, and as he looked at her and raised his eyebrows she felt her cheeks turning pink.

'Your friend, Mr—er—Sheldon did his share, so you'd better make him a pretty speech too.'

Before she could think of anything suitable, Gerald broke in.

'It would be more sensible to make our way home instead of standing about here indulging in polite conversation.'

'Indeed it would, and my motor is not far away. I left it in a quiet street and walked the rest of the way. In spite of my poor attempt at disguise, I had sufficient sense not to arrive in a Hispano-Suiza and leave it at the top of the cellar steps.'

'I'm glad to hear it,' Gerald muttered.

Nicholas offered his arm to Letty. 'I hope you will give me the pleasure of allowing me to drive you home.'

'Th-thank you.' She glanced uncomfortably at her other escort. 'You don't mind, Gerald?'

'Not in the least.' He removed his cap and gave her a curt bow.

'It seems to me your friend suffers rather badly from a stiff neck,' Nicholas remarked when they were alone.

'He's a strange character,' Letty said thoughtfully. 'So very respectable and proper on the surface, and yet I believe he has a genuine interest in the revolutionaries.'

'I dare say, but I hope he will attend those meetings by himself in future,' Nicholas was looking about him with a puzzled air. 'Where the devil did I leave my motor car? These streets look all the same to me, alike in their infernal dreariness.' Apparently getting his bearings, he resumed possession of Letty's arm. 'I believe it is round this corner.'

She had been alarmed at the suggestion that they might be lost, and was greatly relieved to see the bright yellow car standing by the kerb. Fortunately the street appeared to be lined with small factories instead of houses, and was quite deserted.

'It was a good place to leave it,' he said complacently, opening the door for Letty and producing the green chiffon scarf he had lent her before.

How many lady passengers had worn it besides herself? she wondered as she tied her hat on with it. Maybe even her own sister?

Nicholas looked at her critically. 'I must say, Letty, that if you had that particular hat blown away I would only regard it as a good riddance. Never have I seen you looking so frumpish.'

'That was my intention,' she pointed out, smiling. 'Do you know which way to go now that you have found the motor?'

'No, but I expect I can find it.' He swung the starting handle energetically and, after a few attempts, the engine fired. With a spring he leapt into the driving seat and started off down the quiet street.

There followed what seemed to Letty a completely haphazard turning of corners, each of which revealed another look-alike street, the only difference being that some were almost deserted and others had far too many people standing about talking to each other and enjoying the fresh air after the heat of the day—all of whom stared at the alien and obviously expensive vehicle.

Some of them were not content with staring but shouted rudely after it, and once an old woman with her head covered with a black shawl actually spat as they passed.

'Disgusting habits these people have,' Nicholas said, sounding very much the aristocrat.

'You can't blame them for being envious,' Letty protested.

'No, but I do blame them for showing it in such an unpleasant way. It's not my fault I have more money than they have, and if I were to give it all away tomorrow none of them would be any better off.'

They were turning yet another corner and this time there was something familiar about the street in which they found themselves. Letty gave a small exclamation of alarm as she recognised the big shabby old house halfway down, and saw a dozen or so young men milling about outside.

'Oh, Nicholas, we're back where the meeting was held!'

'So I see.' His voice was grim and he put his foot down on the accelerator.

With a puff of black smoke from the exhaust, the car leapt forward, and at the same time the youths spilled out into the roadway so that Nicholas had to brake hastily to avoid knocking some of them down. Clinging to the door, Letty was flung first backwards and then forwards with such force that she landed in a heap on the floor. Scrambling back on to the seat, she only just missed being hit by a stone which whizzed past her and struck Nicholas on the forehead.

It was followed by a rain of stones and, as Letty cowered in terror, she heard the unmistakable sound of shattering glass. Great jagged pieces of the windscreen fell into her lap, inflicting numerous small cuts on her hands which she had instinctively raised to cover her face. Even more afraid for Nicholas than herself, she glanced sideways and saw blood streaming down the side of his face where the first stone had hit him.

Through the hail of missiles he continued to drive as fast as he could, swerving wildly to dodge their assailants who, seeing the tremendous damage they were inflicting, were as though drunk with excitement. The attack seemed to last an eternity, but it was actually not more than thirty seconds before they were able to speed away down the street, leaving the hysterically shouting youths far behind. Fortunately Nicholas appeared to have regained his sense of direction and there was no more of the frustrating twisting and turning which had ended so disastrously. In less than ten minutes they were back in the leafy avenues of the St Petersburg Letty knew and loved.

'Stop!' she said urgently. 'Oh, Nicholas, please stop now we're safe.'

'No! Not until we are back at Natalia's house. I can drive in there and inspect the damage without an audience.'

'It's not the motor I'm worried about—I want to see how badly you are hurt. You may not be fit to drive——'

'Can you not see that I am fit to drive? And if I were not, I would still have to remain behind the wheel.' He wiped blood away angrily from his right eye. 'Or were you intending to take my place?'

Letty relapsed into silence, but she could not help an anguished glance at his head, where blood flowed freely from numerous minor cuts as well as from the major gash on his forehead. He had taken the brunt of the attack, since he had been unable to cower in his seat as she had done. And would have been too proud to do so in any case, she was sure.

What a disaster the whole evening had been, and it was all her fault. If she had not been so foolish as to wish to attend a revolutionary meeting, none of it would have happened. Gerald would have gone by himself and emerged safely at the end without having attracted any unwelcome attention.

But the worst thing of all was telling Nicholas about the meeting and arousing his interest. That, and that alone, had led to the terrible damage to his precious motor, to say nothing of his own wounds. He was so fair-minded, too, and sympathetic towards the grievances of the poorer classes. He didn't deserve to be treated like this!

Letty sighed and stifled a sob. It wouldn't help to burst into tears, though she longed to do so. Instead she sat silently in her seat until they were safely inside the courtyard at the Countess's house. Then, avoiding the broken glass as well as she could, she climbed carefully out and joined Nicholas, who had been in far too much of a hurry to trouble about being careful. Together they walked slowly round the battered vehicle.

Both headlamps had been smashed in addition to the windscreen. The shining yellow mudguards had been kicked and dented, and there were scratches all over the bodywork. The neatly folded hood had been wrenched from its fastenings on one side, and trailed pathetically, almost touching the ground.

'Oh, Nicholas——' Letty was making no attempt now to hide her tears '—how *could* they have done so much damage in so short a time?'

'Class hatred is a wonderfully powerful emotion,' he said bitterly, dragging a handkerchief from his pocket and mopping ineffectually at the blood on his face.

Letty winked vigorously to clear her own vision and banished the tears. 'You need a doctor for that cut. Please come into the house and let me wash it for you while we wait for somebody who can stitch it.'

'I don't need stitching!' he scoffed, brushing some fragments of glass off the long rakish bonnet which had been his joy and pride, and scarcely noticing that he was adding to the scratches he had already received.

Letty took matters into her own hands and approached the doorman who had emerged to see what was going on. 'Fetch your mistress,' she ordered.

But the man shook his head and explained that the Countess was out, after which he returned to his fascinated observation of the scene below.

It was quite clear to Letty that if Nicholas was going to get any medical attention she would have to find some means of getting him away from the Hispano-Suiza and into the house. 'Is there a motor car repairer in St Petersburg?' she asked.

'Yes, of course.' He glanced at her in surprise.

'Then you had better telephone him at once and ask for somebody to come and take the motor away. If you leave it there, the Countess will get a terrible shock when she returns.'

'Yes, indeed. I should have thought of that for myself.' He ran up the steps and into the hall.

Delighted that her plan had worked, Letty followed close behind, and while he was impatiently turning the handle which would summon the operator, she spoke to the doorman.

'When the Count has finished,' she said in her careful Russian, 'I want you to ring up the doctor and ask him to come here as soon as possible. You understand how to use the telephone?'

'Oh, yes. The Countess taught me herself.'

So far so good. But she had still to persuade Nicholas to allow her to put a temporary dressing on his wound. As she debated her next step, he finished his conversation on the phone and turned round.

She did not know how woebegone she looked with her face streaked with tears, blood and dust, and that terrible hat still firmly in place, but Nicholas seemed to see her properly for the first time.

'Are you feeling faint again, Letty?' He came up to her and peered anxiously into her face. Very gently he removed the green scarf, now in rags, and the hat with it. 'Did you get a knock on the head?'

'N-no.' Thoroughly overwrought, she was again on the verge of tears. 'But *you* did and I feel terribly worried about it because there might still be some fragments of glass in that dreadful cut. Do you want to be scarred for life? If not, you'd better come upstairs with me and let me wash it and put a pad on so the blood doesn't keep running down your face. Won't that be a lot more comfortable?'

'I suppose so.' He sighed, cast a despairing glance through the open front door towards his battered car, and followed her slowly up the stairs.

Letty's next problem was where to take him. The Countess had a bathroom but she hardly liked to use it without permission, and her own room seemed the only alternative. Fortunately it was not on the nursery floor but at the back of the house on the first floor, and they reached it without attracting attention.

Nicholas seemed to be suffering from reaction and he sank down on to the nearest chair and leaned his head back, half closing his eyes. Letty guessed that his head was throbbing badly and she doubted whether he was aware of his surroundings. It had been a large, heavy stone which had hit him. She had seen it lying on the floor of the car.

Should she ring for hot water or use what was in the ewer? The question was quickly answered as she remembered the water would be tepid after standing in the hot room all day. Just right for washing wounds.

Using one of her own handkerchiefs, she began work. In spite of the care she exercised, Nicholas flinched as she touched the gaping cut and she found herself murmuring, 'It's all right—I won't hurt you more than I can help,' just as though he had been a child.

Fortunately she found no fragments of glass from the windscreen, and when she had finished the cleansing she made a thick pad with several handkerchiefs. Using his own blood-stained handkerchief to tie it on because it was larger than her own, she fixed the pad in place and stood back to admire her handiwork.

'Does that feel better?' she asked.

He opened one eye and looked at her where she stood just in front of him. Without answering the question he stretched out both arms and drew her close, pillowing his head against her breast.

'Oh, Letty—Letty darling——' The words were borne on a long sigh but she heard them clearly and her breathing quickened. Acting instinctively, she wrapped her arms round him and bent her head until her face was buried in the softness of his hair. Her eyes closed, she allowed herself to drift on an uncharted sea of rapture, conscious only of the joy of holding him. For a few precious moments she could imagine he was *hers*.

After a while Nicholas stirred and twisted his head round. He looked into her eyes, his own strangely sad, and then, with a muffled sound very like a groan, his mouth sought for and captured hers. Their lips clung, the painful pleasure sheer ecstasy, and then Letty felt her mouth being forced open and an extraordinary sensation took possession of her whole body. A strange longing seized her, but she had no idea what it was she longed for.

With an abruptness which startled her, Nicholas regained control. He raised his head and gave her a twisted sort of smile.

'You are very, very tempting, my beautiful Letty,' he murmured softly. 'Do you know what you do to me when I hold you in my arms?' And as she hesitated, uncertain of his meaning, he went on, 'No, of course you do not—you are a well-brought-up young lady. But what would I not give to be the one who teaches you! Oh, Letty, why did we not meet sooner?'

Bewildered, she took refuge in a simple direct answer. 'We met on the train, Nicholas. It was not possible for us to become acquainted any earlier.'

'No, no, of course not. You had better forget I ever asked you that foolish question.' Suddenly he was himself again, standing up and putting on the tweed jacket which he had removed during her ministrations.

'A man and a girl alone in a bedroom!' His eyes danced wickedly. 'It is like a situation out of some naughty French farce, do you not agree? Or are you as ignorant of French farces as you are of—other matters?' He burst out laughing. 'And that is another foolish question. I am quite sure your experience of the theatre is confined to Shakespeare—and the ballet.'

Why did his mention of the ballet strike a discordant note? The answer was easy to find—it had reminded her of Marina—but that should not have been unwelcome.

Deep in her secret heart, Letty knew the reason, but she was not yet ready to acknowledge it.

## CHAPTER FOURTEEN

THE Countess returned just in time to see the doctor driving away from her house. In a panic in case something terrible had happened to Nikki, she rushed indoors and up to the nursery, where she found him peacefully asleep. Downstairs again, she was about to begin an inquisition when the doorman informed her that Count Namorov was in the drawing-room.

Nicholas was stretched out on a chaise-longue, looking very pale and with his head bandaged. His eyes were closed, the long dark lashes lying still on his tanned cheeks, but Natalia's exclamation of horror roused him and he swung his long legs to the floor. With unusually formal politeness he kissed her hand as though she had already been married to the Tsar's brother.

'I warn you, Natalia,' he said tautly, 'I am in an extremely bad temper!'

'What has happened? Has there been an accident?'

He waited until she had sat down and then resumed his former position. 'If you had returned a little earlier and seen my motor car in the courtyard, you would certainly have thought it had been in an accident, but that was not the case.'

He went on to give a full account of the adventure, even managing, in spite of his simmering rage, to make it sound amusing at times.

'If you could have seen the three of us, you would have scarcely credited that a pretty young English girl, a highly respectable bank clerk and I—a Namorov—could have so completely transformed ourselves.'

'Who is this bank clerk?' She frowned in perplexity. 'I did not know Letty had a young man.'

Nicholas started. 'I hardly think Sheldon could be called that.'

Although he had sounded only mildly protesting, the violence of his inner turmoil disturbed him and Natalia's next remark did nothing to help.

'Letty is a very well-brought-up girl, whose father is a churchman. I really don't think she would go out alone in the evening with a young man unless she knew him very well indeed.'

Nicholas's mind flew to the recent scene in Letty's bedroom. The Countess would certainly not approve of that. Even as his lips twisted wryly, he found himself plagued by doubts. She had appeared to enjoy the embrace as much as he had done, which seemed to confirm that there was nothing between her and Sheldon.

Unless she was a flirt? Finding the notion extraordinarily unwelcome, he came back to the present and discovered Natalia was still on the same subject.

'This bank clerk—if he is as respectable as you seem to think—would be very suitable for Letty. She has had a difficult time since coming to Russia and it would perhaps make up for some of her distress over Marina if she could find happiness in a betrothal.'

'What about his revolutionary interests?' Nicholas demanded harshly.

'Surely he was not serious about those? Don't you think it was curiosity which took him to the meeting—as it did yourself?' Receiving no reply except a shrug, she began to talk about the damage to his car, her big limpid eyes full of distress. 'It really is disgraceful that such a thing should happen right here in the city—and to a member of the ruling classes too! Those hooligans deserve to be shot.'

'I must admit I found what they did to the motor car a great deal harder to bear than my wounded head,' he declared savagely.

'Will you be able to get it repaired?'

'Oh, yes, I think so, but it will have to be sent back to the works in France and heaven only knows how long that will take.'

If he had known that it would take six weeks he would have found the prospect quite insupportable. He passed the time somehow, working unusually hard at his shipping business, going for long rides into the country on his favourite horse, and occasionally visiting Natalia's house where he saw Letty only in her presence. He did not go to Liev at all.

The long hot days gradually shortened and the 'white nights' became only a memory. The scorched grass began to show signs of turning green again, before the bitter cold of winter would once more wither it.

Letty received a letter from Ely, referring to her visit to her sister, so she knew Marina had kept her promise to write home. The Canon appeared pleased that his younger daughter was 'doing something useful' and suggested that she should return to England when the Countess and her little son travelled there, assuming that the visit did actually take place. 'If not, we must make other arrangements for you.'

Knowing that Marina wanted her to stay for the baby's birth, Letty shelved the problem. It was extremely unlikely that the dates would fit and this was confirmed one day when she was summoned to the drawing-room. As soon as she entered the room she was aware of a simmering excitement beneath Natalia's composed exterior. The beautiful eyes had lost their sadness and were glowing with happiness.

'I have something to tell you, Letty.' She gestured to her to sit down. 'It is very much in confidence but I am sure you will respect that and keep it strictly to yourself.

My fiancé, the Grand Duke Michael——' she lifted her head proudly '—is weary of waiting for his brother the Tsar to give his consent to our marriage. He is determined to marry me without that consent and I am sure there is no need for me to tell you what the result will probably be.'

'You will have to go away?'

'Yes, though I hope it is only for a time.'

Letty sat tautly on the edge of a delicate little chair upholstered in pink satin. Dared she ask the date of the wedding, or was that a secret? As she wondered whether to put the question, the Countess went on speaking.

'I have told you my news because I know it affects yourself. It seems to me you have two alternatives—either to travel to England with us, or to go and stay with your sister—er—for a time.'

'I very much appreciate being let into the secret,' Letty said impulsively. 'Would it be in order for me to wish you and the Grand Duke every happiness?'

'Perfectly in order!' Natalia laughed. 'There will not be many people in a position to do that, and all good wishes are more than welcome.' She paused and her eyes widened as she gazed for a moment into the future.

Was she wondering whether she would ever be received at court, an acknowledged member of the royal family? Or was she afraid she and her bridegroom would be exiled for ever if the Tsar's heart remained stony?

'There is no need for you to make up your mind in a hurry, my dear,' the Countess went on. 'I know there is much to be considered and, of course, there is still the possibility that we may not be forced out of Russia, in which case I hope you would remain with us as long as possible. I merely wanted to make sure you were warned in advance of the possible effect upon yourself of our marriage.'

'Is the ceremony to take place soon?' Letty ventured to ask.

'Oh, yes—next week! I can still hardly believe it has been arranged at last. We would both have liked to have it in the church at Tsarskoe Selo, but that is obviously impossible. Instead, His Imperial Highness has chosen a small church in the country, not far from Petersburg, where he hopes there will be no publicity. It will be a very simple occasion with only a few friends present. Naturally I want Nikki to be there and I would like you to bring him and take charge of him during the service.'

Taken completely by surprise, Letty almost stammered her thanks. To be present at the marriage of the Tsar's brother—it was something which would have been beyond her wildest dreams when she came to Russia. Of course, it was not a big official occasion, but to be invited to this small secret ceremony was perhaps a greater honour.

'I will arrange for you and Nikki to travel together in a closed carriage,' Natalia added. 'The less attention attracted, the better.'

As she left the room Letty wondered wistfully whether Nicholas would be present. It seemed a very, very long time since that terrible evening which had somehow turned so magical at the end. She did not even know whether his motor car had been returned to him.

She knew nothing about him at all, except that somehow she could not keep him out of her thoughts, no matter how hard she tried.

It did not make her any happier to receive a short note from Marina, complaining bitterly of loneliness. Owing to the damage to the Hispano-Suiza she had not seen Nicholas for weeks, though he had written to explain the reason.

> He told me about the revolutionary meeting. Really, Letty, you must have been crazy to go to such a place! However did you bring yourself to

wear such dreadful clothes? Nicholas made me die laughing when he described your appearance.

The words hurt out of all proportion to their importance. She *knew* she had looked awful and Nicholas had not hesitated to tell her so to her face, causing her no distress at all. Why was it so much more painful when he and Marina laughed over it?

The reason was clear enough, but again Letty refused to recognise it. Instead she tried to occupy her mind by considering what she should wear for the wedding.

When the day came she set out in good time with Nikki for the drive to the village church where the ceremony was to take place. The little boy was resplendent in a miniature Guards uniform, with a tiny and very blunt sword at his side. Letty, determined not to look like a governess, wore a pretty dress of madonna-blue silk, its deep V filled in modestly with a vest of hand-made lace which extended to form the high boned collar. Her only ornament was the gold chain and locket she had worn at the Grand Duchess Anna's party.

She had not even *liked* Nicholas then, she remembered, or, at least, she hadn't at the beginning of the evening, though she had finished up in quite a different frame of mind about him.

A lot had happened since then.

The coachman was taking them in an unfamiliar direction and Letty concentrated on looking out of the window and pointing out things which she thought might interest Nikki. Not long after they had left the city behind they came to the outskirts of a small village, and right in the centre they found the tiny church, resplendent with its bright green and gold onion dome shining in the sunlight.

After the warmth outdoors, the air inside was cold and musty, and the small stained-glass windows were so dark in their colouring that very little light could penetrate. The ornate lamps in their red glass did not do much to lighten the gloom and Letty could not help comparing it with a village church in England. As her eyes adjusted to the semi-darkness, she discovered there were no pews, as there would have been at home, and only a few chairs nearer the altar. Presumably most of the villagers were accustomed to stand throughout the service.

There were about half a dozen people occupying seats and Letty did not know whether she and Nikki should join them or remain in the background. Her mind was made up for her by the little boy, who recognised his grandmother and darted off to join her. Seeing that he was welcomed, Letty decided to stay where she was and only make her presence known if he misbehaved.

She stood very still, absorbing the atmosphere of the alien building and not sure whether she liked it. The smell of incense was overpowering and she hoped the service would not be a long one. Nothing seemed to be happening at present, except that a few village women with shawls over their heads had come in and, after crossing themselves, were lighting candles and placing them in front of the numerous ikons which adorned the walls.

Suddenly someone spoke softly from behind her.

'Would you not prefer to sit down, Letty?'

She started, conscious of instantly leaping pulses, but managed to answer with composure, 'I didn't know whether the chairs were for important people.'

'There will not be many of those.' Nicholas led the way to two unoccupied seats. 'Come—let us be comfortable while we can.'

As they sat down, Letty peeped at him from beneath the wide brim of her pale blue straw hat, anxious to see whether his cut still showed. But unfortunately she was on the wrong side of him and could only see a tanned, unmarked forehead above which the dark hair waved abundantly.

'To what do I owe the honour of this inspection?' he enquired, also peering under the brim.

'Your wound—I wondered if you had a scar.' Stammering, she withdrew her gaze hastily.

'Thanks to your ministrations and the doctor's stitches, it is now no more than a thin red line and will doubtless completely disappear shortly. I had forgotten it.'

'I had not,' she said quietly.

'It is kind of you to be concerned on my behalf.'

'Not at all.' Her tone matched the formality of his. 'How about your poor motor car? Is it quite restored?'

'Oh, yes. I had to send it away, back to the works in France, but it has returned to me looking like new.'

'I'm so glad.'

The stilted conversation had to end there because things were beginning to happen. The choir filed in, singing vigorously in Latin, and a surprising number of gorgeously robed priests appeared, preceded by white-clad boys swinging censers which added to the already strong smell of incense. Everyone stood up and the tall black-bearded groom appeared from somewhere and advanced to meet his bride.

Looking at Natalia, Letty caught her breath in a half-sob. She was as lovely as an angel and in the dim light her beautiful face seemed to glow with an inner radiance.

The service was long, elaborate and totally incomprehensible to Letty. She listened and watched in a half-daze, stood up and sat down when the others did, but an inner streak of stubborn Protestantism prevented her from making the sign of the cross with everyone else. She hoped no one had noticed but did not let it worry her. Her father would have approved anyway!

Afterwards, when she looked back on the occasion, she could remember no details at all, nothing but a kaleidoscope of glorious colour, music that soared to the roof and the choking smell of incense. At the end of it all she retrieved Nikki from the old lady clad in black satin and sparkling with diamonds, with whom he had been sitting. Nicholas was talking to some of the other guests and did not notice when she left the church.

A brilliant splash of yellow caught her eye and she saw the Hispano-Suiza drawn up behind the short line of carriages. As Nicholas had said, it looked like new, and she was glad for his sake. There would be nothing to remind him of that unfortunate evening.

As for herself, the only thing she wanted to remember was the feel of his strong, masculine body in her arms, the hard pressure of his mouth and that strange sensation in her own body which had left her feeling an odd frustration she could not understand.

It would be far, far better to forget these things too.

Back at the house there was a small reception for the guests, at which Nikki was passed from one to another, and kissed and spoilt, and Letty was presented to the Grand Duke. She curtsied deeply, her eyes modestly fixed on his shining black boots, and then faded into the background without having exchanged a single word with him.

Would Natalia now be 'Your Imperial Highness'? she wondered as she stood half hidden by an immense palm in a pot and watched Nicholas apparently enjoying himself in the centre of a circle of flirtatious ladies. It would be hard to remember not to call her 'Countess' any more, and she resolved to avoid using a title in future if it were possible.

She did not have long to wrestle with the problem. Only two weeks after the wedding, Natalia sent for her and informed her—the gentle voice a mixture of sadness and resignation—that they would be leaving for England very shortly, and the governess could either go with them or remain behind and stay with her sister.

'For my part,' said Nikki's mother, 'I would very much like to take you with us. You have taught my little son so well that he now understands quite a lot of English words and can even prattle something of your language in his childish way.' She sighed and the old sombre look returned briefly. 'Will you give me your decision as soon as possible, please, Letty?'

'I can easily give it now. I'm sorry, but I feel I should go to Marina. I know it is what she wants and, after all, it was for her sake that I came to Russia. In many ways——' her voice faltered a little '——I should like to come with you, but I cannot. I'm sure you will find another English governess without difficulty as soon as you are settled in England.'

'I regret your decision very much, but I understand your reasons,' Natalia said kindly. 'How will you get to Liev? If I can be of any help——'

'I thought of going by train. I expect I can find some form of conveyance at the other end.'

'I am sure Nicholas Namorov——'

'No!' Letty's voice was much too emphatic but she feared if she did not immediately crush any suggestion of asking for his help, she would weaken and agree to it. 'I can quite easily manage the journey,' she insisted, 'but if you would be kind enough to tell your coachman to drive me to the station, I would be very grateful.'

'Of course, my dear. Just tell me when you will be ready to leave and I will arrange it.'

Anxious to get the parting over, Letty was ready in three days' time. Nikki cried when he found she was leaving him and she felt like tears herself. Natalia embraced her affectionately and gave her an exquisitely decorated Fabergé egg as a parting present. Letty had often gazed into the famous shop on the Nevski Prospect but she had never expected to actually own any of the delicate gold and enamel ware obtainable there. It would be something to treasure for the rest of her life, a precious memento of these summer months which had brought her both happiness and heartache.

Natalia's coachman delivered her to the station in good time, made sure that a porter had charge of her luggage and then departed. Clutching only her handbag, Letty stood alone, a slender figure in a fawn dust-coat, and waited for the local train. If a trans-European express had been due, the station would have been crowded, but at noon there were few people travelling, and consequently the tall man who came striding along the platform had no difficulty in finding her.

Letty had been having a struggle to keep her composure. She had grown to love St Petersburg and, although it was not really the case, she felt this was the end of her Russian adventure. During the time that remained she would be buried in the forest at Liev, sharing Marina's exile. There would be no more walks along leafy avenues or beside the sparkling Neva, no more drives in the yellow motor car. Worse of all, she would never have Nicholas to herself again. If he came to the dacha it would be to see her sister.

She drew a quivering breath that was half a sob and blinked furiously. When her vision cleared she saw him coming towards her.

'Letty!' He reached her side and seized her unresisting hand, holding it firmly in both his own. 'What the devil do you mean by creeping away secretly like this? Why did you not ask me to drive you?'

She could not meet his eyes, but she kept her voice steady. 'I didn't wish to inconvenience you. Besides, I have far too much luggage for the motor.'

'Your luggage could have gone by train.' His grip on her hand tightened. 'It's not too late, Letty. We can be on our way within a few minutes. It will take longer than by train, but what does that matter? You have weeks ahead of you for being with Marina.'

Letty did not think she had ever been so tempted. With all her heart she yearned to accept his suggestion, to snatch at this heaven-sent opportunity to be in his company—just the two of them—once more.

Somehow she managed to find the courage to refuse.

'It's extremely kind of you, Nicholas, but I already have my ticket and it would be a pity to waste it. Besides, I was quite looking forward to the railway journey. There will be people getting in and out at every station and I shall be able to listen to their conversation and see how much I can understand. I'm sure it will be very interesting.'

'So you would rather have a Russian lesson than drive with me?' he flung at her. 'I never heard such utter nonsense! Give me your ticket and I will tear it up before your eyes, then you can blame me for the wastage and your conscience will be clear.'

'On the contrary, my conscience would be greatly disturbed,' she assured him, daring to steal a peep at his face.

She found him looking thunderous. 'For heaven's sake, Letty,' he exploded, 'let us stop talking this rubbish! Forget the wretched ticket and come with me now. My motor car is outside the station——'

'No!' She wrenched her hand free. 'Why can't you simply take "no" for an answer, Nicholas? I have made up my mind to be independent and go by train and there's no more to be said. It was very kind of you to offer the lift but I'm not in need of any assistance.' She turned her head as a train chuffed slowly into the station. 'I think that is probably the one I'm waiting for, so I'd better say goodbye.'

He was looking at her as though he could still scarcely believe what she had been saying. In making her choice, she had insulted both the Hispano-Suiza and his male pride.

'If that's how you feel, Letty——' his eyes were steel-grey with barely suppressed anger '——then there is no more to be said. I wish you a pleasant journey.' And with that he turned on his heel and strode back down the platform.

She watched him until he was out of sight and then got into the train. As it drew slowly out of the station her eyes filled with tears. She must have been crazy to refuse his offer and she could not imagine why she had done it. It had been instinctive, as though something deep within had urged her to say farewell to him as well as to St Petersburg, and there was no point in regretting it now.

Nevertheless, she continued to do so and it was not until the train had nearly reached Liev that she succeeded in convincing herself that she had been right.

There was a shabby carriage awaiting her, presumably arranged for by Marina, and a rough-looking countryman retrieved her luggage and piled it in. Sitting in the old but comfortable vehicle behind a plodding horse, Letty banished the unhappy start to her journey from her mind, and looked about her with interest as they entered the woods.

There were signs of autumn already. Some of the fluttering leaves on the birch trees were turning yellow and dropping to the ground, and the atmosphere where the track was shaded was noticeably cool and damp. But it was still hot in the sun and when they reached the clearing the little house sat basking in the strong light, just as she remembered it.

As on the previous occasion Marina was sitting in her rocking chair on the veranda and this time she had some difficulty in struggling up to greet her sister. There was no doubt about her welcome and the two girls clung together, both overcome by emotion. After a while they regained their composure and began to talk, ignoring the pile of luggage which would have to be stowed away somewhere.

'I expect you'll be glad when your waiting time is over,' Letty ventured. 'Has it seemed very long?'

'Interminable!' Marina sighed and glanced down at her misshapen figure. 'I hate myself like this—so fat and ugly. It seems so awful that it was caused by a few minutes of madness which I imagined to be love. How could I have been such a fool?' She looked across at her sister, neat and slender in her plain blouse and linen skirt. 'Never let it happen to you, Letty. It's just not worth it.'

'It doesn't seem to be.'

Marina hesitated and seemed to have difficulty in deciding whether to put into words what was in her mind. She sat watching a rabbit which had emerged on to the rough grass and was sitting upright, his nose wrinkling anxiously. Eventually she asked diffidently, 'I suppose you do understand what I'm talking about?'

Letty started and felt herself colouring. 'Well—not exactly. I mean, I know you're talking about something that happens on the wedding night, only with you it wasn't, if you know what I mean.'

'I know exactly what you mean. There's no denying I got completely carried away by my physical sensations and I should have had more control. I'm not talking about the moral side, Letty, in spite of having been brought up in the church. What I'm trying to say is that being landed with an unwanted baby is a heavy price to pay for those brief moments of bodily pleasure.' She broke off and sat brooding, and then added bitterly, 'It was only once. I could hardly believe my ill luck when I found I was pregnant.'

Letty's mind flew back once again to the extraordinary sensations she had experienced during those few minutes alone with Nicholas in her bedroom after she had attended to his cut. All her instincts had told her that her body was needing something more, and that he shared that longing. Had she been in danger then?

In danger of *what*?

'Marina,' she said suddenly, her voice sharp and incisive, 'will you please tell me what you have been talking about?'

Her sister stared at her. 'You really want to know?'

'Yes, I do. I can't see that being ignorant is any help to a girl. How can you be sure of avoiding something if you don't know what it is? Mama always said we must wait until we were married, but I'd like to know *now*. After all, *you* must have found out some time—I mean, you've never once excused yourself by saying you were ignorant.'

'Not many theatre people are.'

'I suppose not.' Her cheeks were uncomfortably hot but her resolution remained firm. 'Go on—tell me!' she commanded.

So Marina told her.

When she had finished Letty made no comment. She sat very still, staring out across the clearing towards the birch trees beyond, and Marina saw no more than her profile. Only a pair of goldfinches, feeding on the dry seeds of a thistle, could have seen her expression and they were no more aware of her than she was of them.

The birds finished their eager pecking and flew away, and Letty stirred. Her shocked mind floundered hopelessly and she could think of no comment to make. Instead she picked up her lighter luggage and said over her shoulder, 'I'd better go and start unpacking.'

'Tell Varya to come and fetch the rest,' Marina called. 'She's very strong.'

Letty's room was small and very old-fashioned, and she could not avoid comparing it with the two pretty bedrooms she had occupied in the city. Trying to make the best of it, she unpacked some of her possessions and left most of her summer clothes in the trunk. There seemed little point in trying to find a place for her pretty hats, and the leather hat box also remained as it had arrived. As she tried to make everything tidy, it occurred to her there was no obvious way of taking a bath.

Appealed to, Marina laughed and directed her to the bathhouse behind the dacha. Peeping in, Letty was amazed to see a low-ceilinged room with a space in the roof covered by a sliding panel. The floor consisted of large uneven stones and there was nothing else. Puzzled, she applied to her sister for more exact information.

'Varya lights a fire of brushwood and when it has died down, she slides back the panel in the roof and pours in a bucket of cold water. It's as well to stay out of the way while this is going on. The cold water and the hot stones combine to make a great deal of steam, and that's how you bathe.'

'In steam?'

Marina smiled. 'That's right. Of course you have to remember that a dacha is really only intended for summer living.'

Again Letty made no comment but her heart was heavy, and she was obliged to remind herself that her sister had been putting up with this sort of thing for months.

It would be terrible in winter.

Letty shuddered at the thought of cold weather and tried to accustom herself to life in the wilds. There would not be many baths, she discovered, because all their water was brought in barrels by a man named Sergei who came twice a week with a cart. He brought other supplies too and, although the food was monotonous, there were always fresh vegetables and huge quantities of mushrooms.

'All Russians go out looking for mushrooms at this time of the year.' Marina produced a special basket shaped like a shallow trough. 'I can't pick them now, but I'll show you where the best ones grow.'

They wandered in the woods every day, enjoying the cooler weather and watching the trees gradually assuming their full autumn colouring. And every day Marina talked about Nicholas.

'It's such a long time since he came to visit,' she complained.

'Perhaps he doesn't think it's necessary now I'm here,' Letty suggested.

'I don't see that makes any difference. He likes coming—he told me so when I was saying something about how kind it was of him to take such care of me. He said it was no trouble at all and it was the least he could do after what his brother had done to me. But I don't think he's doing it just because of Paul.'

'Don't you?'

Marina lowered herself carefully on to a fallen log. 'Once when he came he found me in an awful fit of the blues. I burst out crying and he held me in his arms and comforted me, and then he kissed me.' She paused, her eyes wide and thoughtful. 'I think it was then that I fell in love with him.'

Letty spun round, almost upsetting her basket. Rearranging the mushrooms gave her a chance to hide her face. 'I didn't realise you were in love with Nicholas—at least, not *really* in love. I knew you were fond of him but——'

'It's been coming on gradually all through the summer months, and at first I wondered whether I just felt grateful to him. But I know now it isn't only gratitude, but something much stronger and deeper. I do truly love him.'

'You're quite sure? I mean, you believed you were in love with Paul——'

'That was absolutely different. I told you it was only physical attraction.'

'Yes, you did.' Letty turned her back and bent to pick a particularly luscious mushroom. 'What about his feelings?' she asked, her voice barely audible.

'I can't be sure about those, of course,' Marina admitted, 'but I'm hopeful. I know he's very fond of me, but he'd hardly be likely to propose to me in the present circumstances. I think he's just biding his time.'

And amusing himself with Marina's sister, Letty told herself bleakly. No doubt he considered it highly humorous that he had captured the hearts of both the Mayfield girls!

No... that wasn't fair. He had probably guessed how Marina felt about him, but he had no reason to believe that she herself had been indulging in anything more serious than a mild flirtation. At least, she hoped so.

'Do you think Nicholas would want to be a father to his brother's illegitimate child?' she asked.

'Why not? The baby's a Namorov, after all. It would be the perfect solution.'

There was a long silence. Letty continued with her task, but her mind was totally unaware of what her hands were doing.

'Don't you think,' she said at last, 'that if Nicholas wanted to marry you he would have suggested it right at the beginning?'

'He hardly knew me then,' Marina said impatiently. 'I told you, it has been gradual with both of us.'

It had been gradual with her, too, Letty thought sadly but she didn't think it was likely to bring her any happiness. Perhaps her sister would be more fortunate.

## CHAPTER FIFTEEN

NICHOLAS did not come for a long time. The mellow fruitfulness of September turned into wind-tossed October, and then cold November mists swirled round the trees like ghosts, and still he did not appear.

Marina complained loudly and, at times, very crossly, but Letty kept her longing for him to herself. It was better that she should not see too much of him, she knew that perfectly well, but nevertheless her need of him was as great as her sister's though she never mentioned it.

It was on a cold frosty morning that he came at last, crushing the brown carpet of leaves with his car wheels, and drawing up with a flourish below the veranda. Marina and Letty were in the living-room, warm and cosy beside the big porcelain stove which Sergei kept well supplied with wood. They were sewing, for no better reason than that there was nothing else to do. Marina's baby already had enough tiny garments for twins.

The previous week, their handyman had spent all day sealing the windows ready for winter. Putty, which would have to be chipped out in the spring, held the extra sheets of glass in place and kept the outside world at bay. Neither of the girls heard the noise made by Nicholas's car although, until the double-glazing was done, they had both been listening for it for some time.

Suddenly he was there, standing in the doorway, wearing a long fur-lined coat and holding a tall astrakhan hat in his hand. 'What a charming domestic scene,' he drawled.

His face looked cold and, although he was smiling, it seemed to Letty that his eyes were sombre. But Marina noticed nothing, except that he was there at last. With an exclamation of delight, she scrambled to her feet and greeted him enthusiastically, standing on tiptoe to put her arms round his neck.

He bent his head and kissed her lightly. As he straightened up again his eyes were on Letty and she thought he might be wondering why she was not taking part in the exuberant welcome. Instead, she continued to embroider the cot-cover which Marina had given her to work at, and no one but herself could have been aware that her hands were shaking.

'Good morning, Nicholas,' she said coolly. 'I expect you have had a cold journey.'

He nodded. 'Because it was sunny, I started out with the hood down and had to stop halfway to put it up. By that time I was thoroughly chilled.' He looked at Marina. 'I should greatly appreciate it if your servant could produce some mulled wine.'

'I'll see to it myself.' She went out to the kitchen.

Although her eyes were on her work, Letty was conscious with every nerve in her body of Nicholas sprawling in the vacated chair, his long legs in high boots stretched out to the warmth of the stove. It was the first time she had seen him since Marina had imparted to her that alarming, and yet exciting, information about the extraordinary way ladies and gentleman behaved when they were married. And on other occasions too, apparently, or her sister would not be in this mess. Her guilty knowledge had lain heavily on her mind ever since. She preferred not to think about it, yet found it impossible to forget.

'Since you have no telephone,' Nicholas was saying, 'I will give instructions that in another week or so Sergei is to remain here at night instead of going to his own home. No doubt Varya will find some sort of bed for him. Perhaps a share of her own—who knows?' For a moment the wicked gleam was back in his eyes.

Letty bent her head further over her work, hoping her heightened colour would be attributed to the heat of the room. 'How will Sergei get about when the snow comes?' she asked.

'He is very capable on skis and will soon get in contact with the doctor and nurse when the time comes. As for the ordinary necessities of life, those will come by sledge instead of cart, so you have nothing to worry about.'

'The Russians seem to cope very efficiently with winter,' Letty said politely. 'In England a few inches of snow flings us all into confusion.'

'That is because the English can never be sure whether there will be snow or not. If they were as certain as we are, they would doubtless cope as well.'

'Perhaps.'

She had never discussed the weather with Nicholas before, but she was thankful to have that great conversational standby available to her now. Unfortunately, after they had dealt with the snow there did not seem to be much else to say, and while she was searching in her mind for a new topic, while appearing to concentrate on threading a needle, Nicholas startled her by asking a personal question.

'Have you been happy here, Letty?'

'Happy? Yes, of course—I mean, I came to Russia to see my sister, so naturally I've been happy after finding her at last.'

'I would have expected anyone with your lively mind to be somewhat bored in this dreary little dacha.'

'It won't be for much longer anyway,' she said, leaving the question unanswered.

Marina came back at that moment, bringing hot spicy wine for them all, and the small party inevitably became gayer, though in Letty's case it was only a superficial gaiety. With the other two it appeared to be perfectly genuine.

When Nicholas prepared to depart after lunch, she bade him a composed farewell and kept in the background, watching her sister's loving embrace with as much detachment as she could muster. Over the top of Marina's head, Nicholas's eyes met hers and her control slipped briefly so that her hurt and bewilderment showed for a moment. As she yearned for some sign from him, some tiny secret indication that he had not completely relegated her to the position of Marina's sister—a sort of nurse-companion—the fragile link between them was broken. His gaze dropped as Marina raised her head, offering her lips, and he took them with a casual tenderness which pierced Letty's heart.

Shortly after his visit the snow came. All night the wind howled round the snug little cottage, and in the morning the two girls awoke to see a white world beyond the windows. When the sun eventually rose it was so huge and red that it tinged everything with a pinky glow, and the scene was so beautiful that Letty forgot her unhappiness and stood entranced by the window.

'I wish I could ski,' she said when Marina joined her. 'It must be wonderful to swoop over the snow as a bird swoops through the air.'

'I hate snow.' Marina shuddered. 'If I had to get landed with a baby, why ever could it not have been in the summer?'

'You would find the heat even harder to bear,' Letty pointed out, receiving only a shrug and a pout in reply.

During the days that followed, she found herself withdrawing more and more into the role of listener as her sister grumbled about her physical discomfort and—a recurring theme—her misfortune in getting pregnant when she had only transgressed once.

There were times when Letty's patience gave out completely.

'You should be looking to the future, not moaning about the past,' she snapped one day when she had been shut up in the house for a week without exercise or fresh air.

Marina dissolved into tears. 'You don't know how horrible it is to feel like a pregnant elephant when you're used to being slim and lissom and as light on your feet as thistledown.'

Letty bit her lip hard and just managed not to point out that the situation was as least partly Marina's own fault. 'Never mind,' she said at last, 'it's not long now.'

'Perhaps the baby will be late.'

'You *are* looking on the black side!'

But the baby was not late. Three days prior to the expected date, Marina felt the first warning.

There had been several heavy falls of snow, but for a while now the skies had remained clear and frost had laid a thick solid carpet over the white depths below. Sergei went about on his skis without difficulty and kept them well supplied with water—which had to be melted—and logs for the stoves, all brought on a small sledge.

Varya, who seemed to know something about childbirth, kept a reserve barrel of water 'because there will be much needed' and she happened to be present when Marina complained of backache.

'Ah!' Her broad peasant face was alight with interest. 'I think perhaps it is the baby. You would like that I rub your back for you?'

'You mean it might be the beginning——?' Marina's expression was a mixture of excitement and fear.

Her back was still aching at bedtime but Letty persuaded her to go to bed as usual. Some time later she awoke from a light sleep to find her room illuminated by a wavering candle flame and Marina's grotesque shape flung upon the ceiling.

'I've started having real pains, and I've timed them as the doctor told me. They are twenty minutes apart.'

'That doesn't sound very urgent,' Letty protested. 'Why don't you try and get some more sleep?'

'I have tried, but it's no good. Do come along to my room, Letty, and at least keep me company.'

So Letty got up and dressed, though she left her hair in two plaits, and went to the kitchen to see if she could persuade the samovar to provide them with tea. Varya was snoring somewhere nearby, and a deeper note confirmed that Sergei was also at hand. Whether they were together, Letty neither knew nor cared, a state of mind which would have shocked her deeply a few months ago.

She had learnt a lot since coming to Russia, and she had changed, too. She had been an excited, carefree girl when she left England, totally ignorant of life. She would return—presumably quite soon now—a grown-up young woman with a hidden core of sadness deep within her and a new awareness of life's problems.

That night it seemed that the dawn—always very late—would never come. The pains continued to be regular, but were in no hurry to become more frequent. Letty made innumerable glasses of tea, rubbed Marina's back, tried to encourage her flagging spirits, and occasionally fell asleep in her chair from sheer exhaustion.

Varya exclaimed in surprise at finding her up and dressed, assessed the situation and announced that the baby was progressing. 'It is better he not come too quick,' she assured them.

'How do you know so much about it?' Letty asked curiously.

'I am eldest of twelve. Much experience.'

Halfway through the morning, Marina announced that the pains were increasing and the doctor ought to be sent for. Letty, by now beginning to feel an urgent need for professional support, agreed with her, though the servant looked doubtful.

'I am quite sure Count Namorov would not want us to take any risks,' Letty said firmly.

The mention of the Namorov name had a magical effect and a few minutes later Sergei set off on his skis.

They were prepared for him to be a long time but it seemed an eternity before Letty, venturing out to the veranda for a reviving breath of fresh air, heard in the distance the jingle of sleigh bells. It was a magical sound, wafting over the frozen trees and for a moment her imagination painted an enthralling picture of herself and Nicholas, wrapped in furs and snuggling in delicious intimacy beneath a vast fur rug, gliding through the forest behind a team of high-stepping horses.

The picture faded and Letty was back in the real world. The sleigh coming towards the dacha, its bells growing ever more distinct, would be bringing two strangers, a doctor and nurse of unknown appearance and temperament, who were to help Marina's baby in its struggle for birth.

Doctor Lipka was a jolly-looking man with a red face and Father Christmas beard, and the middle-aged nurse was short and plump, and seemed much more approachable than the two dragons who had attended Mrs Kemp.

After a brief examination, the doctor sat sipping vodka by the stove and telling Letty long stories about his past experiences in the snow, while in the bedroom the nurse took charge completely, organising both the patient and the furniture until everything was to her liking.

The pains were coming much faster now and, when Letty ventured to ask when the child was likely to be born, she was told it would probably be soon after midnight.

'I should get some sleep if I were you,' the nurse advised. 'There's nothing you can do that your servant can't manage better, if you will forgive me saying so. She's a good girl and has agreed to stay up. Besides,' she added with a smile, 'Childbirth is not a suitable occasion for a young unmarried lady—enough to put her off for life!'

'I'll lie down for a little while anyway,' Letty agreed.

Having been awake nearly all the previous night, she was asleep almost at once, although she had not intended to do more than rest her weary limbs. Some hours later she awoke abruptly, startled into awareness by some sound.

There it came again—a high-pitched scream, which cut through the hitherto silent cottage and fiercely demanded how Letty could dare to sleep when her sister was in such agony. Deeply ashamed, and shaking with nervous tension, she was obliged to lie for a moment before her trembling legs could summon the strength to enable her to get out of bed.

As she thrust her feet into slippers the noise came again, but this time she was braver and she hurried out to the living-room, half expecting to see the doctor still sipping vodka by the stove while Marina laboured to give birth with only the nurse to help her.

There was no one there, and as she tried to find the courage to tap on her sister's door, Varya came in from the kitchen.

'It not be long now.' She seemed quite unperturbed. 'Poor lady—she suffer much, but she will forget when her child is placed in her arms.'

Refreshed by her short sleep, Letty longed to do something useful but there was nothing, and after Varya had left her she could only walk up and down the room and resist an urgent desire to cover her ears every time Marina cried out.

Suddenly she realised that everything was quiet, and somehow that seemed even more frightening. Holding her breath, she strained her ears to catch some sound— any sound.

Almost immediately there came the high, thin mewing of a very new baby.

The relief was enormous. It was over, all the long, long wait and the final agony. Now Marina could begin to rebuild her life. Alone as she was, Letty gave a small cry of exultation, and when she heard the door opening she advanced to meet the nurse with an expectant smile on her face.

But the nurse was not smiling. Her head was bent over the small bundle in her arms but, as she became aware of Letty's presence, she thrust it towards her and said tersely, 'It's a female child. Take her—she's yours.'

The bundle was heavier than Letty had expected and, as her arms folded round it, she spared only a moment to wonder at the woman's strange greeting. Carefully, she moved the shawl aside and peeped at the little puckered face. There was a tuft of black hair and two unfocused blue eyes, which nevertheless seemed to look up into her own, and her throat constricted with emotion. Illegitimate as the child undoubtedly was, she had as much right to a happy childhood as any born in wedlock, and she hoped Marina intended to see she got it.

The baby whimpered and Letty began to walk up and down, crooning softly. She was delighted when the whimpering ceased, and ventured to sit down by the stove, rocking the child gently in her arms. She was so absorbed that she did not immediately notice the bedroom door had opened again.

This time it was the doctor who emerged.

His face was grave and he had quite lost his jolly Father Christmas look. He stood for a moment just inside the room and Letty looked at him hopefully, thinking he had come to tell her she could now see Marina.

Instead he said quietly. 'I am sorry to have to tell you to brace yourself for a great shock. Your sister——'

'Yes?' Letty's eyes dilated in fear. 'Is Marina—ill?'

'Not ill. I very much regret to inform you she did not survive the birth of her child.' He crossed himself. 'She has gone where there will be no more pain or suffering, and all is forgiven.'

'You mean——' Letty's mouth felt dry and she had to start again. 'You mean—she's *dead*?'

He bowed his head. 'I'm very sorry. There was nothing we could do.'

There was a sick feeling at the pit of her stomach and her whole body seemed to be trembling. 'I don't understand!' The words were a cry of anguish. 'Why did she die? What happened?'

'She had a severe haemorrhage and went rapidly into a coma. After the loss of so much blood, we were helpless to save her.' He was silent for a moment and then added gently, 'The child is a fine healthy infant. You can at least be thankful for that.'

The attempt at consolation meant nothing to Letty, and the little bundle in her arms was no more important than a bundle of old clothing. Tears were streaming down her face, but she was not aware of them. Her thoughts whirled round inside her head like leaves in the wind.

Perhaps they had made a mistake—perhaps Marina had only fainted and she would come round eventually and ask for her baby.

But two experienced medical people would not make that sort of mistake. Marina must indeed be dead and she would never, never see her again, except lying cold and marble-pale in her coffin.

She began to cry properly, with great choking sobs like a child, and the nurse came and put her arms round her and said, 'There, there, dear, don't try to control yourself—the tears will do you good.'

When she eventually recovered her composure, Letty felt as though her eyes were no more than slits between hugely swollen lids and her head ached so much she could hardly hold it up.

The doctor gave her a pill and put vodka in her glass instead of water. 'Go and lie down for a while,' he advised.

Letty had just enough strength left to crawl under the thick padded quilt before sleep overtook her and she sank into total forgetfulness.

When she awoke her mind felt completely empty and she lay for a moment enjoying the warmth and the wonderful feeling of relaxation. Vaguely she wondered if it was time to get up. That the room was dark meant nothing, for the sun was reluctant to rise these December mornings.

It was then she realised she was already dressed, and she remembered she had gone to bed some time during the morning. Instantly everything came flooding back—the terrible, tragic end to her long search for Marina. For a moment she tried to thrust it away from her and a desperate longing for her home swept over her. If only she had never left it, never come to Russia...

But she *had* come to Russia. She had no one to blame but herself, that she had got involved with this unhappy situation.

Dry-eyed and quite calm, her hand trembling only a little, she lit the candle and struggled out of bed. There must be all sorts of things she ought to be doing. Someone, she hoped, was caring for the baby, but there was the funeral to arrange and she had no idea how to go about it. What a good thing she had learnt to speak passable Russian!

She was standing by the mirror staring in disgust at her dishevelled appearance—her blouse crumpled and her two long plaits all fuzzy where she had lain on them—when a sound at the door made her spin round. Someone was opening it very cautiously. It would probably be Varya, she reasoned, come to see if she was awake.

But it was not Varya.

'May I come in?' Nicholas paused and, receiving no answer, entered and halted just inside, his hand still on the latch.

They looked at each other and Letty saw twin candle-flames reflected in his eyes, but they hid his expression and she only noticed that his mouth was grimly set.

The man spoke first. He said quietly, 'Oh, Letty, what can I say? I am so terribly, terribly sorry.'

She longed to fling herself into his arms and feel the comfort of his strength holding the world at bay. Instead she deliberately whipped up anger she had not known existed until that moment.

'What do you want?' she demanded furiously. 'Hasn't your family done enough harm?'

Her attack seemed to startle him, but before he could speak Letty went rushing on again.

'Your brother killed my sister as surely as though he had stabbed her with a knife, but *he*'s safe in Venice, enjoying himself pretending to be an artist. Isn't that enough to make me feel I never want to see any of you again?'

'That's ridiculous!' Nicholas flung back at her. 'I am not responsible for my brother's actions.'

She was being unfair, Letty knew that quite clearly with the cooler, less emotional side of her mind. Marina had never claimed she had been taken by force; she had admitted she had had a whirlwind romance with the glamorous Paul Namorov. Nevertheless, she continued to feed the quarrel with bitter words simply because she dare not show her real feelings.

'You must have felt responsible,' she accused, 'or you would not have spirited Marina away to this hidden dacha, and kept an eye on her all this time.'

'You think not?' His tone was as bitter as hers had been. 'So you give me no credit for common humanity? Am I not allowed to feel sympathy for a talented dancer swept from her normal environment and faced with long months of boredom and physical discomfort because of an—er—unfortunate lapse?'

Tongue-tied, Letty dropped her gaze. Of course he was allowed to feel sorry for Marina. What she couldn't bear was the suspicion—almost a certainty—that his sympathy had, during those same long months, turned to love.

And all the time he had been pretending to be attracted to herself.

She said icily, 'I should be glad if you would leave my room so that I may tidy myself. There is a great deal to be arranged.

'On the contrary,' he told her coolly, 'it is all done.'

'Done?' She looked at him blankly.

'You have been asleep all day. I came as soon as I heard the sad news, which was just before lunch. Fortunately I happened to be at my great-grandmother's house so it did not take long to get here by sleigh. When I had established that Varya is quite competent to tend a newborn infant, I sent the nurse off with the doctor and returned to the house to telephone.'

'Telephone?'

His expression softened. 'There were funeral arrangements to be made, but there is no need for you to worry about them. As I said, it is all done.'

Stubbornly determined not to show her immense relief, Letty thanked him stiffly. 'Perhaps you will be kind enough to tell me what you have arranged?' she added.

She was astonished to learn that Marina was to be interred in the Namorov vault at the little church on the estate. When she protested she was told it would be much easier on account of the ground being frozen hard.

'We have another vault on our main estate,' Nicholas explained, 'and this one has not been used for some time. There are a great many coffins there and one more will not be noticed.'

He had probably only meant to reassure her, Letty knew, but she chose to regard the remark as unacceptably flippant.

'How dare you joke about it?' she flashed.

The dark eyebrows lifted fractionally. 'My dear Letty, I can solemnly assure you I find nothing amusing in the whole unhappy affair. However, you seem determined to misjudge me this evening——'

'Evening! Is it really evening?' she broke in, forgetting for the moment she was quarrelling with him.

'Past nine o'clock and high time I was returning to the big house.' He paused, looking at her doubtfully. 'I have a suggestion to make, but in your present mood I am not sure if it is wise.'

As she said nothing, but merely waited, he continued speaking. 'If you would care to pack an overnight bag, I should be glad to take you with me so that you do not have to spend the night here in this house of sorrow.' His lips twisted in a wry smile. 'I can promise that nothing untoward would happen to you—as on your previous visit.'

'How dare you remind me of that occasion?' There was no need for Letty to pretend. This time her rage was perfectly genuine. 'I shouldn't dream of spending the night at your grandmother's house. I really can't understand how you could have imagined that I might. And now will you *please* go away?'

He went without another word. But when she was sure he was no longer nearby, Letty crept out to the veranda and heard, drifting on the night air, the sound of his sleigh bells. She listened until they had died away in the distance and nothing was audible except the intermittent hooting of an owl, and then went slowly and sadly indoors.

She had had her opportunity to ride with him in his sleigh behind prancing horses whose tinkling bells rang out over the snow, and she had refused it with scorn. There was no sense at all in feeling such bitter regret.

# CHAPTER SIXTEEN

NONE of the difficult letters which Letty had written to her parents during her stay in Russia had been as bad as this one. On previous occasions she had been distressed by the necessity of deceiving them, but at least in the beginning it had been to spare them worry. Then Marina had flatly refused to let her tell them about the coming baby, and she had been obliged to respect her wishes.

This time it had to be the truth, and as Letty picked up her pen she shuddered to think of the double blow she must inflict. Slowly and carefully, at times struggling with tears, she recorded the whole unhappy story, ending:

> I am writing to Aunt Eugenie by this same post, to ask if I may stay with her for a while. I am, of course, making myself responsible for the infant—I'm sure you would wish that—but in view of Papa's position I do not think it would be right for me to arrive at Ely with a baby.
>
> Please do not worry about me on the journey as I shall have Varya, Marina's servant, with me. She is eager to visit England and most competent in caring for a young child.

When both letters were finished and ready for the post, Letty leaned back and closed her eyes. Her head ached with the effort of finding the right words but, in pouring it all out to those whom she loved, she seemed to have eased her own pain a little. Just possibly she might be able to sleep tonight.

'I will see that those reach the post office,' said Nicholas.

Letty started and her eyes flew open. He was standing in the doorway looking grim and pale in his dark fur-lined overcoat.

'Why have you come?' she demanded.

'I have a good reason or I would not have inflicted myself on you. I came to tell you that the funeral is arranged for tomorrow. The priest has promised to make it as brief as his conscience permits and asks if he may christen the child afterwards.'

'No!' Letty sat up with a jerk. 'Whatever would my father think if I allowed Marina's baby to be christened in your heathenish church——?' She broke off abruptly. 'I'm sorry, I should never have called it that. I meant only that the infant will be brought up a Protestant.'

'Have you thought of a name?' Nicholas asked after a pause.

'She is to be called Mary. It seemed appropriate so near to Christmas.'

'I agree.' He hesitated, studying her face with sombre eyes, and then said quietly, 'I should like to see the child—if you have no objection.'

How could she object? Bitter as her feelings were, she had to admit he had been more than generous in shouldering his brother's responsibilities during Marina's pregnancy. He had earned the right to inspect his small niece if he so wished.

'Wait here. I will fetch her.'

She went out to the warm kitchen where the baby lay asleep under Varya's protective eye. With a word of explanation, she bent over the painted wooden cradle, wonderfully carved, and picked up the tiny shapeless form, well swathed against the cold.

Back in the living-room, she held her out to Nicholas. 'You may hold her if you wish.'

He stretched out his arms and she placed the little bundle into them. Together they looked down at the sleeping face. So might they have stood looking at their own child, Letty thought suddenly, and a terrible choking emotion tore at her throat so that she could scarcely breathe. As she struggled to hide her distress, Nicholas broke the silence.

'Already she has a look of the Namorovs. That dark hair and——'

Saved by his words from breaking down, Letty whipped up her anger. '*I* wanted her to look like Marina. I hate to think there might be anything of her father in her.'

His lips tightened and he said tersely, 'I suppose that is natural, but I fear I cannot share your regret. Illegitimate this baby may be, but she is the first child of a new generation of my family and——'

'The child is *mine*—even the nurse said so!'

They glared at each other above the innocently sleeping infant and then Nicholas thrust her back into Letty's arms. Turning his back, he picked up the letters.

'I will call for you tomorrow morning at eleven,' he informed her curtly over his shoulder, and the door slammed behind him. With a long-drawn-out sigh, Letty went to the kitchen and replaced little Mary in her cradle.

When Nicholas came the next day he brought with him a black sealskin coat, immensely thick, heavy and warm. Letty was already shivering with nerves as well as cold and she made no protest when he held it for her to put on. During the sleigh ride to the small church in the grounds, they sat far apart, sharing the fur rug but not touching each other at all. Everything seemed very silent and suddenly Letty realised the jingling bells on the horses' heads had been replaced by black plumes.

Afterwards she remembered nothing at all of the service except the awful chill of the vault in which Marina's coffin was placed. How far, far away was this cold, dead world from the light and colour and music of the life she had loved! And how strange that she—Letty—had during her stay in Russia attended both a wedding and a funeral.

'When do you intend to leave for England?' Nicholas asked on the return journey.

'As soon as it can be arranged.'

'Will you go straight to your home?'

When she told him she hoped to stay for a while with her aunt in London, he immediately offered to obtain tickets and reservations for her all the way to Liverpool Street.

'It is extremely kind of you, but I would prefer to see to it myself,' Letty said stiffly.

His reply was half a groan. 'Oh, Letty, why do you have to be so independent? Can't you see that I wish to try to make amends?'

'Make amends? You know perfectly well that is impossible!' she flashed with a sudden return of her old spirit.

'The words were ill-chosen. Naturally I am as well aware of the impossibility as you are, but there is a great deal I can do to ease your present stony path.' Nicholas paused to brush off a small cascade of powdery snow which had descended on them from an overhanging branch, and then finished coolly, 'I have every intention of making the arrangements for you and the servant, and I will not accept any further opposition.'

Too exhausted by the grief she had suppressed during the funeral, Letty gave up. When they reached the dacha, she slipped out of the warm coat and returned it to him with a brief word of thanks, after which she went into the house and closed the door firmly behind her.

Three days passed before she saw him again.

She was occupying her mind by trying to teach Varya a few words of English when he appeared with the tickets and asked if she could be ready in twenty-four hours.

Since she had already done most of the packing, she assured him that she could.

'You have a private first-class compartment all the way to Holland, a cabin on the night boat, and another reservation from Harwich to London. I have also arranged for the express to stop at Liev to pick you up.'

Letty gasped. She could never have managed all that by herself. For a moment she allowed her guard to slip and her genuine gratitude showed through the barrier of reserve which had built up between them.

'It's extremely kind of you to take so much trouble,' she told him warmly.

'Not at all.' He had not followed her example and his tone remained businesslike. 'Is anyone meeting you at the other end?'

Sergei had the previous day brought her two telegrams sent in answer to her letters. They were strangely alike. Both began with the words, 'Deeply shocked,' after which the senders confined themselves to practical matters. Her Aunt Eugenie, who had done so much to encourage Marina in the early days of her career, would willingly take her and the baby in at her home, and her father proposed to meet her at Harwich. Both ended in the same way. 'Wire details.'

'My father will meet the boat,' she said in answer to Nicholas's question, 'if I let him know when to expect me. Now that you have so kindly brought me the train and boat times I shall be able to telegraph him.'

She could sense he was on the verge of offering to do it for her but he restrained himself, and the tiny spurt of independence gave her a brief lukewarm satisfaction. But she was obliged to accept his offer of transport to the station.

'Since you will undoubtedly have a great deal of luggage, you will require a larger sleigh than the one I normally use. Please remember to take Sergei with you to help with transferring it all to the train, since the halt will be only short. He and the coachman should be able to manage.'

So he did not intend to escort them to Liev. Letty knew she ought to be glad and found it totally impossible. Perhaps he would put in a brief appearance at the station? She stole a peep at his face and found him staring out at the desolate scene beyond the window, where the snow was trampled and brown. She could not guess at his thoughts.

'Do you wish to be kept informed as to the welfare of—your niece?' she asked diffidently after a moment of silence.

Nicholas started and turned round, his expression giving away nothing. 'Naturally I shall keep in touch. My bank will see to the financial side——'

She lifted her chin proudly. 'There is no need for assistance of that kind.'

'I am not interested in whether you need it. It is my plain duty to provide it.'

If only he would not talk so much about duty. If only he would give her a glimpse of his real feelings.

But perhaps this hard practical side was all that was left of the Nicholas she had known during the summer. If he had loved Marina deeply he might be too much hurt by her death to be able to show any feeling for those who were still alive.

He was speaking again and Letty forced herself to listen. 'I do not intend to see you off at the station. It would be extremely distressing for us both.' He held out his hand. 'I wish you a comfortable journey.'

They had never shaken hands before and Letty could hardly believe it was happening. As his hand clasped hers, she felt herself drawn gently a little nearer. He bent his head and kissed her lightly on the lips. It reminded her of the first kiss she had had from him, at the Grand Duchess Anna's party, yet even that had had more feeling in it than this cold impersonal salute.

With a small strangled sound she wrenched herself free and fled from him to her own room, there to lean back against the closed door and allow the tears to flow unchecked down her cheeks. They were the first she had shed since her sister's death which had nothing to do with mourning for Marina.

When she emerged she was dry-eyed and calm. With care and precision she supervised Varya's preparations for taking the baby on such a long journey at so tender an age. Fortunately Mary was strong and healthy, and the curious Russian habit of wrapping a young child in swaddling clothes would ensure she was well protected from the cold.

When she enquired about the nursemaid's own luggage, she found it to be almost non-existent and for a moment she wondered whether Varya was sewn into her clothes for the winter, which suggested a distinct lack of hygiene. Deciding that tackling this delicate problem was something which could be postponed until they reached England, Letty concentrated on ensuring that they were ready and waiting when the big sleigh arrived.

Throughout the loading she was calm and businesslike, all her emotions firmly battened down beneath a frozen exterior. Not for one moment must she allow herself to think about anything except the matter in hand. Memories hammered at the walls of her mind without avail and the ice in which she had encased her heart remained as hard as stone. It was made easier because she had never really been happy at the dacha; happiness belonged to St Petersburg, for it was there that she had found love, and she was grateful that she had already suffered the anguish of saying goodbye to the lovely, romantic city with its leafy avenues and beautiful waterways.

At the station she had plenty to think about, for Varya had apparently never seen a train before, and when it drew up before them, puffing and panting and belching out steam, she stood transfixed, staring at it with wide eyes and clutching the baby tightly in her arms.

If she should panic now...

Fortunately her devotion to the infant saved the situation and soon she was settled in the roomy compartment and gazing entranced from the window. So quickly did she adapt that, except when attending to Mary, she slept peacefully through the night, unaware that her snores were keeping Letty awake. By the time they left the train to board the ship, late the following evening, she considered herself such an experienced traveller that she compared their cabin very unfavourably with the comfortable railway compartment.

It was a smooth crossing and Letty slept fitfully, both dreading and longing for the coming meeting with her father. Yet the sight of his tall clerical figure standing on the quay in grey, misty and snowless England instantly banished all her doubts and fears so that she felt nothing but a desperate need to fling herself into his loving arms.

But the Canon was not accustomed to displaying emotion, even in private, and this was a very public place indeed. He kissed Letty's cheek, said a courteous 'Good morning' to Varya, who stared at him wide-eyed, and ignored his granddaughter who, in any case, was invisible in her wrappings. With cool efficiency he devoted himself to seeing that his little party was transferred to the London train with a minimum of disturbance.

It was just like coming home from an ordinary holiday, Letty reflected as she settled in her corner seat. No one would guess she had returned after eight months' absence, bringing with her an illegitimate half-Russian baby who must be absorbed into the Mayfield family. Her father's control enabled her to regain her own and to remember she was grown-up now, no longer the excited and carefree girl who had left England, but a sober young woman who knew about life as well as death. When he began cautiously to question her about her plans she was able to answer him in a calm and practical tone.

'For the present I intend to stay with Aunt Eugenie. She has already said she is willing to take us in.'

'No doubt her well-trained staff will cushion her against the upheaval in her household, and her husband left her well provided for——'

'I shall not require any financial aid from her. The—the Namorov family are making arrangements with their bank in St Petersburg.'

'I am very glad to hear it. It is the least they can do.' The Canon's lips tightened, betraying for a moment his inner distress. 'I hope you will visit Ely in due course, Letty,' he went on. 'Your Mama is suffering very much from the palpitations just now and does not feel up to journeying to town to see you.'

'Does she not want to see Mary?' Letty demanded.

'Mary? Oh, yes—the infant.' He removed his pince-nez and polished them with a silk handkerchief. 'I regret not at present, but she will, I am sure, change her mind when she has had more time to get used to the idea. It is, in a way, fortunate that you are going to stay in London. If you brought the child home, she would not find it easy.'

'I have no intention of doing that and my reason is that I don't think it would be fair to *you*, Papa.'

He smiled faintly. 'It would give me a great opportunity to demonstrate practical Christianity.'

'No doubt, but I'm afraid your demonstration must wait until the Mayfields are prepared to present a united front to the more narrow-minded inhabitants of the Cathedral Close.'

Aware that her father was looking at her in astonishment, not altogether unmixed with displeasure, Letty stared out at the small flat fields of Essex, so different from the vast European plain she had been travelling across yesterday. She had not meant to speak out quite so plainly, but perhaps it was a good thing for him to realise right from the beginning she was different from the lively but obedient daughter he had said goodbye to at Ely station last April. In taking charge of the baby, she had also assumed responsibility for the management of her own life.

They did not speak again until the train was nearing Liverpool Street, not because there was nothing to say, but because there was too much.

At the big Georgian house in a quiet London square they were welcomed with copious tears, for Aunt Eugenie saw no reason for hiding one's feelings. She was as plump as her sister Charlotte was thin, and tightly corseted in a black satin dress ornamented with jet. When she had pressed Letty against her ample bosom, she glanced in horror at Varya and then inspected the baby, mopping her eyes as she did so.

'I had so hoped she would be blonde like Marina but we must hope the poor little mite has inherited her mother's talent. Would that not be wonderful?'

Letty could not look that far ahead. There were so many practical matters to attend to, for her aunt had never had any children and had not thought to set aside two rooms for a day and night nursery. That was easily sorted out, but it was only the first of many problems she had to deal with before they could get settled in, and also during the weeks which followed.

The Canon stayed only twenty-four hours and then returned to Ely, saying that he would do his best to persuade his wife to travel to London when the weather improved. In the meantime, Letty was to be sure to let him know if there was anything he could do.

It seemed unlikely, for the worst of her problems was Varya.

'I really don't think I can keep that Russian girl in my house much longer,' Eugenie complained at the end of the first fortnight. 'She's upsetting the other servants with her outlandish ways and some of them have been with me for years—I don't want them to start giving notice.'

'I would hate that to happen when you've been so good taking us in,' Letty said gratefully.

'I've done it for the sake of poor dear Marina, though I must say I never thought she'd be such a naughty girl as to produce a baby when she shouldn't.' Eugenie sighed and then continued with her complaints. 'I do wish she didn't insist on feeding Mary on goat's milk. It's very difficult to obtain in London and I have to make special arrangements.'

'The baby is certainly thriving on it, Auntie.'

'Well—yes, but she would probably do even better on an English patent food.' She paused, looking unusually embarrassed. 'There's something else I must mention, Letty. That girl *smells*! Surely you must have noticed it? I don't think your mother would approve of your employing anyone like that.'

'Varya is devoted to Mary,' Letty said quietly, 'but I will introduce the subject tactfully and find out if she would like to return to Russia.'

It was easier than she had expected. To her surprise, Varya burst into tears at the mention of her homeland and at once confessed to homesickness. And so it was arranged for her to leave, and she went one cold January morning with the precious tickets hidden somewhere in her clothing. Letty hoped she would agree to produce them when required by various officials, and that she would eventually arrive safely in Liev.

Liev... She must not think about the place where so much had happened to her at the beginning and end of her stay in Russia. To do so would be to allow Nicholas to occupy her thoughts and she had spent much time trying to build a barrier to keep him out. There had been no word from him though she had hoped—unreasonably—for one during the first week or two. Instead there had come a letter from his bank, informing her in stilted English that a substantial sum would be forwarded to her every three months to cover the expenses of the infant Mary Mayfield.

How had they known her London address? she wondered, and then remembered the letters Nicholas had posted for her.

At the beginning of March there was a spell of warm weather and Charlotte at last ventured to London. At the sight of her granddaughter, sleeping peacefully in the elaborate muslin-trimmed cot which had been bought to please the starchy English nurse, she had an attack of palpitations and, even after a few days' rest, declared she dared not return to Ely by herself. Letty must accompany her. 'Leaving the baby here, of course,' she added hastily.

It seemed a long, long time since Letty had occupied a 'ladies only' compartment on the London and North-Eastern Railway—nearly a year, in fact. Then she had been alone, excited, nervous and eagerly looking forward to the immediate future. Now she felt five years older at least, and quite capable of taking charge of her mother.

The train was slowing down and, looking from the window, Letty saw the Cathedral perched on its hilltop, with the houses of the little town clustered round it like chicks surrounding a mother hen. It was wonderful to see it again, and to drive in her father's carriage up the steep hill from the station towards the prim houses in the Cathedral Close, and to note that nothing had changed.

But pleased as she was to see it all, it no longer felt like coming home. Her home now was wherever Mary was.

That afternoon she went for a long walk through the fields, noting signs of an early spring all around. There were catkins in the hedges and the blackthorn would soon be out, violets nestled in the long grass on the edges of ditches, and sparrows rushed about trailing long pieces of nesting material. At the top of an oak tree a thrush poured out all the joy in its tiny heart.

As usual, Letty had only the cows for company, but when she turned round to begin the homeward stroll she saw in the distance a man's figure approaching. He did not look like a farm labourer; in fact, he did not look as though he belonged in Ely at all. Although she was at first too far away to see details of his clothing, she could tell there was something vaguely foreign about him.

They walked steadily towards each other. And suddenly Letty's heart began racing as though she had run all the way, the colour flooded her face and then receded, leaving her deathly pale.

For the man approaching with long strides was Nicholas.

She was trembling so much she was afraid her voice would betray the state of her feelings, but the pallor of his face and the grim set of his lips told her that he was not unaffected by the meeting himself. No doubt it had brought back all the unhappiness he had suffered at Liev.

'What are you doing here? Why have you come?' she challenged him.

'To see you,' Nicholas said simply. 'I hope that is not a crime?'

'Please don't be absurd. I only meant that I don't understand your being here. I—I thought we had said goodbye at the dacha—for ever.'

'Did I say that?'

'N-no.' Letty faltered a little, some of the fire of her greeting dampened by his coolness. 'But I certainly believed it to be the case.'

'Was that what you wanted?'

The question flung her into a turmoil. Of course she had not wanted to part from him for ever, but she had no intention of admitting it. Instead of answering she tried to steer the conversation on to a safer, more ordinary level.

'I'm sorry I had to send Varya back, but she did not fit in with my aunt's household.'

His lips twitched with the old ironic smile she remembered so well. 'Having met your aunt and seen her house, I can understand that.'

'You've met Aunt Eugenie? But how——'

'Naturally I went there first, hoping to find you, but you were already on your way to Ely. When I explained who I was, I was permitted to see the infant. I thought she looked well, but I am no judge of babies and did not spend much time in the nursery——'

'She took a little time to settle down with an English nanny but she's doing very well again now,' Letty interrupted.

'As soon as possible,' Nicholas continued, 'I excused myself and took a cab to Liverpool Street. Then when I reached Ely I found the pursuit was not yet over and I must chase you through these exceedingly damp fields.'

'There was no need,' she said crisply. 'If you came to make sure Mary was being adequately looked after, you were able to satisfy yourself on that score at my aunt's house. Why did you find it necessary to follow me here?'

'It was not in the least *necessary*.' Nicholas took a step forward and put both hands on her shoulders. 'I followed you because I wanted to and I can think of no better reason.' His grip tightened painfully and it seemed to Letty that his eyes burned into hers with such power, she feared he must be able to read her every thought. Hastily she dropped her own gaze. 'I came to ask you to marry me,' he finished quietly.

'M-marry you?'

'It would be a most excellent arrangement,' he urged. 'The child is related to both of us and our marriage would give her two parents and a settled home. As she grows older, a secure background will become increasingly important. A young, unmarried woman could not possibly supply that.'

For a moment Letty could scarcely believe she had heard aright. Outraged, she had no difficulty now in meeting his eyes and at the same time she furiously wrenched herself free.

'So you did come because of Mary! Why did you bother to deny it? I presume you thought if you offered me marriage for the sake of Marina's baby I would jump at the chance of being a Countess and having an assured position in society—and because of giving me all that, I suppose you would consider yourself free to amuse yourself with—with other women——'

'How dare you accuse me of that?' Nicholas was as angry as she was. As they faced each other, he reached for her again and shook her, and this time she was unable to escape. 'Have I ever given you any reason to make such a monstrous suggestion?'

How could she explain to him that if she didn't keep whipping up her anger she felt sure she might weaken and accept his proposal?

'If you are anything like your brother——' she began wildly.

'I am not like my brother.'

'But you can't deny you don't love me...'

He stared at her blankly. 'I most certainly do deny it!' he flung at her passionately.

Letty's heart was thudding so fiercely that she was sure he must hear it. 'I believed you to be in love with Marina,' she faltered. 'I know she loved you and it seemed to me you felt the same about her.'

'I was very fond of your sister and extremely sorry for her. I did not love her as I hope to love—my wife.' His voice deep with feeling, he added quietly, 'That very special love is all yours, Letty.'

She made a strangled sound that was half a sob, and suddenly she was in his arms, deliriously aware of the strength of his body and the heat of his desire for her. Breathless, their hearts beating fast in total harmony, they exchanged the first kiss of their new relationship, and Letty's lips were eager and her natural maidenly modesty forgotten as she pressed herself against him and felt his response. The forbidden knowledge that Marina had imparted to her was both ecstasy and anguish.

'Has it occurred to you that I still do not know whether you love *me*?' Nicholas asked after a while, laughter glinting in his eyes.

'Have I not shown you that I do?' Letty leaned her head back and stroked his lean, slightly rough cheek with her forefinger.

'I would still like to hear it in words.'

'I—love—you, Nicholas,' she said obediently.

'And you will marry me?' he enquired when he had finished demonstrating his delight in her assurance.

'It is the one thing I truly want.'

After another interval, he said thoughtfully, 'I don't wish you to feel you are abandoning your own country. My shipping business can be run as easily from Grimsby as from Petersburg. We could spend quite a lot of time in England. You would like that?'

'Of course I would!'

He smiled at her enthusiasm, but suddenly became grave. 'It will not always be easy for us, Letty. We belong to different churches as well as different nations, but those are not insuperable problems.' He hesitated and then continued even more seriously, 'I am not sure what sort of future I am asking you to share. For one thing I believe there may be war in Europe before many years have passed.'

Her eyes dilated. 'You don't mean our families might be on different sides?' she asked fearfully.

'Not that. Russia and Britain are friends—it is the German Emperor who may be the enemy, but that is not all. As you already know there are rumours of coming revolution in Russia and it may be that I shall never inherit the estates which my father has devoted his life to managing. Would you mind that, Letty?'

'Oh, Nicholas, how can you ask such a question?' She snuggled her head against his shoulder as they turned and began to walk slowly homewards. 'Don't let's worry about the future now. Today is ours, and I am quite sure there will be many more weeks and months—and years too—before any of these terrible events can possibly threaten us.'

Above their heads the thrush began a new paean of joy and the sun came out from behind a cloud and touched them with its gentle English warmth. And it seemed to Letty, at that moment of sublime happiness, that together she and Nicholas could face the world and not be defeated.

# *TWO COMPELLING READS FOR MAY 1990*

**TESS**  *Katherine Burton*  **£2.99**

In the third book of this sensational quartet of sisters, the bestselling author of *Sweet Summer Heat* creates Tess. Tormented by the guilt of her broken marriage and afraid to risk the pain again, Tess is torn by desire. But was Seth Taylor the right choice in helping her to get over the pain of the past?

**SPRING THUNDER**  *Sandra James*  **£2.99**

After a traumatic divorce and the unfamiliar demands of a new born son, Jessica is determined to start a new life running a garden centre. Tough, reliable Brody was hired to help, but behind the facade of job hunting is hidden the fact that he was being paid to destroy Jessica…whatever the cost.

# W●RLDWIDE

*Available from Boots, Martins, John Menzies, W.H. Smith, Woolworths and other paperback stockists.*

# GREAT SPRING READING SELECTION

**ADORING SLAVE**
*Rosemary Gibson*

**AFTER THE AFFAIR**
*Miranda Lee*

**CONDITIONAL SURRENDER**
*Wendy Prentice*

**STUDY IN LOVE**
*Sally St. John*

Don't miss out on this unique presentation of four new exciting Mills & Boon authors, carefully selected for creating the very best romantic fiction. Packed with drama and passion, these novels are guaranteed to keep you turning the pages.

**Published: April 1990    Price: £5.40**

*Available from Boots, Martins,
John Menzies, W.H. Smith, Woolworths
and other paperback stockists.*

### **GIFT OF GOLD**  *Jayne Ann Krentz*  £3.50

One dark night in Mexico, Verity Ames tantalized a knight in shining armour – Jonas Quarrel. To release himself from a tormenting nightmare, he was compelled to track her down and discover all her secrets...

### **A WILD WIND**  *Evelyn A. Crowe*  £2.99

Ten years ago, Shannon Reed and Ash Bartlet had planned to marry, but disaster struck. Now they have been given a second chance, until Shannon is accused of murder...

### **SHARE MY TOMORROW**  *Connie Bennett*  £2.75

It was a dream come true for marine biologist, Lillian Lockwood – not only working with the renowned submarine pilot, Neal Grant, but finding such happiness together. But only by confronting his ghosts could Neal bury the memories which were crippling their love.

**These three new titles will be out in bookshops from April 1990**

# W●RLDWIDE

*Available from Boots, Martins, John Menzies, W.H. Smith, Woolworths and other paperback stockists.*

# HELP US TO GET TO KNOW YOU

and help yourself to "Passionate Enemy" by Patricia Wilson

**FREE BOOK!**

Patricia Wilson's classic Romance isn't available in the shops but can be yours FREE when you complete and post the simple questionnaire overleaf

## Romance Survey

If you could spare a minute to answer a few simple questions about your romantic fiction reading, we'll send you in return a FREE copy of "Passionate Enemy" by Patricia Wilson.

The information you provide will help us to get to know you better, and give you more of what you want from your romance reading.

Don't forget to fill in your name and address – so we know where to send your FREE book!

### SEE OVER

# Just answer these simple questions for your FREE book

1. Who is your favourite author? _____

2. The last romance you read *(apart from this one)* was? _____

3. How many Mills & Boon Romances have you bought in the last 6 months? _____

4. How did you first hear about Mills & Boon? *(Tick one)*
   - ☐ Friend  ☐ Television  ☐ Magazines or newspapers
   - ☐ Saw them in the shops  ☐ Received a mailing
   - ☐ other *(please describe)* _____

5. Where did you get this book?
   _____

6. Which age group are you in?
   - ☐ Under 24  ☐ 25-34  ☐ 35-44
   - ☐ 45-54  ☐ 55-64  ☐ Over 65

7. After you read your Mills & Boon novels, what do you do with them?
   - ☐ Keep them  ☐ Give them away
   - ☐ Lend them to friends
   - ☐ Other *(Please describe)* _____

8. What do you like about Mills & Boon Romances?
   _____

9. Are you a Mills & Boon subscriber?  ☐ Yes  ☐ No

---

*Fill in your name and address, put this page in an envelope and post TODAY to:* Mills & Boon Reader Survey, FREEPOST, P.O. Box 236, Croydon, Surrey. CR9 9EL

**NO STAMP NEEDED**

Name (Mrs. / Miss. / Ms. / Mr.) _____

Address _____

_____ Postcode _____

  You may be mailed with offers as a result of this questionnaire

PWQ1